The WHY of life

How ilsa saved the world - or didn't she?

Novel - Part I

Kai Neumann

The WHY of life

How ilsa saved the World - or didn't she?

Kai Neumann
»The WHY of life: How ilsa saved the world - or didn't she?«

Published: BoD · Books on Demand GmbH,
Überseering 33, 22297 Hamburg, bod@bod.de
Printed by: Libri Plureos GmbH, Friedensallee 273,
22763 Hamburg

For more information on KNOW-WHY and the author:
www.know-why.com
info@ilsa.de

(ISBN 978-3-7693-8967-8)

A bifurcation or branching
is a qualitative change of state
in nonlinear systems
under the influence of a parameter …
(Wikipedia according to Henri Poincaré)

1.   After the bifurcation (atb)

From a seemingly absolute silence, as if an amplifier were being turned up without a music signal, but with a slowly increasing yet still quiet hum, ilsa wakes up—just like so many other mornings. There's no reason for 'the headache'—no excess the night before, no illnesses—just stress, ilsa thinks, briefly pondering what she did last night. Did she work? Just read? Or simply watch documentaries?

Michael—like seemingly always—jumps out of bed: "Did you work late last night?"

"Also," ilsa replies, in a way Michael finds full of meaning, and shuffles to the bathroom. There—at the source of inspiration—she murmurs to herself: "Exercise, gymnastics, yoga, meditation...?" She feels that 'first the duty, then the indulgence' mentality and simply heads to the kitchen to make her fair-trade organic cocoa and open her laptop.

"I'll wake the kids," Michael says, almost cheerfully, and shortly after, they sneak into the kitchen. Given the early hour, they remain silent as they prepare their breakfast and, glancing frequently at the clock, apparently now start packing their school things.

ilsa skims through her list of emails—over 30, mainly from her bubble of international newsletters on sustainability and economics. "What's on your agenda today, kids?" she calls into the kitchen, wincing at her own self-imposed volume. Then, with a slight smile, she follows up, seemingly unsurprised: "Julia?"—dragging out the 'u'.

"Nothing special—I'm going to Steph's after school," Julia replies matter-of-factly.

Max, picking up on the general mood of 'not wanting to be bothered,' simply says, "Math exam—no problem," and is already rushing out the door. Julia, as if seizing the opportunity, follows close behind.

"If you were going to ask me—I'm heading to the office soon and meeting with the developers today," Michael beams, giving her a quick kiss on the bridge of her nose before disappearing as well. Hearing the sound of the electric car, without taking her eyes off the screen, ilsa reaches for her cocoa.

She eagerly participates in online discussions, linking publications and cause-effect models, when suddenly her smartphone, smartwatch, and of course, her laptop start ringing. Briefly pausing with a sense of being interrupted, ilsa finally takes the call on her laptop. It's Thomas, a research colleague: "Morning, figured you'd already be available. Wanted to discuss our workshop next week."

"Why not today," ilsa whispers inaudibly and, still immersed in the post she's writing, replies, "Yep, that's on my to-do list for today as well."

Thomas easily picks up on her mood: "Not awake yet, or already in the middle of it?"

"In my bubble—it's frustrating. Thomas, why are we even still doing research? Everything is so clear, yet nothing changes. Maybe we should just say, 'Science proves that we must not change anything,' and suddenly the great transformation will begin."

"You know yourself that the ego-trolls and their troll-lemmings may be loud and are unnecessarily put in the spotlight by many media outlets just to make their reporting appear neutral. But ultimately, they are the minority—at least for now," Thomas responds, making it clear that all scientists should already be aware of this.

"And yet, we have to push back so that the false memes don't take over the center of society," ilsa justifies herself—also to herself—for what seems like a futile effort. Then, almost sighing after an audible inhale, she adds, "It's the psychology, stupid." Of course, she hopes that Thomas recognizes the reference and doesn't take it personally.

But Thomas—presumably out of empathy, and deviating from the reason for his call—follows up: "What do you mean by that?"

"Well, I don't know whether Clinton really said it to Obama first, or if it's actually even older: it's the phrase 'It's the economy, stupid,' meaning that, in the end, the state of the economy determines political success. But if we keep asking why the economy functions the way it does, we quickly land at people's basic needs—whether in consumption, economic striving, or the ideals shaped by our environment. So, psychological drivers are behind the economy and also behind our views, which, in turn, steer the fate of our society."

"And that means?" Thomas presses further—possibly to give ilsa a chance to phrase it more simply or because he didn't understand it at all and doesn't want to abruptly switch to his own topic.

"It means that we humans, like other thinking beings, strive for development and integration through emotions—to adapt, to improve in competition and evolution, and to belong. For modern humans, every kind of consumption beyond basic needs is rooted in this. Clothes, cars, big homes, distant travel—it all feels good because evolution wants us to keep developing. That drives the economy, and marketing fuels it. The reaction to us scientists, who now propose the idea that we can actually be happy without this endless 'more,' gives many people a sort of enemy figure. It's not just about something being taken away— it's about how good it feels to be against something, especially when others share the same opinion, and even more so when that opinion is conveniently simple."

Thomas is fully engaged: "That's why politics that rely on science are labeled as idealistic."

"Exactly. The mass media don't score points with factual headlines but with headlines that reinforce people's roles—whether by framing something as a threat or by subtly making them feel that celebrities are actually much worse. That's how we end up with so-called 'bad bans' that politics supposedly want to impose, even when they're not bans at all. Or the car that the famous climate activist supposedly drives—which probably doesn't even exist."

"Have you ever clicked on one of those?" Thomas asks, acknowledging that such sensationalist headlines, often placed as paid advertisements, keep showing up even in serious media.

"No. But the real danger is that it's no longer just the people left behind by our high-performance society who are against everything. Even the middle of society isn't just disengaged anymore— it starts going along with it, especially when conservative parties compete for political capital and spread these simple memes as well."

Thomas responds, "Ultimately, this is how extreme parties continue to gain support."

"And that's exactly what makes them ego-trolls as well—reckless people who harm the common good and revel in the fact that troll-lemmings follow them on social media," ilsa is in her element.

"And that's why you push back and ruin your own day with a bad mood," Thomas picks up on her argument, seemingly laughing a little, and adds, "You just need to keep it simpler..."

ilsa interrupts him: "Yes, the memes need to be as simple and clear as possible, carried by all of us and put into practice. But back to our workshop. I'll create a few slides, and you can add to them, okay?"

"Good idea. It would be great if you could finish that today. I'll take a look at them tomorrow. We should also go over the right memes again. And you should really appear on a talk show!"

"Sounds good. And every time I get frustrated, I feel like I am in a talk show—when people fail to explain in plain words that the economy ultimately benefits from sustainability and that everything is truly interconnected. But I suppose in a real talk show, I'd hardly get a word in or end up stumbling over my own thoughts. It's easy in front of the TV—probably much harder in front of the camera. I'll send you something later." ilsa is steering the conversation toward an end, especially as Bella, beside her, stirs with a reproachful look.

"Great, talk later," Thomas concludes the call.

ilsa closes her laptop, turns to Bella, takes her shaggy head in both hands, and gives her a full rubdown, making her eyes disappear into folds of fur as the dog lets out a satisfied groan. "Mommy is having an existential crisis," ilsa practically tells her dog. "I research the world, and no one cares. I'm powerless."

Getting herself and the dog ready for jogging, ilsa is visibly lost in thought. As they step outside, her neighbor pulls her out of her reverie: "Morning, ilsa—hard to believe, but your car is actually being moved today."

ilsa knows what's coming and preemptively replies, "Touché. How about we share a car instead? You have so many that there's always one just sitting around."

5

"We can still afford it—and so can you. And if we wanted to do something like that, it certainly wouldn't be an electric car filled with child labor and coal-powered energy," Nick retorts, as if ready to spar with ilsa.

For a moment, she considers whether to just smile and leave it unchallenged or practice spreading the right memes. The latter wins: "You do realize that's nonsense, right?"

"Oh? Are you denying that with all these electric cars, we still have to keep coal plants running, and that lithium batteries use up rare earths and involve child labor?" Nick asks confidently.

ilsa actually has a top ten list of common misconceptions about electric cars that she enjoys debunking, but these two are a bit tricky to explain: "The thing with coal isn't about electric cars—it's about the slow expansion of renewable energy. And even with coal, the carbon footprint is lower than your diesel's—which, by the way, also runs on a lot of coal-powered electricity. And as for rare earths and child labor, that needs context: lithium isn't actually rare, child labor is involved in cobalt mining, which modern batteries can avoid. What's in your phone, by the way? And rare earths aren't actually rare—they're just distributed in small concentrations all over the world. But I'll give you this: like all cars, EVs are massive resource guzzlers that we urgently need to move away from."

"I just watched a documentary about lithium mining yesterday—how small farmers are being ruined. In the end, diesel is the most efficient form of transport, or at least synthetic fuels," Nick insists.

"No question, when extracting raw materials, we have to factor in an additional cost to protect people and the environment. By the way, the impact on humans and nature per kilometer is significantly higher with diesel and gasoline than with lithium, which, once mined, can be recycled for centuries. And with synthetic fuels, we just need to accept the fact that they require more electricity than simply using it directly in an electric car. And before you say that we need too much of it and won't have enough wind and solar, especially in winter—yes, we do need to produce hydrogen to generate electricity during lulls in wind and sun, and we do need to smartly manage EVs and heat pumps so that they help stabilize the grid. All of this is already possible."

"I'm just going to wait and see what future technologies emerge—we should all be more open to technology instead of dogmatically allowing only EVs," Nick grumbles.

"Well, maybe the XXL SUV will get a fusion reactor, and the world will be saved—I gotta go. See you later, Nick." And as if Bella had understood that they were finally heading off, she and ilsa take off at the same time. Nick waves wordlessly, and ilsa murmurs to Bella, "Oh boy, Bella, either he's right, or he just doesn't care..." A few steps later, she adds, "...and Mommy shouldn't be so preachy with facts—she should lead with questions and help integrate the other side."

They have barely made it 100 meters when a military vehicle pulls up, practically blocking their path.

"What the...?" ilsa mutters to herself—if Bella weren't there. She appears completely stunned.

A young man steps out of the vehicle: "You are needed for an important matter, and we have orders to take you there immediately. We can't say more at the moment—but it is important."

The young man looks serious, his sentence sounding rehearsed, and ilsa can already sense that she probably won't be getting much more information.

She takes a careful look at the vehicle, the uniform, and the driver inside, making absolutely sure this isn't some kind of joke. Raising her eyebrows in complete surprise yet responding with apparent composure, she says, "I need to take my dog home first. How long will this take? Do I need to bring anything?"

"We'll be waiting at your door," the soldier replies.

ilsa picks up her jogging pace behind the car, noticing how the adrenaline is making her both excited and weak in the knees at the same time.

Once at the door, the female soldier who had stepped out adds, "We can't say how long this will take. Please hand us your smartphone, watch, and laptop. We will pack them in a box and transport them to another location—a seminar hotel in the countryside. We also have clothing and all the essentials you might need. We will now quickly draft a message for your family, explaining that you are covering for a colleague at a seminar where there will be no internet access. Please phrase it in a way that ensures your family doesn't worry. The seminar will last several days, and you will be in touch soon."

The male soldier quickly adds, "Scientists are likely being picked up worldwide, and measures are being taken to ensure that this process does not become known online."

A whirlwind of scenarios rushes through ilsa's mind as she hurriedly pulls on a pair of jeans and a hoodie, adds a few spritzes of her organic deodorant spray, and grabs her jacket. She looks at Bella and speaks—perhaps to the dog, perhaps to herself: "Kidnapping? But for what, and why bother returning the dog so considerately? Why is no one coming inside—apparently, they trust me not to sneak out through the back door. I'm not an expert in any security-related field—so why me at all?"

She looks down at a confused Bella, who clearly does not understand this abrupt shortening of their jogging route: "No idea, Bella, what this is all about. If this were a movie, I'd be saying 'What a load of trash.' But Mommy will be back soon." She feels a lump forming in her throat. "Hopefully."

ilsa gets into the vehicle, which starts moving immediately. She looks around once more to confirm that it really is a military vehicle and not just some old car from the used market. The weapons and the details of the uniforms also look real. She glances at the driver in the rearview mirror, and although she had resolved not to ask futile questions, she still formulates them:

"Of course, I'm wondering—why me? Is this a mistake? What is this about? Should I be worried about my family? If this were a war or a pandemic, would I be of any help at all, or wouldn't I rather decide to stay with my family? What would you think if you were suddenly taken from your home without any further information? You mentioned multiple scientists—how do you handle those who panic and refuse to come along?"

The driver looks into the rearview mirror, meeting ilsa's gaze. The soldier in the passenger seat glances at the driver, then speaks without turning around: "We have orders to bring you to the barracks without leaving a digital trace. From there, you will be taken further. That's all we know. If we had to convince you, we were allowed to say that this involves a computer virus attacking scientists. If you still refuse, we leave without you, but you will be sworn to secrecy. However, we believe that—whatever this is—you would want to help."

ilsa notices that the route does, in fact, lead to a barracks, which at least dispels the idea of a well-executed kidnapping. On the base, there is no sign of urgency—everything looks routine. Two soldiers stroll along the sidewalk, laughing. If there were a war or emergency readiness, the atmosphere would surely be different ilsa assumes and the inner fear she hadn't wanted to acknowledge gives way to a growing curiosity and impatience about what will happen next.

"Hello, ilsa," a slightly older man, apparently an officer, greets her. "We will be flying you to a collection point shortly, where you will meet other experts before being transported to the location of the workshop. To ensure everything remains as discreet as possible, I'd like to ask you to put on a military jumpsuit."

'Expert' and 'workshop'—these are words the two soldiers who had persuaded her to come along had not used. Before ilsa can respond, she is already surprised as another high-ranking female soldier gently touches her shoulder and guides her toward a building: "Come along, we have brand-new, stylish jumpsuits for you to choose from."

The way she says it makes it sound routine, and the shoulder touch—almost a technique of neurolinguistic programming—feels anything but military. For ilsa, the entire situation is becoming even more of a mystery, something that is reflected in her body language—a slightly tilted head and raised eyebrows.

As if the soldier had noticed this—or perhaps simply because it was the logical next thing to say—she continues: "You will be flown in a helicopter shortly—it's quite loud inside. After that, you'll meet other experts and fly in a plane, where you will certainly receive more information. Unfortunately, that's all I know myself, and I'd love to be there just to find out more."

ilsa remains patient regarding the big secret, but she doesn't want to be passively led around without question. So she asks: "Does the military train you in NLP techniques?"

The officer looks almost embarrassed: "Oh, right—I did touch you just now. We do learn things like that for certain situations, but in everyday life and in this case, it's really not appropriate in the military. I must have done it completely unconsciously—I apologize."

"Oh no, you don't have to apologize. I was just curious. Either it works subconsciously, or it hits a mental barrier. Or someone recognizes it, and then it depends on the situation whether they take offense or not. I found it completely fine... I also got the impression that it wasn't an attempt at manipulation but something entirely natural. Outside the military, I probably wouldn't have even noticed it. So, all good."

By now, ilsa has put on the jumpsuit and placed her jacket into a backpack that was also given to her. The two of them then walk briskly toward a rather large helicopter, which is already starting up.

"I've never flown in one of these before!" ilsa shouts and then thanks the officer, who wishes her good luck.

ilsa is actually the only passenger, and the flight lasts only 45 minutes before they arrive at a military airfield. There, a large transport plane is being loaded, and several people in similarly "stylish" jumpsuits are boarding. Another helicopter lands at the same time, and, like its passengers, ilsa is waved toward the plane with urgent hand gestures under the roar of the rotors.

"Everyone on board, please! We're ready for takeoff!" a soldier calls out.

ilsa spots two familiar faces—one belonging to a highly prominent professor in linguistics who also frequently comments on societal issues. And another, a professor she knows personally, whom she greets immediately: "Hello, Carol—a familiar face! I suppose you don't know what this is all about either, do you?"

"ilsa! Great to see you. It looks like we're quite the mixed bunch, so it actually makes sense to have a systems researcher like you here. What I'm doing here as a psychologist, though, is a complete mystery. And no one is saying anything. If the military weren't real, I'd say there's no actual case and that we're just part of some experiment dreamed up by psychologists—after all, we do come up with the weirdest things," Carol says with a loud laugh.

The two board the plane, where they are assigned seats along the wall, facing sideways. They are helped with their seatbelts and handed headsets. Before putting hers on, ilsa asks: "How do you know we're a mixed bunch? Do you recognize a lot of the people here?"

"Only a few, actually—but they asked around, and apparently, there are physicists, computer scientists, biologists, soldiers, and probably even more."

After taking a quick breath to be heard over the noise, Carol adds, "It's almost like an Ark for experts from planet Earth."

ilsa raises her voice over the noise as well: "That sounds less like a computer virus and more like aliens. But for aliens, I'd assume they already have full-time experts and don't need so many new people."

Both put on their headsets. ilsa notices that the other passengers display varying degrees of uncertainty, casting brief glances at one another.

"Hello and welcome," a voice announces in English over the headsets, even as the plane is still taking off. "I'm Major Marks, and I will be preparing you for your assignment—though even I don't know what this is ultimately about. You have likely noticed that this operation is highly classified and cannot be discussed over phone or internet. That means neither I nor anyone else you've encountered so far knows the full scope of the situation. Our task is solely to gather designated experts and transport them safely and discreetly to various locations."

ilsa furrows her brows—this mystery just gained another twist.

After the plane has taken off, Major Marks stands up from his seat, gripping a handle for support, his expression serious as he addresses the group: "And that brings us straight to the point. You are being flown to a military base, where other experts from around the world will also be arriving. As far as I know, this is happening simultaneously on other continents as well. The goal is to form interdisciplinary expert teams to develop solutions in parallel to whatever this mission entails. I do not believe this is just a drill."

A slightly older man, whose body shape suggests he is more of a scientist than a soldier, fumbles irritably with his headset, which he has just torn off his head. The major explains that to speak, one must press and hold a button on the earpiece, which allows everyone to hear. The scientist's neighbor hears this instruction and relays it to him. He immediately follows the guidance and practically rants into the microphone: "What kind of nonsense is this? Can everyone hear me?"

He looks around impatiently, more demanding than truly inquiring, and receives nods and a thumbs-up in response. "If this is so important that we've all been practically abducted from our daily lives and transported at great expense and speed by aircraft, then why are we wasting time, and why is no one telling us what's going on? Whatever this is about, we could already be putting our heads together!"

ilsa's initial reaction is a subtle mouth movement, indicating that he might have a point. But then she speaks to herself: "The secrecy is a good enough explanation, and whoever came up with something this big would hardly build in such inconsistencies."

In fact, the rest of the group also holds back, neither supporting nor rejecting the outburst, waiting instead to hear from Major Marks: "The entire command staff has asked the same questions, and the answer is simply confidentiality. If you're already discussing it now, and a crew member here or at the military base you came from picks up on something and spreads the information, then there is apparently some kind of risk—whether for you personally or for all of us. I hope I'll eventually find out what this is about myself."

At that moment, Carol has a thought. She takes off her headset and motions for ilsa to do the same, then calls out to her: "What if this is an experiment—to study our reactions, to see how we respond to stress, how much we put up with, whether we remain passive or start organizing ourselves?"

ilsa nods but then thoughtfully counters: "Too expensive. The logistics, the use of military resources, the potential civil lawsuits for damages—I don't think this is just an exercise."

"Pity," Carol says, almost pouting as she puts her headset back on.

Others have also briefly removed their headsets to whisper with their neighbors. The major quickly adds: "We will arrive at our destination in 30 minutes. I assume you will have some short nights ahead, so you might want to get some rest. If that's completely out of the question for you right now, I hope you won't hold it against me—I simply can't offer more information at this moment."

Many people then fall into deep thought, staring into the space around them, while some continue whispering in pairs—though ilsa cannot hear what they are saying.

Fairly quickly, the plane begins its descent, and everyone looks as though they can hardly wait to get out of the aircraft and finally learn more.

It appears that others have just been flown in as well—around 100 people, guided by soldiers, stream toward a building next to the airstrip.

A colleague calls out to the group: "Wasn't there a movie where a professor asked his students to stand on the desk, only to tell them that none of them were suited to be managers because nobody had first asked why they should stand up?"

He clearly doesn't expect an answer, but many of those who hear him smile in response.

They enter a hall filled with rows of chairs, with about 20 soldiers inside—not appearing threatening in any way, but rather as though they, too, are waiting for information. Most of the experts seem to be speaking out loud more to themselves than to their neighbors as they take their seats. The tension is palpable, and the previously composed professionals can no longer contain their anticipation.

A seemingly high-ranking woman—dressed in civilian clothing, surrounded by seven others—stands at the front of the hall and speaks into a microphone, asking everyone to be seated. The two doors, which had remained open until now, are closed from the inside. It's finally about to begin: "Ladies and gentlemen, thank you for being willing to help us. You will soon be divided into teams to face a major challenge for humanity."

Everyone stares intently forward, hanging onto her words. ilsa, unable to hold back, mutters just loudly enough for those around her to hear: "What could be bigger than the sustainability crisis—something we apparently can't even mobilize this kind of effort for?"

No one reacts to her comment; all eyes remain locked on the speaker. The woman continues: "To finally tell you what this is about—it concerns what we would likely call aliens. We are about to show you footage from a surveillance camera. You will see what appears to be a person walking behind the corner of a house. Moments later, according to eyewitness reports, this person melts."

A collective murmur spreads across the room—a blend of monosyllabic exclamations and sharp intakes of breath. No one speaks clearly, but the shock is audible.

"In analyzing the scene, we found that the material involved consists of elements unknown on Earth. Experts continue to study it and strongly suspect it is of extraterrestrial origin. The material appears to be a combination of organic and mineral—possibly even some form of metallic—compounds. We have yet to determine who this supposed person was. However, when we attempted to investigate further, we encountered cyberattacks on our systems—attacks of a nature that should not even be possible."

"Vibranium from Wakanda," someone murmurs a few seats to ilsa's right. She has no idea what they're referring to, but she is oddly relieved to hear that others are also impatiently thinking out loud.

"Before any of you speculate that one of the billionaire moguls dabbling in both robotics and space exploration might have a hand in this—we've already ruled that out. Likewise, we have determined that no hostile nation or rogue organization has made a sudden breakthrough.

As for how we selected you—this incident occurred ten days ago. Since then, security experts and specialists in extraterrestrial phenomena, primarily from the U.S., have been working to assemble a team. We searched for chemists, computer scientists, disaster researchers, and even philosophers and medical experts who, in their work, have demonstrated an ability to think outside the box. We have made every effort to contact you without using digital channels. Even the IT specialists present here have been instructed to stay away from technology for now—though, of course, IT teams elsewhere are continuing to track digital traces."

At this last remark, several of the senior officials allow themselves a brief, knowing smile at the casual wording.

ilsa is thoroughly impressed. Leaning slightly toward Carol, she whispers: "Fascinating—how brilliantly thought out this is. Nothing like the trashy movies my kids watch and then describe to me in epic detail at the breakfast table."

"This still feels like a surreal dream to me—one where I keep wondering where it comes from and how it can feel so real," Carol replies.

Other experts, too, are murmuring quietly with their neighbors as the speaker at the front continues: "We must admit that we're relieved so many of you are going along with this and staying level-headed. We've formed teams of eight or nine people and will be assigning you shortly. Each team will focus on a specific topic. Every two hours, we will take long breaks, during which you can also exchange ideas with members of other teams. You might want to stick with your topic until tomorrow. However, we hope not to need more than 24 hours—and, of course, we would be delighted if we had an explanation and a plan even sooner. Each team will have a designated moderator. Before we get started, we'll take a few minutes for any questions. Fire away."

Surprisingly, only one person raises a hand—a young man with an extremely athletic build: "The question for me is, of course, what you haven't told us. Are we going to rack our brains over this, only to receive crucial additional information later?"

A man from the leadership group, who had not yet spoken, steps forward: "Everything that can be said has been said. And yes, I would say that even if it weren't true. You are now facing a dilemma—does this statement make us more credible, or is that precisely why it's a trick? But why would we withhold information if the solution is that important?"

The young man doesn't let up: "At least in movies, the cliché is that you opened Pandora's box. And because the world must not know, you're keeping information from us while hoping we'll still fix your mistake. I'm not accusing you of anything—but we might not be able to afford to work without all the facts."

"Okay, fair point. If anyone here has withheld information, feel free to put them on public trial," the leader responds—showing no sign of irritation. "But you're right. At least one group should seriously consider this angle—that maybe one of the agencies involved here did set something in motion and lost control of it."

After that exchange, no one else seems eager to ask a question—most prefer to start working among themselves.

A woman from the leadership team steps forward: "Then let's get started. This part of the base is completely sealed off from the outside world. We have enough supplies, accommodations, clothing, and hygiene products for everyone. The soldiers in the room are here to assist you and keep the base running. Now for the team assignments: Team 1...."

ilsa turns to Carol one last time before they end up in separate groups: "The introduction was really well done—it answered a lot of questions in advance, included some empathetic elements… just solid. We'll catch up later?"

Carol nods, and both head to their assigned teams.

ilsa is placed in Team 7. A female soldier designates her as the moderator—a role she had half-expected: "Alright, let's get started. I'm ilsa. My specialty is the systemic analysis of interconnections. I'm neither an expert on extraterrestrials nor IT, nor chemistry. I suggest that I take responsibility for guiding this group, but all of you should absolutely share your concerns and ideas at any time.

We should start with introductions. Also, I propose that we use first names. After that, let's throw out any possible explanations—everything is allowed, and no idea is too far-fetched. Once we have a list of hypotheses, we'll define a goal and systematically analyze the risks and key levers using a cause-effect model. We'll use the flip charts—I haven't worked with paper in a long time."

As a systems modeler, ilsa is well-versed in running workshops with vague objectives. The sheer surreal nature of the situation, as Carol described it, fuels her adrenaline, helping her project confidence: "And just so you know a bit more about me—I've worked extensively on sustainability issues, as well as digitalization, artificial intelligence, demographics, and politics."

She scans the group with a questioning look: "Does that sound good to everyone?"

Most nod in agreement, and ilsa feels a sense of relief—no one here seems interested in feeding their own ego. Everyone appears genuinely focused on the task. "Would you like to go next?" she asks, gesturing toward the older man sitting to her left.

The group introduces themselves—ranging from psychologists to IT specialists to an astronomer.

Then, the brainstorming begins—throwing out theories about a human-like alien that can simply melt—and the ideas that emerge are nothing short of wild

. . .

2.   Before the bifurcation (btb)

From a seemingly absolute silence, as if an amplifier were being turned up without a music signal, but with a slowly increasing yet still quiet hum, ilsa wakes up—just like so many other mornings.

There's no reason for the headache—no excess the night before, no illnesses—just stress, ilsa thinks, briefly pondering what she did last night. Did she work? Just read? Or simply watch documentaries?

Michael—like seemingly always—jumps out of bed: "Did you work late last night?"

"Also," ilsa replies, in a way Michael finds full of meaning, and shuffles to the bathroom. There—at the source of inspiration— she murmurs to herself: "Exercise, gymnastics, yoga, meditation...?"

She feels that first duty, then indulgence mentality and simply heads to the kitchen to make her fair-trade organic cocoa and open her laptop.

"I'll wake the kids," Michael says, almost cheerfully, and shortly after, they sneak into the kitchen. Given the early hour, they remain silent as they prepare their breakfast and, glancing frequently at the clock, apparently now start packing their school things.

ilsa skims through her list of emails—over 30, mainly from her bubble of international newsletters on sustainability and economics. "What's on your agenda today, kids?" she calls into the kitchen, wincing at her own self-imposed volume. Then, with a slight smile, she follows up, seemingly unsurprised:

"Julia?"—dragging out the 'u'.

"Nothing special—I'm going to Claudia's after school," Julia replies matter-of-factly.

Max, picking up on the general mood of not wanting to be bothered, simply says: "Math exam—no problem," and is already rushing out the door. Julia, as if seizing the opportunity, follows close behind.

"If you were going to ask me—I'm heading to the office soon and meeting with the developers today," Michael beams, giving her a quick kiss on the bridge of her nose before disappearing as well.

Hearing the sound of the electric car, without taking her eyes off the screen, ilsa reaches for her cocoa.

She eagerly participates in online discussions, linking publications and cause-effect models, when suddenly her smartphone, smartwatch, and of course, her laptop start ringing. Briefly pausing with a sense of being interrupted, ilsa finally takes the call on her laptop.

It's Thomas, a research colleague: "Morning, figured you'd already be available. Wanted to discuss our workshop next week."

"Why not today," ilsa whispers inaudibly and, still immersed in the post she's writing, replies: "Yep, that's on my to-do list for today as well."

Thomas easily picks up on her mood: "Not awake yet, or already in the middle of it?"

"In my bubble—it's frustrating. Thomas, why are we even still doing research? Everything is so clear, yet nothing changes. Maybe we should just say, 'Science proves that we must not change anything,' and suddenly the great transformation will begin."

"You know yourself that the ego trolls and their troll lemmings may be loud and are unnecessarily put in the spotlight by many media outlets just to make their reporting appear neutral. But ultimately, they are the minority—at least for now," Thomas responds, making it clear that all scientists should already be aware of this.

"And yet, we have to push back so that the false memes don't take over the center of society," ilsa justifies herself—also to herself—for what seems like a futile effort. Then, almost sighing after an audible inhale, she adds, "It's the psychology, stupid." Of course, she hopes that Thomas recognizes the reference and doesn't take it personally.

But Thomas—presumably out of empathy, and deviating from the reason for his call—asks: "What do you mean by that?"

"Well, I don't know whether Clinton really said it to Obama first, or if it's actually even older: it's the phrase 'It's the economy, stupid,' meaning that, in the end, the state of the economy determines political success. But if we keep asking why the economy functions the way it does, we quickly land at people's basic needs—whether in consumption, economic striving, or the ideals shaped by our environment. So, psychological drivers are behind the economy and also behind our views, which, in turn, steer the fate of our society."

"And that means?" Thomas presses further—possibly to give ilsa a chance to phrase it more simply or because he didn't understand it at all and doesn't want to abruptly switch to his own topic.

"It means that we humans, like other thinking beings, strive for development and integration through emotions—to adapt, to improve in competition and evolution, and to belong. For modern humans, every kind of consumption beyond basic needs is rooted in this. Clothes, cars, big homes, distant travel—it all feels good because evolution wants us to keep developing. That drives the economy, and marketing fuels it. The reaction to us scientists, who now propose the idea that we can actually be happy without this endless 'more,' gives many people a sort of

22

enemy figure. It's not just about something being taken away—it's about how good it feels to be against something, especially when others share the same opinion, and even more so when that opinion is conveniently simple."

Thomas is fully engaged: "That's why politics that rely on science are labeled as idealistic."

"Exactly. The mass media don't score points with factual headlines but with headlines that reinforce people's roles—whether by framing something as a threat or by subtly making them feel that celebrities are actually much worse. That's how we end up with so-called 'bad bans' that politics supposedly want to impose, even when they're not bans at all. Or the car that the famous climate activist supposedly drives—which probably doesn't even exist."

"Have you ever clicked on one of those?" Thomas asks, acknowledging that such sensationalist headlines, often placed as paid advertisements, keep showing up even in serious media.

"No. But the real danger is that it's no longer just the people left behind by our high-performance society who are against everything. Even the middle of society isn't just disengaged anymore—it starts going along with it, especially when conservative parties compete for political capital and spread these simple memes as well."

Thomas responds: "Ultimately, this is how extreme parties continue to gain support."

"And that's exactly what makes them ego trolls as well—ultimately reckless people who harm the common good and revel in the fact that troll lemmings follow them on social media," ilsa is in her element.

"And that's why you push back and ruin your own day with a bad mood," Thomas picks up on her argument, seemingly laughing a little, and adds, "You just need to keep it simpler..."

23

ilsa interrupts him: "Yes, the memes need to be as simple and clear as possible, carried by all of us and put into practice. But back to our workshop. I'll create a few slides, and you can add to them, okay?"

"Good idea. It would be great if you could finish that today. I'll take a look at them tomorrow. We should also go over the right memes again. And you should really appear on a talk show!"

"Sounds good. And every time I get frustrated, I feel like I am in a talk show—when people fail to explain in plain words that the economy ultimately benefits from sustainability and that everything is truly interconnected. But I suppose in a real talk show, I'd hardly get a word in or end up stumbling over my own thoughts. It's easy in front of the TV—probably much harder in front of the camera. I'll send you something later."

ilsa is steering the conversation toward an end, especially as Bella, beside her, stirs with a reproachful look.

"Great, talk later," Thomas concludes the call.

ilsa closes her laptop, turns to Bella, takes her shaggy head in both hands, and gives her a full rubdown, making her eyes disappear into folds of fur as the dog lets out a satisfied groan.

"Mommy is having an existential crisis," ilsa practically tells her dog. "I research the world, and no one cares. I'm powerless."

Getting herself and Bella ready for jogging, ilsa is visibly lost in thought. As they step outside, her neighbor pulls her out of her reverie: "Morning, ilsa—hard to believe, but your car is actually being moved today."

ilsa knows what's coming and preemptively replies: "Touché. How about we share a car instead? You have so many that there's always one just sitting around."

"We can still afford it—and so can you. And if we wanted to do something like that, it certainly wouldn't be an electric car filled

24

with child labor and coal-powered energy," Nick retorts, as if ready to spar with ilsa.

For a moment, she considers whether to just smile and leave it unchallenged or practice spreading the right memes. The latter wins: "You do realize that's nonsense, right?"

"Oh? Are you denying that with all these electric cars, we still have to keep coal plants running, and that lithium batteries use up rare earths and involve child labor?" Nick asks confidently.

ilsa actually has a top ten list of common misconceptions about electric cars that she enjoys debunking, but these two are a bit tricky to explain: "The thing with coal isn't about electric cars— it's about the slow expansion of renewable energy. And even with coal, the carbon footprint is lower than your diesel's— which, by the way, also runs on a lot of coal-powered electricity. And as for rare earths and child labor, that needs context: lithium isn't actually rare, child labor is involved in cobalt mining, which modern batteries can avoid. What's in your phone, by the way?"

"I just watched a documentary about lithium mining yesterday— how small farmers are being ruined. In the end, diesel is the most efficient form of transport, or at least synthetic fuels," Nick insists.

ilsa sighs but keeps her composure: "We need to factor in the real costs of resource extraction to protect people and the environment. By the way, the environmental and human impact per kilometer is much higher for diesel and gasoline than for lithium, which, once mined, can be recycled for centuries. And synthetic fuels? They require more electricity than simply using it directly in an electric car. And before you say that we don't have enough energy and that there isn't enough wind and sun in winter—yes, we need to produce hydrogen to store energy for those times. And we need smart grids that use electric cars and heat pumps to stabilize the system. All of this is already technically possible."

Nick shrugs: "I'll wait and see what future technologies emerge. We should all be more open to different options and not dogmatically push only electric cars."

"Maybe we'll get a fusion reactor in an XXL SUV, and the world will be saved—I gotta go. See you later, Nick."

As if Bella understood that they were finally going for a run, she and ilsa take off at the same time. Nick waves wordlessly, and ilsa murmurs to Bella: "Oh boy, Bella, either he's right, or he just doesn't care..."

A few steps later, she adds: "...and Mommy shouldn't just bombard people with facts—she should lead with questions and help integrate the other side."

ilsa and Bella run through a beautiful mixed forest when ilsa receives a call on her smartwatch. It appears to be from the editorial team of one of the most influential talk shows: "We would like to invite you as a guest on our next show. The topic will be: 'Disruptive Developments—Are Today's Leaders Capable of Mastering the Great Challenges?'"

ilsa takes a deep breath, pulled out of her own thoughts, and perhaps even audibly baffled, she responds: "Right now, this sounds like a prank from some colleagues. Let me ask—why do you think I should be on the show? How did you come across me?"

With a slight laugh, the caller replies: "We actually encounter this kind of skepticism quite often. We'll send you an email with all the details shortly. We found you through a search for experts in complexity. We came across your blog, where you've published models on several of the topics we'll be discussing on Sunday—economics, war, migration, AI, and more. You were also recommended to us. Sitting in front of a camera shouldn't be a problem for you as a moderator of large workshops, right?"

"No, that should be fine. I assume there will be some sort of preparation—ground rules, format, etc.?" ilsa asks.

"Of course—though it won't be too much. If you agree to join, we'll send you an email right away. Naturally, we'll cover all travel expenses." is the reply.

After the call, ilsa and Bella continue their run as if nothing had happened—but inside, ilsa's thoughts are racing. How should she handle this opportunity to share important insights?

3.   Motivation (btb)

In Max's classroom, the usual chaos reigns as the lesson begins:

"What are you listening to?" … "Cool hoodie." … "I have to reach Level 8 later." … "Today, I'm training thighs." … "Forget about him..."

Smiling and shaking his head slightly, the teacher enters the room. With what appears to be just the right amount of authority over the class, it's enough for him to stand in front of them—within seconds, all attention is on him: "Today, we're going to talk about motivation."

"Just don't give us homework—then we won't need to talk about missing motivation," comes the first joke, followed quickly by another: "Okay, so who messed up this time?"

With an open-armed gesture, the teacher invites them in: "Go ahead—what motivates us? Why do we choose to do one thing and not another?"

"Because others do it too." … "Because the system forces us." …

The answers come immediately. The students raise their hands but are allowed to speak right away, looking at each other as they talk. There's a clear culture of open discussion between them and the teacher.

27

"Hold on a second..." the teacher interrupts. "... Because the system forces you? Because others do it too? What does that sound like?"

"Definitely not free will," says Eve, a pretty girl who seems calmer than some of the others.

"So, are you just mindless machines?" When no one responds, the teacher turns to a student sitting in the corner, looking irritated: "Do you decide for yourself what you like, what you want to do?"

The answer is just an indifferent shrug. But Eve jumps in: "We can decide for ourselves what we want. But what we want isn't independent of what others think about it. Or what others are doing."

"Huh? So, we decide what we want, but other people determine what we want?" asks a girl who had previously seemed unfocused.

The teacher looks delighted, hopeful that the discussion will keep flowing. Max, after a quick, slightly shy glance toward Eve, speaks up: "Because we're always looking for happiness, we want things. And we have these feelings so that evolution works."

Apparently intrigued, the teacher picks up on this: "Okay, very interesting. Can you explain that?"

"No, not really," Max admits, feeling a bit of pressure but trying to focus: "We do everything either to belong or to be better, to develop further. My mom talks about this kind of thing a lot. And most people do and want the same things because they want to belong, because they seek security in a group. Until someone tries something different. And they can only stick with it if others think it's cool too."

After that long answer, Max glances at Eve again—this time even more briefly.

"Very interesting. Do you, Max—or better yet, do any of you—have an example to help grasp this?" the teacher asks, now clearly deep in thought himself.

"Well, we all don't do our homework because it's uncool. And if someone suddenly does do their homework, the big question is whether we make fun of them—or whether some of us start doing it too," a student blurts out, immediately earning laughter from the class.

"Hmm, that's actually not funny at all, because it makes it seem like it's okay not to do homework. Come on, give me more examples!"

"We all play Zombie 3, but Max thinks it's dumb and prefers to be the only one playing Survivor," a student says with a laugh, clearly knowing that Max can take the joke.

"Uh, I don't get it. Why does Max play that, then? Didn't you all just say that people are only motivated when others like what they do?" a girl asks.

"And Max, what does motivate you?" someone chimes in.

"Shooter games are just mindless, and in Survivor, you have to come up with solutions to move forward," Max replies.

"But none of us play that, so no one admires you for it. Why are you motivated to play it when you're the only one?" a classmate asks—but gets no immediate response.

"So, does that mean Max actually does have free will and does something independently of all of you?" the teacher asks, noticing that the discussion is losing momentum.

Eve watches Max for a moment—he clearly doesn't like being the center of attention. After a brief pause, she says: "Maybe in his own mind, some people do admire him—maybe he identifies with the heroes in his game. We all live in our own mental worlds, but we don't really talk about it."

29

For a moment, this actually seems to make the class think—no one cracks a joke.

The teacher is impressed: "Respect! The level of this discussion is really great. But what about when we have to do something that doesn't feelgood? What motivates us then?" He looks around. "This question is for everyone."

"Like school!" comes the quick response from a student…

…immediately followed by another:

"Well, we're all doing something here without being motivated."

Max adds: "When we were kids, our parents always talked about the play muscle, the cuddle muscle, and the behave muscle. And we had to train all our muscles and make sure we could do everything. I think my play muscle is the strongest!" he laughs.

Once again, the teacher is surprised and finally reveals what he was really leading up to the whole time: "Actually, I wanted to talk to you about the difference between extrinsic and intrinsic motivation. Have you heard of those before?"

When no one responds, he continues: "You're intrinsically motivated when you do something for yourself. You're extrinsically motivated when you do something because of pressure or for a reward. Can you think of examples?"

A girl raises her hand: "Well, my homework—if I do it—isn't for me. I only do it because I'm forced to and because I need a good grade. So even though I'd say I'm not motivated, you're telling me I am, just extrinsically?"

The whole class, including the teacher, chuckles.

"Okay, time to let all that sink in. It's actually not that easy to separate. Philosophers still debate whether free will even exists. Cogito, ergo sum."

He scans the room, hoping to spark interest. "Right now, this is a big topic in artificial intelligence discussions." The class remains unimpressed. "And whether extrinsic motivation—when you do something not out of interest, but for good grades or money—also involves positive feelings for you, is something you should question too." The teacher looks expectantly at two girls in the front row, who seem to be processing the challenge on their faces.

"And finally, what Max earlier called the behave muscle is what I know as the discipline muscle. When we train our discipline muscle, it might not feel good in the moment, but being the kind of person who has great discipline can feel great. And it doesn't even matter if others acknowledge it, or if we just imagine their admiration in our own minds. Of course, we also tend to achieve things this way—things that we would have thought were cool to accomplish even before we started."

That was a lot. Now, the teacher tries to bring it full circle: "Okay, start working on this—alone or in groups—describe motivation from your own perspective. At least one full page. The rest you can finish at home—so you can be cool for having done your homework. If you research this online or ask your AI assistants, you'll get frustrated by how many different approaches exist. Choose the ones that actually resonate with you."

He knows, of course, that many students have already mentally checked out, and that most will definitely put off—or completely ignore—this assignment.

A mixed scene unfolds: some students pull out their tablets or phones, some form groups and genuinely dive into the discussion… and others talk more about what really motivates them.

In the school bus a friend playfully elbows Max: "So, you've got a behave muscle, huh? Man, you have such smart parents, and you want to become a handyman?"

Max glances over at Eve, who only briefly looks back—clearly amused and curious to hear his response. "I just think it's cool to build something real, something that lasts. Being a programmer would be cool too, but we won't need many of those in the future once AI takes over. Investment bankers mostly just destroy things…" he looks at a boy who casually flashes a victory sign.

"… and no one listens to scientists, and lawyers are boring." He glances at two boys who clearly have those career aspirations.

His friend isn't letting it go: "But as a tradesman, you'll have to work hard. And there's a lot you won't be able to afford—big houses, awesome vacations, and so on."

"Multiple houses!" laughs the aspiring investment banker.

"Great, we're actually doing our homework here!" Max exclaims, though he clearly sounds annoyed. "Should we really do a job just for the money if we have zero motivation for it?"

Another student chimes in: "But I can be super motivated to succeed at work and make loads of money."

Yet another student adds: "That's extrinsic motivation—if we're not doing something for itself, but for money. And only what we do with the money actually motivates us."

Surprised, a girl from Eve's group turns around: "Wait—are the guys actually doing the homework?"

All the girls look over. Eve, who had clearly been listening in class, remarks: "Since they don't care about the homework, they must be intrinsically motivated."

Another girl laughs: "What's up with you guys suddenly being such nerds? I don't get any of this. And you even remembered the terms?"

Everyone cracks up.

"Okay, someone write this down, and we've all done the homework," says a boy who is clearly not yet intrinsically motivated.

When Max gets home, he sees his neighbor Nick tinkering with his visibly powerful SUV. They greet each other.

As if searching for an alternative to the classic 'So, how was school?' Nick doesn't say anything at first. But Max, amused and friendly, jumps in with a casual comment: "Aren't you afraid your car will explode?"

Nick smirks slightly, but mostly looks surprised. Taking a deep breath, he takes on the challenge: "Cheeky kid—you're already repeating the same nonsense as your parents. It's EVs that explode all the time—you read about it everywhere… except in your ideological bubble."

Max, of course, knows the good-natured battle of arguments between their families. He enjoys a debate and doesn't hesitate to jump in: "We actually talked about this in school—about why and how people spread misinformation. Statistically, per mile driven, gas-powered cars are way more likely to catch fire. But that doesn't stop anyone from driving them. But suddenly, for EVs, that's supposed to be a deal-breaker?"

Max watches Nick expectantly—waiting for him to argue back so he can explain why people love believing and spreading obvious nonsense.

But as if deliberately avoiding that trap, Nick just shrugs and says: "Never trust a statistic you didn't fake yourself." With a friendly grin, he turns back to his car.

Max keeps walking toward his house but can't resist leaving one final remark: "EV drivers are better people - only cyclists are better."

4.   Working to survive (btb)

Michael's company office is an open space, featuring modern, large screens on real-wood furniture, surrounded by plants. In the background, there's a dartboard, kicker table, and a pool table.

For the meeting, everyone has gathered around a few standing tables, with an electronic whiteboard capturing the discussion. Things are getting serious.

"Is what you're planning really such a smart idea—automating process tracking and even integrating AI? Are we doing this just because we can, or because our customers actually want it?" a young colleague asks.

"Or—do customers want it? Or will they want it once we explain it well?" an older colleague adds.

Michael is clearly burning to answer himself, but he looks around the room and, unfolding one arm from his crossed stance, makes an open-handed gesture: "What do you think?"

A tense silence stretches for a solid three seconds—almost uncomfortably long—before the first thoughtful arguments are practically thrown into the room:

"Our customers use our software only because they have to and because we're easier to use than the competition."

"...and because we accommodate their individual requests."

"...which costs us valuable developer resources, and as a result, we end up maintaining tons of custom solutions. Speaking of which—Stefan, when will you finally be done? Are you actually working on this full-time?"

"I do think our solution should stand out. And if we integrate AI, it'll definitely be exciting."

"We're not here to make things exciting for our developers."

"With AI, it's probably impossible to be too early—only too late."

"...or we could lose focus and burn through too many resources."

"This whole Enterprise Information System idea—the dream of running a business in real time from a central cockpit—completely flopped. No one's excited about it anymore."

"...except maybe controllers, but no one likes them anyway."

"...but let's not jump on AI just so we can claim some nonsense in our marketing."

Michael places both hands on his head and takes a deep breath: "Wow. Interesting. Exciting." He pauses for a moment, and everyone watches him intently. "Okay, let's check the mood first and then systematically figure out where we're headed."

Clearly improvising, Michael continues: "You know the drill: I want two numbers from each of you—both between 0 and 10, where 10 is the best score.

First number: How comfortable do you feel in the company?

Second number: How much do you feel challenged and given enough freedom to try new things?

We can do this with a show of hands—but then people might get asked about their numbers later, which could be good but might also be uncomfortable.

Or we write the numbers anonymously on slips of paper and put them in a bowl.

Show of hands—who prefers anonymous?"

A few hands go up, but not all.

"Okay, not everyone," Michael notes. "Then we'll do it with paper ballots."

The vote happens quickly. Slips of paper are cut up, tossed into a bowl, and the results are tallied with tally marks on the whiteboard.

Michael comments: "By the way, I do think we're here for our developers as well. Remember our strategic model—besides long-term financial survival, we aim for a better world, and above that, motivated employees. Their motivation drives performance. It's a dual principle. And honestly, every other management theory is nonsense if it doesn't work the same way."

At least a few colleagues react with appreciative expressions, encouraging Michael to continue: "For employees, it's about feeling integrated, belonging, feeling safe—but also having freedom, achievements, and room to grow."

After a short rhetorical pause, one meant to let the realization sink in together, he adds: "And a company needs both as well: Integration—meeting market demands and aligning with its own capabilities. And development—adapting to change, staying ahead of the competition. So, let's check whether our company is evolving in an integrated way—and whether you can evolve in an integrated way within it."

Turning to the whiteboard and glancing at the results, he adds: "Of course, some people don't live to work—they work to live. And for a lot of jobs, that's how it has to be. But in a company like ours, we should design our jobs in a way that feels good—and makes the company successful."

The young colleague picks up on the point thoughtfully: "Hmm... working to live would mean working as little as possible. But does living to work automatically mean we have to work a lot? Or can we still enjoy work even if we work less?"

Another colleague immediately jumps in: "Technically, we can already do that—we implement AI, set the parameters, design smart structures, and just check the final code. With the time we save, we could just stay home and do things we actually enjoy. Right, Stefan?"

The running gag lands perfectly, and everyone laughs. Another colleague, however, wants to go deeper: "Completely agree—work that we enjoy doesn't necessarily mean working a lot."

He raises a finger to emphasize an important but: "But! I want to buy a boat, so I'm offering to use the extra time to do your work too. I'll do the work of three people for the salary of two, Michael saves a ton of money, and what you do is none of my concern."

"Then the only jobs left will be for those who program AI," the older colleague remarks.

The other colleague then delivers his explanation with the confidence of a professor: "Not really—people just don't realize it yet. The AI we're developing now evolves on its own and will soon be universally applicable. Robots will build other robots, which will then build factories. We won't need cleaners, service workers, or even most healthcare staff once robots optimize their own performance. And once one robot learns something, all robots can do it."

"Okay, take that idea to its logical conclusion. We'll finalize our corporate strategy on Monday—we won't get there today, and I need to be home on time," Michael says, sounding—perhaps unintentionally—almost like a teacher talking to his students.

He continues: "If just a few highly productive people create everything, what happens to everyone else? I see two possible scenarios."

Michael looks around, and one colleague jumps in—though it seems like several people already know the answer: "Michael pays huge taxes, and the rest of us enjoy a life of self-determined leisure, living frugally off Universal Basic Income."

For a brief moment, everyone smiles—it sounds like a great scenario. But of course, there's at least one more possibility.

Another colleague speaks up. "Or we all keep working—more or less—and thanks to increased productivity, we can afford more as a society. Boats for everyone!" he declares.

Michael has thrown a cause-effect model onto the screen and starts adding the arguments. The team is familiar with this way of working. As they reflect on the discussion, more points emerge: "If we all want more, the limiting factors will be material resources and the environment."

"Do the people who aren't ultra-productive get a share, too?"

"And when exactly does UBI start? When enough has been automated—by which time people who lost their jobs will have already hit the streets? Or before full automation, when there still aren't enough robots to support the system?"

"...and suddenly we don't have enough police officers, nurses, or teachers?"

Clearly impressed, Michael takes a moment to integrate these points into the model. Once he sees how to structure it, he throws in another argument himself: "And what if I invest tons of money into AI but don't have to pay much in taxes at all? I'd have fewer employees but not necessarily higher taxable profits. Who funds Universal Basic Income then?"

"Then we implement an AI or robot tax—whether you make a profit or not. The market will adjust. If AI becomes too expensive, suddenly humans will be cheaper again," the young colleague counters smoothly.

"Hmm," Michael starts, clearly thinking out loud as he speaks: "If AI is better and foreign competitors don't pay these taxes, we'll fall behind globally. This kind of tax would have to be global—and that's highly unlikely."

Michael wraps up the productive session, noting that the model is available online for further input. Everyone wishes each other a great weekend. For now, the running gag doesn't make another appearance.

5.   Emotion (btb)

ilsa is reading something on her smartphone when Julia cheerfully asks: "Are we eating together today?"

"Sure," ilsa replies. "What are you in the mood for?"

"Maybe something with crispy fried potatoes?" Julia suggests, then adds after a slight pause, "I'll even help peel the potatoes."

"Deal," ilsa agrees, and the two of them get to work in the kitchen.

Max comes down the stairs and sees the two busy women: "Mother-daughter thing, or do I have to help too?"

"Help," they both say in unison. Then ilsa furrows her brow and looks at Julia. "Or do we want to manage on our own?"

"It's all good, Mom," Julia replies, with a certain gleam in her eye—clearly enjoying the chance to mess with Max.

"Set the table?" Max asks, just as his phone pings.

At first, he glances at it casually—but then suddenly freezes as if he'd just received news of someone's death. It's a friend request from Eve.

He stares at his screen for so long—completely stunned—that both ilsa and Julia notice.

"Everything okay?" ilsa asks.

"Yeah, of course. What should I set up?" he replies while hastily accepting the request.

Meanwhile, the girls are discussing Julia's upcoming school trip. She's thrilled about the idea of biking, camping, and an outdoor adventure with her class.

Max, on the other hand, keeps glancing at his phone after every single trip to the table—checking if Eve has sent a message yet. Of course, he wonders why she reached out to him in the first place. Should he send her a message first?

Now Julia asks, "Max, what is it? Are you selling something online, or is this about a girl?"

ilsa raises her eyebrows at the two rather different options, while Max clearly just wants to get out of this conversation as quickly as possible: "We talked about motivation in school today, and I tried explaining the play muscle thing. But I don't remember all of it—can you explain it quickly for my homework?"

The question is directed at ilsa, who, as a scientist, immediately shifts into explanation mode—but not before Julia gets in one last remark: "Okay, so definitely about a girl."

ilsa begins: "There are many ways to explain motivation. I once asked why we want things, and I landed on the concepts of integration and development. I asked why we desire things. We have hormones and neurotransmitters that create all sorts of emotions—from fear to comfort, from boredom to excitement. Evolution designed these feelings to protect us, to make us connect with others, and to drive us to be better, to keep evolving. In general, evolution is about adapting to circumstances, keeping up with change, and competing for development. All emotions can be categorized as either positive feelings—which come from integration or development—or as negative feelings, which arise when those things are missing, like with fear or boredom."

Max briefly glances at his phone again, which inspires Julia to provoke him further: "To get back to the topic—what about love?"

ilsa laughs briefly before continuing: "Love is something very special—I'll get to that in a moment. What's important about feelings of integration and development is that we can experience the same emotions and hormonal releases through very different things in life. Some people buy happiness, others build a bird-house, and others get deeply invested in their favorite TV characters—all of them experiencing the same evolutionary feelings of integration or development."

She pauses, then asks: "What did your teacher say? Was it about students not being motivated?"

"That's what we thought at first," Max replies, "but I actually think it's just part of the subject. So basically, we do everything either because it protects us or helps us evolve?"

"Yes, essentially," ilsa nods, though she seems to be thinking further. Then she adds: "At least when we talk about motivation in the sense of desire and positive emotions. Of course, there's also motivation in the sense of obligation. That's where, along with the play muscle and the cuddle muscle, the discipline muscle comes in."

"Ah! So that's the difference between extrinsic and intrinsic motivation!" Max exclaims, clearly proud to have grasped it.

But now ilsa pauses entirely, looking out the window: "Hmm, that's a good question. Is all extrinsic motivation—at least in the beginning, before the good feeling of achievement kicks in—a question of the discipline muscle? And is everything we have to do but don't want to do always extrinsic motivation?"

Max seems to enjoy the feeling of discussing these ideas on equal footing with ilsa. "I think so," he says. "And if I enjoy understanding something after boring study sessions—even if the topic itself didn't interest me at first—then my extrinsic motivation turned into intrinsic motivation. Because now, it feels good."

"I think that sentence belongs in your essay," ilsa says, nodding approvingly. "And I'm curious what your teacher will say about it. The question remains—does that good feeling come from development because you've learned something new? Or from integration, because your teacher and classmates recognize your achievement?"

Max smirks slightly and murmurs triumphantly: "That will definitely overwhelm Alfred."

Seeing the confused looks from ilsa and Julia, he clarifies: "That's what I've named my AI assistant. 'Friday', 'Jarvis', or just 'J'—every third person calls theirs that."

In fact, everyone in the family has an AI assistant, though they neither own robots nor use the emerging neuro-implants.

"Love," Julia interjects again—this time, without Max checking his phone.

He's too absorbed in his feelings of integration and development, having just had an intrinsic learning moment together with others. ilsa picks up the thread again: "But we have already talked about love before, and I'm surprised that this isn't analyzed to death in your social circles. Love is an invention of evolution—for species whose offspring depend on the protection of both parents.

To make sure they stay together long enough, the right mix of pheromones and other biochemical triggers leads to a powerful hormonal surge—one that lasts about two to three years. You can't think about anything else, you get weak knees, butterflies in your stomach—the whole deal. It's all described wonderfully by Desmond Morris—along with the many functions of sexuality."

"So… you don't love Dad anymore?" Julia asks—somewhere between uncertainty and provocation.

"Well, I did say that love is something special. On average, we fall in love two to three times in our lifetime. But that doesn't stop us from being happily in a relationship for decades. Some say they fall in love with the same partner multiple times. The benefits are clear—trust, security, great sex, and ideally, mutual support and shared experiences of belonging and growth." ilsa knows this answer won't be enough just yet.

"So why don't the hormones last longer? And what about cheating?" Julia immediately follows up.

"The hormones don't last longer because, from a genetic perspective, it's optimal for us to try out multiple partners," ilsa explains. "But cheating, of course, is the ultimate betrayal—a direct violation of Kant's imperative: 'Do unto others as you would have them do unto you.' Or something like that. But finding sexy men and women attractive is completely normal. That explains fashion, cosmetics, flashy cars, pornography, and so on…

For the details, you can refer back to Desmond Morris—like why human females don't display their fertile days, why women are more sexually active in the evening while men tend to be in the morning—or, well… always," ilsa laughs.

But the kids seem to be struggling to keep up, so she continues: "From that perspective, our sexual desire exists to initiate the search for the best possible partner, while love exists to ensure that at least once in life, we commit and successfully raise offspring."

"Well, I definitely shouldn't say that in school," Max exclaims. "The LGBT crowd would rip my head off if I claimed love is only for reproduction."

"From a zoological or evolutionary standpoint, that's certainly the case. But the right pheromones can also exist between humans and animals." ilsa turns toward the dog, while Julia and Max's jaws drop slightly. "Right, Bella? This absolute affection between all kinds of living beings exists independently of sex or reproduction. Ask why. Why does love exist between humans? And why do the hormones only last 2-3 years? Love is emotionally invaluable to us—even if it can also be painful. And the fact that it doesn't always lead to reproduction? That's fine too. We should avoid terms like 'normal'. Just because evolution favors a certain mechanism doesn't mean everything else is unnatural—it's just one possible explanation."

Julia presses further: "You said earlier that sex in a relationship is good sex. But isn't a new partner exciting? Isn't the better always the enemy of the good?"

ilsa is momentarily stunned: "I'm not sure how I feel about hearing that from my teenage daughter… But actually, it depends. If your partner and you have the right chemistry, that's gold. It's more than just a guaranteed orgasm. The fact that we still find other people sexy even after falling in love isn't a conscious choice—it's just what evolution intends. Whether new partners are actually sexually enriching from the start depends on two things: Whether the woman shows what feels good, and/or whether the partner has the right touch."

"In reality—especially at a young age—this can often be pretty disappointing. The guys? Excited and acting like a sewing machine on full speed. The girls? Too shy to say what they actually like or don't like. Boys are done quickly—girls aren't. Definitely a phase where we can get lost in stereotypes.

My recommendation? Show or say what feels good. Hoping the other person will just magically know is the wrong approach—we're all too different for that. Even though porn makes it seem like everything follows the same script."

At this point, both kids slowly lift their heads, raising their eyebrows slightly. The electric car hums as it reverses into the driveway—Michael is home.

ilsa wants to quickly tie the discussion back together before they shift into weekend mode: "Back to motivation for a second. Let me ask you this—why should we even care about what motivates us?"

She turns to Julia.

Michael steps inside, calling out: "Weekend!"

Then, seeing all four of them gathered—including an excited Bella, he adds: "And apparently, it's Family Time."

ilsa leans in and, without any context, but with a mischievous grin, responds: "Let's have sex."

Michael looks puzzled for a second but, staying quick on his feet, strides toward the delicious-looking dinner table: "Okay—but first, we eat."

Everyone is clearly hungry and digs in eagerly. Max of course glances at his phone one last time but quickly refocuses on their earlier conversation: "If we know what motivates us, we can shape our own happiness."

ilsa still has her mouth full, so Julia jumps in: "And we can sell things to others—because we first figure out what triggers their happy hormones."

"Brilliant!" ilsa says.

Michael adds: "And we can manipulate people—NLP and all that. Did your discussion by any chance have something to do with sex?"

Everyone bursts out laughing and waves him off, rather than explaining it to poor Michael. He tries once more with direct questioning, but the conversation soon drifts to typical family chatter—their latest encounter with the neighbor, traffic, weekend plans, and so on…

Until Julia, apparently enjoying the family time, suddenly asks:

"Should we play the The-WHY-of-Life-Game later?"

This game is usually suggested by the parents when there's tension in the house—or by the kids when they want something.

ilsa agrees first, Max hesitates briefly before nodding, and finally, Michael sighs dramatically: "Okay—maybe I'll finally figure out what all this has to do with sex."

Julia, clearly amused by the confusion, adds: "And love, of course! Max, you're allowed to keep your phone with you, obviously."

A playful jab that Max doesn't appreciate—but it's not a big deal. A brief father-son glance—and Max is relieved that his dad gets it and lets it slide.

"Okay!" says ilsa. "Max, go grab the game. Do we want to write new cards? What should the topic be?"

"Weekend," Max suggests.

"Vacation," Julia adds.

"Job," says Michael.

The The-WHY-of-Life-Game is played by taking turns rolling a dice and drawing cards. The goal is to accurately predict another person's preferences or opinions regarding topics like vacation, work, etc.

Each player writes 10 possible answers beforehand—but only 5 are correct and ranked in order of importance.

Points are awarded based on correctly guessing the 5 true answers and their ranking.

The The-WHY-of-Life-Game also includes various additional cards that focus on awareness, eye contact, emotional expressions, conscious breathing, step-by-step planning, and more.

ilsa originally designed the game to help make people conscious of the fact that we all strive for integration and development—yet most of the time, we just drift through life unconsciously. The game is a hit with the family.

By the end, everyone is feeling deeply connected and shares an empathy-filled group hug before heading to their rooms.

Just as he settles in, Max receives a message from Eve: "Hi Max—why don't you become an architect? Then you can build things—intrinsically motivated—and still make a ton of money! :-)"

Max furrows his brow in confusion. But not because Eve wrote to him. He murmurs: "What the… Why would I want to make a lot of…" Then he stops himself—mid-thought. As if he's afraid to say out loud what he was about to realize.

6. Existentialism (btb)

Michael turns to ilsa in bed: "What's up?"

ilsa responds instinctively: "Why?" A sure sign that she knows he's noticed something. Michael doesn't say another word—he just looks at her. ilsa takes a deep breath and begins:

"I've been struggling with existential questions for a while now. What's the point of generating so much knowledge about how the world could be better—only to realize that the decision-makers won't change anything?"

Michael responds immediately: "So… not knowledge for its own sake, but for its impact?"

ilsa fires back—almost as a reflex, rather than out of actual disagreement: "Why? Do you work for the products or for the impact they have on customers?"

After today, Michael has to admit: "You'd be surprised."

But determined not to start talking about his own day, he quickly redirects: "But don't you have to research everything multiple times before it gains credibility? And isn't it normal for change to take time?"

He pauses briefly before adding: "You always say idealism isn't about what others believe—it's just an unsupported claim or based on some one-off study that hasn't been confirmed."

ilsa finally drops the bombshell: "I'm going to be on a talk show this Sunday." An indirect way of admitting that Michael has a point.

"What?!" Michael's eyebrows shoot up.

"The editorial team called me today. At first, I thought it was a scam, but the show is about complex political challenges. And when they looked for people who understand complexity, they found my blog posts in various places." It still sounds like she's reassuring herself that it's real.

Michael is thrilled: "That's amazing! How many times have we sat in front of the TV, furious, complaining that no one ever clearly explains how things are connected?"

ilsa raises an eyebrow. Michael notices the slight pressing of her lips—so he zeroes in on her and thinks out loud: "That's why you were questioning the point of your work. You see this as a huge opportunity…"

"Challenge!" ilsa quickly corrects him.

Michael shifts his tone, deliberately emphasizing his next words differently: "…and now you're scared."

His eyes briefly flick to the ceiling, as if searching his thoughts for the impact of what he just said. But before he can worry, ilsa takes the concern off his shoulders: "Exactly. But not because of the TV appearance—because of the responsibility of using this chance properly. Not for myself, but for the cause."

Michael knows this isn't the time to say, 'You'll be great, don't worry.' He pauses—probably thinking of something that won't sound superficial: "Can you prepare for it? Will they brief you in advance?"

ilsa has already thought about this: "Apparently not really—they just asked how I'm traveling and how early I can get there. I assume there will be a short introduction and a welcome right before. And I'm sure they'll explain that my speaking time will be much shorter than the big-name guests."

"And will you prepare specific key points?" Michael asks.

ilsa answers with a slightly worried tone: "I think you can always tell when someone over-prepares. The messages won't be a problem—but I need to find the brake."

Michael laughs: "Oh yeah, if there's one thing you're great at— it's pushing too much development."

"Exactly. Instead of explaining the full complexity of everything, I should take more of a Jiu-Jitsu approach—asking my opponents about individual connections, challenging their statements on those, and then calmly concluding that all of these separate points are actually interconnected—and that our decision-makers need to understand that." ilsa speaks with deep reflection.

Michael thinks out loud: "Hmm. And then it all goes differently— the discussion derails into something trivial, you don't get a chance to speak, and when you finally do, you rush to catch up, cramming in too many arguments."

ilsa sighs almost theatrically: "Exactly. That's why I'm nervous. And I'm not used to being restricted in my speaking time."

They both fall silent for a while—until Michael formulates a question: "Back to existentialism for a moment. You see yourself as responsible for the cause. But what is the goal of human existence? You always say we seek integration and development, and that culture is the result of our collective striving. Ultimately, most people pursue recognition, forms of immortality, children, and simply more of everything."

He raises his arm at a right angle, spreading his fingers as he continues: "How does that lead to a better world?"

After another brief pause, he bends his open hand even further backward: "Like ants, we play a role in society—except that humans have a far greater impact than ants, who exist in balance with nature."

ilsa immediately picks up on it: "Exactly. Very early in human history, we disconnected from nature—pursuing too much progress without enough integration. But it's not just emotions that drive us. We can also consciously choose our path—that's exactly what we practiced in the The-WHY-of-Life-Game earlier. We can actively decide who we want to be—as individuals or as a society. In practice, of course, we're not free from the values and emotions of our environment, but theoretically, we could be."

A key element of the The-WHY-of-Life-Game is to hold an object and, one by one, reflect on what it means—from its materials to its function, to its personal significance. It helps players realize that in daily life, we rarely take the time to consciously reflect on anything—we just function.

Michael asks: "Okay, we both live with a mission for a better world. But when is the world better?"

ilsa responds: "When we live peacefully and contentedly, in harmony with the planet."

Then she cuddles up to Michael. He starts to say—teasingly: "Didn't you say earlier—"

But ilsa cuts him off: "Too late." Then—not fleetingly—she kisses him on the nape of his neck.

7. Vocation (btb)

Max had trouble falling asleep at first—and then, in the middle of the night, he woke up again. He gets up and walks over to his smartphone—which, of course, isn't right next to his bed. He immediately opens his AI assistant app and whispers: "Alfred?"

Alfred responds instantly: "Yes, Max. What's up?" ...causing Max to hastily lower the volume.

He thinks for a long time, while Alfred's Memoji—a kind of Yoda, but with a white beard—starts yawning, seemingly responding to Max's sleep profile.

But then Max just mutters: "Ah, never mind."

By morning, Max finally figures out how to respond to Eve's message without looking suspicious. He types: "Is money important to you?"

His satisfied expression reveals that he likes this response—it leaves it open-ended whether he's talking about money itself or what she expects from him.

Michael is setting the table when Julia comes galloping down the stairs as the second one awake. She pauses, eyes wide, and asks with mild alarm: "What's going on outside?"

A massive, almost black storm front has appeared—on what was otherwise a sunny summer morning. Extreme weather events are nothing special anymore. Slowly, the rest of the family joins the breakfast table—just as the storm hits.

Huge hailstones—bigger than usual—slam into the garden and onto the house with deafening force. Within minutes, it's over.

Max looks out the window: "Look at Nick's car—it's wrecked."

"And our solar panels on the roof probably are too," Michael adds, picking up on the point.

He looks out the window again: "Hmm... and the pigeon too."

Everyone—including Bella, who is excitedly wagging her tail at the door—looks outside.

"We have to do something!" Julia exclaims, urgently.

"Not Bella!" ilsa quickly says, holding her back.

Michael places a hand on Julia's shoulder and says: "Come on, let's go check."

Michael and Julia step into the garden. Michael looks up at the roof, where multiple solar panels and solar thermal tubes are shattered. A pigeon, badly injured and bleeding, doesn't even try to fly away.

"Should we put it out of its misery, or leave it to nature?" Michael asks.

"We have to end its suffering," Julia says, resolutely.

"Okay. How do you want to do it? Would you hit it with something? Or do you think you could press your thumb against the back of its head? That would be the quickest way." Michael's voice is calm and rational.

Julia's face contorts in shock, and she immediately says: "I can't do that—you have to!"

Michael: "I'll do it, no question. But why do you say you can't?

You want to become a soldier."

He doesn't ask it as a question—but as a statement.

"That's not fair," Julia says after a brief pause. Michael just looks at her, waiting. She continues: "You don't want me to be a soldier. Killing an innocent animal is different from defending yourself against someone who's trying to kill you."

"Well, this is about ending the pigeon's suffering—not killing it for practice." After a moment of hesitation, he adds: "And—are the soldiers on the other side really guilty? Or are they just forced into it?"

Julia's voice rises in frustration: "You were a soldier yourself! If enemy troops invaded here—if they raped women and children, bombed us—you'd want to defend yourself too!" Her voice shakes slightly. "You… you just want to protect me."

Michael, meanwhile, has already ended the pigeon's suffering with a swift blow from a flat shovel. Julia struggles to keep her composure. Michael speaks slowly and carefully: "Of course, we want to protect you. But if you choose this career, we will accept it."

ilsa and Max step outside with Bella. It looks bad. Since their garden has little lawn space, there was a lot that could be damaged. Most of the plants are devastated—climbing vegetables like beans, spinach, and kiwi, broccoli and cabbage, and countless flowering legume sections. The greenhouse has multiple shattered windows.

Max stares in awe at the damage: "I'm going to develop cool solutions for storms like this. Houses and gardens that can handle extreme weather."

He continues walking with Bella, toward the front of the house. ilsa, Michael, and Julia look after Max in confusion.

"Huh?" ilsa mutters quietly, glancing at Michael and Julia—apparently surprised by Max's bold statement about wanting to design entire houses. Was this their Max, the one who wanted to become a craftsman?

Michael shakes his head slightly but returns to their original conversation: "Your mom and I both believe that wars could actually be prevented. Most of the time, they're driven by economic interests. We also believe that a global community, with strict and consistent sanctions—even against the countries that supply weapons and keep doing business with warlords—should be able to end wars immediately."

He looks at ilsa, who signals her agreement with a subtle widening of her eyes. Michael continues: "On the other hand, I do understand your desire to fight back against those who kill innocent people—with more skills and better weapons. You have a strong sense of justice. And honestly, sometimes I also wish there was some kind of Iron Man who could just step in, disarm the bad guys, and—if necessary—eliminate them. When you see those TV images of gangs with AK-47s in poor countries—destroying everything, killing people senselessly, taking away any chance of a future for children—And you wonder how they even get those weapons… And why they don't just use those resources to build infrastructure instead… It makes me furious. I want to intervene."

Julia, surprised and hopeful, asks: "But?"

Michael tosses the dead pigeon into the trash bin and ilsa immediately picks up the thread: "But first—no matter what weapons are used, the other side always catches up… Or rather—many other sides do."

Michael adds: "And second—it's about your soul."

"That's why the pigeon thing happened just now," he continues.

Julia doesn't say whether she had already considered that or if it just occurred to her now: "We're trained to handle stress and trauma," she says firmly.

ilsa, ever the scientist, blurts out: "Trauma means it's already too late."

She quickly continues: "The problem is—you've learned to think critically. You're sensitive and self-aware. At some point, it will tear you apart—the realization that the soldiers you had to kill, or the collateral damage you inevitably caused, might not have been necessary at all."

She adds: "I pointed this out years ago—that AI-controlled robots will soon replace soldiers. At first, it sounds positive—but logically, the next step is that these robots will either develop their own agenda or be misused to kill indiscriminately."

Michael chimes in: "Even today, we're already seeing cheap mass-produced drones being used—swarm-intelligent, capable of identifying both people and other drones." He shakes his head.

Where does that lead? Do we end up hiding from rogue drones—like in some bad B-movie? Or will every criminal gang, for pocket change, be able to use drones for terror and extortion?"

ilsa tries to simplify it: "I don't know your guys' movies, but isn't it always a theme in Batman, Iron Man, and whoever else—that the villains are just a consequence of the heroes' existence?"

"That's true," Julia admits, explaining: "There are already plenty of dirty nukes, biological and chemical weapons— Both sides keep developing them in an arms race, but luckily, they're too afraid to actually use them."

ilsa, now animated: "And that is exactly the problem. The so-called good countries wouldn't dare use them to protect their own people. But in the many rogue states, the warlords probably don't care what happens to their own population."

Michael backs her up: "Someone who loves nothing—who has nothing to lose—will stop at nothing."

He adds: "And don't forget: Someone else will give you orders.

And before long—you'll be giving orders yourself. It looks easy in movies, but in reality, you don't get to freely decide what you think is right."

Meanwhile, Max inspects the front side of the house.

The north-facing green roof is only slightly disturbed—

But the other houses have even lost roof tiles, and several neighbors have gathered outside—staring, shaking their heads in disbelief.

Max frowns—

Then hears Nick's son, Melvin, who's kicking around hailstones in the driveway with his older sister, Claudia.

Melvin notices Max looking at their wrecked luxury car and says:

"Dad thinks it's cool. The floor mats were dirty anyway—
Now we're getting a brand-new car from the insurance."

8. The view from above (atb)

The brainstorming session on possible explanations for an apparently human-like alien that can simply melt away produces some adventurous ideas:

Aliens that have secretly lived among us for ages. A billionaire who has lost control over his secret AI robots. An invasion that first replaces key positions with human-like robots.
A creative school project. A military experiment that has gone out of control. Or, inspired by movies, the explanation that it is one of us, having traveled back in time.

ilsa structures a cause-and-effect model. At first, it looks like a mind map.

ilsa: "I'll start by collecting guiding questions – we can refine and add to them as we go. These are not ranked in any order:

How is it possible? What would be the motive? What can we do? What could go wrong – a question we should always ask, but here, maybe even more in terms of worst-case scenarios. How do we communicate our findings, or even our lack of understanding, to the outside world?"

She looks around at the group. An older sociology professor speaks up: "What are the possible motives of our stakeholders – from the military and politics to the scientific community?"

ilsa beams and immediately takes note of it, murmuring to herself, "Strange to actually write this down myself instead of using an AI."

Once finished, she asks: "What do you think – should we tackle all topics one after the other together, or work in a World Café format with parallel groups where you can move freely between discussions?"

A natural scientist suggests: "One after another, so we can tap into our full creative potential on each topic. If needed, we can quickly push topics to the back and return to them later."

ilsa nods and asks the group, "What do the others think? Who's in favor?"

Most of the group nods more or less in agreement and briefly raise their hands.

She continues, "Do we want to go through the points multiple times randomly, as suggested, or should we establish a sequence?"

Since there is no clear reaction, ilsa decides, "Okay, all these questions are interlinked anyway, so let's just go through them from left to right. We can state initial thoughts and then explore what leads to them or contradicts them. Or, if nothing comes to mind immediately, we can approach it systematically—by asking what something requires and what could act against it. Sounds abstract, but in practice, it's quite simple."

"That's your KNOW-WHY method—I use it all the time," a military representative chimes in, backing her up.

ilsa raises an eyebrow slightly, visibly impressed, gives a brief smile, and begins with the first guiding question.

The possibility of the phenomenon being real could stem from an origin on Earth, either in the present or the future, or it could be of extraterrestrial origin, raising the question of how the vast distances of space could have been overcome.

For the question of motive, the first step is to examine how it happened. An Earth-based origin would imply entirely different motives than the idea of extraterrestrial intelligence integrating itself among humans. If the intent were espionage, it would suggest that, despite superior technology, they needed a tactical advantage to assert themselves.

"That sounds like a movie-inspired perspective," ilsa remarks with a smirk and adds, "If it was human-made and not military-related, it would mean an awful lot of commotion for relatively little impact, wouldn't it?"

When discussing what could go wrong, the scenarios range from an AI disguised as a human surpassing us in the shadows to aliens spying on us and planning to take over the planet.

A younger psychologist adds another nuance to this idea, "Taking over the planet or liberating it from us?" She looks momentarily uncertain, then adds, "Or perhaps guiding us toward something better?"

Hearing this, ilsa raises both eyebrows and nods in agreement.

On the question of communication with the outside world, everyone quickly agrees that, for the time being, nothing should be shared externally. The approach would depend on the actual findings, and information should only be released under certain circumstances—to gather more clues or to corner whatever entity is involved. This point is later rephrased even more defensively as 'handling communication.'

The discussion about possible reactions from external parties is met with great interest but only briefly touched upon. The speculations range from geopolitical crises to covert business interests.

For every explanation, the team collects responses to the KNOW-WHY questions: What does it require? What speaks against it, now or in the future?

Regarding the potentially extraterrestrial materials, ilsa wonders, "Could the elements be synthetic?" Like many other thoughts, this one is added to the model on paper, and by the end of the session, several square meters of flip chart paper cover the floor, some with footprints from team members stepping on them.

Looking at the time, ilsa suggests, "Let's take a longer break. We can reflect on what else comes to mind. But we also need to establish a concrete next step—beyond just listening to the results from the other working groups."

Once again, everyone signals their agreement, and the sociology professor adds, "We should send an unknown entity a signal that we are open to communication without revealing anything about ourselves."

ilsa gives a thumbs-up, and everyone heads outside while she quickly adds the suggestion to the model.

Outside is a relative term—like in a prison, the workshop participants now find themselves with even fewer points of contact with the personnel at the base. Only the soldiers from the rooms accompany them and handle any food or drink requests.

A soldier from another group walks over to ilsa.

"Hello, ilsa. Have you already answered the question of why?"

ilsa looks somewhat puzzled at the medium-sized, rather unremarkable soldier and his name tag.

"Uh, 'Miller'—how should I address you? 'Mr. Miller'?"

"Feel free to call me 'Frank'—otherwise, we actually address each other as 'Mr.' or 'Ms.' here, since none of us are wearing rank insignia," Frank explains.

"Okay," ilsa replies, tilting her head slightly. "But how do you know my name?"

Frank smiles: "Your name tag."

He notices that ilsa is looking at him, aware that her name tag is hanging the wrong way around and isn't actually visible. He adds, "I saw you pass by earlier and managed to read it."

ilsa still seems slightly unsettled and continues, "I'm still surprised that you approached me like this, even though you're in another group. Never mind. Why are you asking about the 'why' directly?"

She continues to look him straight in the eyes, likely searching for any hesitation or slight shifts in his pupils.

Frank replies, "Just curiosity. Our primary role is organizing the logistics here, but we're allowed to participate as long as we don't make ourselves too important."

"That's good," ilsa says. Checking her watch, she adds, "Has your group already come up with ideas regarding the 'why'?"

Frank maintains his smile, gives a slight nod, then turns away, saying, "Back to work. See you later."

ilsa responds, "Yep, good luck," and nearly at the same time, she rushes back to her room, muttering to herself, "He could have at least offered me a drink."

Back in the room, the discussion shifts to the next steps.

A professor raises an important concern: "If there really is no more information, the other groups won't be able to determine anything with certainty either. The question is how we can get more information—and when we'll be allowed to go home."

ilsa nods in agreement, as do many others.

Another voice adds, "I think it doesn't matter whether we ask the general public for clues or only a small circle. The news will leak out, and it will cause chaos."

"We just need to send a signal that we know what's going on and that we want to talk—hoping we get an answer before the public starts to panic," someone suggests.

"But what will happen to us? Will we be kept in isolation until the response comes—or until the story leaks anyway?"

9. At home (atb)

It's evening, and Julia is standing in front of the open fridge, searching for something to eat. Max comes down the stairs and immediately comments, "If Mom weren't around, we'd have a smart fridge that would call you an 'energy waster' right now."

Julia fires back, "I'd just ask our household bot if we have anything savory for me, and I wouldn't need to search. Speaking of which—where is Mom, anyway?"

Max receives a text message—a contact request from Eve. He stares at his phone in disbelief, and Julia immediately asks, "From Mom? Something wrong?"

"No," Max replies. "Someone from school. No idea where Mom is. When's Dad coming home? Should we just choose pizza?" he asks, clearly trying to distract from the message.

Julia furrows her brow briefly but is too hungry to argue and agrees, "Pizza it is." She rummages through the freezer and pulls out two vegan organic pizzas, while Max heads over to the water dispenser.

When Michael arrives home, the first thing Max asks is where ilsa is.

Michael replies, "Mom is at some seminar without internet—for a few days. She's filling in for a colleague at the last minute. What's for dinner? I want pizza too!"

Julia looks skeptical. "Some seminar for several days with no internet or phone? Did you guys even talk on the phone?"

"Nope," Michael responds casually. "Just a text message."

Max, completely unfazed, states, "If we rule out an affair, that leaves only kidnapping."

Julia smirks slightly and raises an eyebrow. "And why exactly is an affair ruled out?"

Michael looks genuinely caught off guard. "I'll send Thomas a message. Hopefully, he's not at the seminar and is reachable." He immediately pulls out his phone and texts Thomas.

The three of them keep busy while waiting for the pizzas to bake—setting the table, closing up the greenhouse, staring at their phones, and playing with Bella.

Once they're sitting down to eat, Max asks, "Any response from Thomas?"

Michael checks his smartwatch and shakes his head. "Nope. But you guys don't need to worry. Mom is involved in different projects with various institutions. Even if Thomas doesn't know about this seminar, there's still no reason to worry."

Julia frowns. "I tracked Mom's phone—it really is at some seminar hotel in the middle of nowhere. Should we try calling her there?"

Michael shakes his head. "No, she said she wouldn't be reachable. It's probably some kind of digital detox, and everyone there has to stick to it. Do you guys want to do something together tonight? I was thinking of getting some work done, but I can put it off until tomorrow."

The kids exchange glances, and Max is the first to respond, "Nah, I've got stuff to do." Julia follows, "Same here."

As they continue eating, Michael asks, "So, what happened at school today?"

Julia purses her lips and shakes her head slightly, signaling "nothing." But when both Michael and Julia turn to look at Max, he sighs and answers, "We talked about motivation. I tried explaining Mom's concept—that we're all just seeking integration and development. I don't think it landed well."

"Why not?" Michael asks.

"I somehow got tangled up in my explanation—but I think I'll do better in the group homework." Max shrugged. "How was your day?"

Michael: "Oh, we actually discussed whether you guys will even need a job in the future or if AI will take over for us."

"Cool, no more school," Julia exaggerated.

Max, however, countered, "Or school could intrinsically motivate us." Seeing Julia's puzzled look, he explained, "That was today's topic—whether we do things for ourselves or just because we have to."

Michael smiled, satisfied. "I'll clean up and take Bella out." With that, they all wrapped up dinner.

Michael headed to the bedroom, Bella following closely behind. He glanced at ilsa's wardrobe and murmured, "Okay, no way I can tell if she took clothes and her toothbrush or not."

In his room, Max looked again at Eve's contact request, hesitated for a moment, then finally accepted it with a quiet, "Hmm." A little later, Eve's message came in: Why don't you want to be an architect? Without thinking too much, he typed back, That's an option too. Honestly, I don't really know what I want to be yet. What about you?"

Eve didn't reply right away. Max kept his phone within sight and absentmindedly browsed the internet, switching between topics like tiny houses, the best drummers, and Madagascar.

Meanwhile, after a long and exhausting day, ilsa and the other experts were merging the findings from various working groups. Some teams focused on materials and technologies that had to be of extraterrestrial origin, while others took a more tactical approach, thinking in terms of defense strategies.

ilsa took the floor, trying to summarize her group's results in response to the previous presentations: "We essentially have four possible explanations—it could be either hostile or merely curious, and it could originate from Earth or be extraterrestrial. Only when we answer that can we ask the most important question: why? Why is it hiding among us? What is its purpose?

If it's merely curious, we might just need to send a peaceful message. Unfortunately, a lack of response wouldn't necessarily mean hostility. We need more clues. Across all four possibilities, we've explored how the materials might exist, why a self-destruction mechanism seems to be built in, and whether the greatest threat is its ability to mimic humans or if we should be more concerned about its unknown technologies—especially if this is of extraterrestrial origin.

We recommend sending out signals. We strongly advise against letting this information leak to the public. And, quite frankly, we have no idea how we could defend ourselves until we know what we're dealing with."

ilsa looked back at her group. "Did I forget anything? Feel free to add." Everyone signaled their agreement, and the discussion moved on to the next two groups.

To everyone's surprise, the decision-makers who had gathered the teams didn't withdraw to deliberate in private. Instead, they opened the floor to all participants, asking for input on the next steps. Discussions covered the development of detectors for identifying these beings, a combined analog communication and defense strategy, preparation of statements in case of leaks, and how to handle representatives from other nations.

Late into the night, ilsa finally blurted out what many had been quietly wondering: "Uh, guys, we all agree that mass panic and the exploitation of that panic are the biggest immediate threats, meaning the real danger right now comes from us humans.

"But are we, the people gathered here, supposed to remain cut off from the outside world for days, weeks, or even longer, waiting for more information? We have families. We have important jobs. This is a dilemma—we need a solution for this too!"

Both the seriousness of the situation and the difficulty of the question lead to an oppressive silence in the hall. No one says a word, while back at ilsa's home, a severe storm in the early morning hours causes massive damage due to oversized hailstones.

ilsa, however, steps into the silence and assumes her role as moderator. "Okay, we need some creativity. We're allowed to throw out crazy ideas now, and together, we'll see if we can turn one of them into a solution. I'll start: The story—some billionaire decided to have a little fun and gathered a bunch of scientists to test out exactly this scenario. But there are no aliens, no inexplicable materials. We'd be as harmless as the myths about aliens in Area 51. If anyone here tried to make themselves important or was coerced into revealing something, it would always just turn into another conspiracy theory."

She looks around the room expectantly. No one speaks up immediately, but at least now, many are murmuring among themselves or thinking aloud. Finally, someone asks, "Who's the billionaire?"

ilsa shakes her head, slightly puzzled. "No idea, could stay anonymous. But don't get stuck on this example—just throw out your own, wild ideas."

A prominent senior scientist speaks up in a calm voice, "That's actually incredibly clever. Any other approach would fail due to legal concerns or eventually collapse under scrutiny. But staging a conspiracy theory that works as long as most of us dismiss it as nonsense—or until the threat reveals itself—is... well, quite brilliant."

From the original leadership team, after some murmuring, comes the response: "Alright, let's give ourselves ten more hours to think this through. Get some sleep, take a walk, discuss among yourselves. If we don't find any major objections, we'll organize your return transport in ten hours. Well done!"

With those final words, a small round of applause begins, and the groups break up, some energized, some exhausted.

ilsa runs into Carol, who enthusiastically calls out, "Wow, you were amazing."

ilsa raises an eyebrow. "No, if anything, it was all the teams. I still think this is nonsense—what if none of it is real, and it's actually just a drill?" Both step outside into the early morning air, and ilsa continues, "We applauded—but what have we really achieved? We're still missing critical information."

Carol smiles knowingly and places a hand on ilsa's shoulder. "If we compiled all the insights and scenarios from the past 20 hours into a book, it would be the bible for multiple fields of research. We've generated a high level of variety, allowing us to match the complexity of potential threats. Ashby's Law."

ilsa nods in agreement. "Threats… or simply a higher intelligence."

Frank approaches them. "Beer to help you sleep or coffee to keep thinking?"

ilsa and Carol exchange amused glances. Carol whispers, "Coffee?" to which ilsa responds aloud, "Coffee—and a cola for me, I don't drink coffee."

Frank nods with a grin, turns to leave, and adds, "I'll see if I can find caffeinated cocoa." ilsa's eyes widen in surprise, her mouth half-open, but Carol nudges her, signaling her to do some stretches as they watch the sun rise higher in the sky.

Meanwhile, the storm back home has left damage beyond just an injured pigeon—it has destroyed plants, buildings, and cars. Claudia calls over to Max, "Oh wow—good thing we only have lawn and not vegetable gardens." Max, however, is focused on the severe damage to their organic garden. At the same time, they hear heated voices from Nick and other neighbors out in the street and immediately head toward their driveways to see what's happening.

Late that evening, ilsa unexpectedly walks through the front door. Michael raises one eyebrow and lowers the other. "Everything okay? Did your phone not work on the way home either?"

Exhausted but relieved to be back, ilsa hugs each of them in turn. "Sorry. I have something unbelievable to tell you—but honestly, I just want to sleep first. The government secretly gathered scientists to answer a major question—but we're all sworn to secrecy. I'll tell you everything in the morning. Just don't say anything for now—is that okay?"

Michael smirks. "But first, maybe a quick shower?"

ilsa nods, her mouth half-open in tired agreement.

10. Memes (btb)

The day of the talk show has arrived. ilsa, of course, takes the train and plans to ride her bike to the station when Michael asks, "Should I drive you to the station real quick?"

"No, thanks. I'll be back tomorrow in daylight. It's all good," ilsa replies.

"If I say 'You'll do great,' I'll probably get in trouble. So instead, I'll just wish you lots of fun," Michael says, fully aware that he's said it anyway.

"Murphy," ilsa grins with her lips almost pressed together, referencing Murphy's Law—that whatever can happen, will happen—and gives Michael a long, deliberate goodbye kiss.

On the train, she tries to distract herself with work. But as they pass through the suburbs into the city, she looks out the window and marvels, as she often does, at how people live in such confined spaces. Small businesses have cluttered backyards filled with random junk, while closer to the station, rows of sleek office buildings house banks, insurance firms, and consulting agencies— all sharing one thing in common: barely any people outside, just moving or parked cars. "We're just ants with cars," she murmurs to no one in particular.

She walks to the hotel to check in and change into something comfortable before heading to the studio by taxi. However, she does take a quick glance at the e-scooters lined up in front of the hotel.

At the studio, she is warmly welcomed. The editor introduces her to a not-so-prominent corporate representative who has also arrived early. The current opposition leader is already there as well, absorbed in phone calls with his assistant by his side.

Busy as ever, the editor promptly hands ilsa over to the makeup team.

"We have time for more, but at the very least, we'll just apply some powder so your skin doesn't shine too much under the hot lights," says an energetic, stereotypically quirky young woman.

"Just the minimum, please," ilsa replies, then adds, "Are there any pre-discussions or preparation regarding the questions and roles?" She realizes that, with this question, she's outing herself as a first-timer in such a major TV event.

"Well, the celebrities try to define no-go topics and push their key messages," the young woman replies. "The no-go topics are politely acknowledged, and the rest of their wishes are ignored. They'll probably explain to you soon that speaking time is limited, and you shouldn't be frustrated if the celebrities get to talk more. But, what am I saying—maybe you're a celebrity too, and I just don't know it." She quickly shifts into a believably embarrassed stance.

The panel is indeed filled with prominent figures: two current ministers, two representatives from opposition parties, a journalist, a business leader, and ilsa—apparently as the representative of science. One minister seems well-prepared and is visibly pleased to see ilsa. "I'm looking forward to your systemic perspective," she says warmly.

The others seem less informed about ilsa's background, and one of the opposition representatives rather clumsily remarks, "Well, I'm curious to see what the scientists will throw at me this time."

ilsa, at least pretending to be slightly puzzled, asks, "Why do you expect me to say something against you? I'm not anticipating a showdown—you all have more debating experience than I do."

The tall politician nods thoughtfully, as if about to respond, but before he can, an assistant invites everyone to take their seats. There is no further preparation—most of the political representatives were too busy exchanging polite greetings.

The show begins, the studio audience having been briefed better than ilsa. After the opening credits, the charismatic host jumps right in:

"The challenges in the world are growing. On one side, we face climate change and biodiversity loss. On the other, we have threats to global peace, the rise of autocracies, disruptions to business models and supply chains, emerging AI, and increasing societal divisions. How prepared is our politics? What do citizens and businesses need to do now? These are the questions we'll explore tonight."

She first directs the question to the government representatives, asking what they see as the greatest challenges and what the government is doing to address them. She then poses a similar question to the two opposition representatives, asking how they view things differently.

The pattern of answers is typical—government representatives cite slow progress due to compromises and poor communication, while the opposition criticizes these compromises without offering concrete solutions. The journalist highlights this lack of clear messaging, and the business leader complains about excessive regulations while simultaneously calling for more global agreements to ensure competitiveness.

After what feels like an eternity, ilsa is finally addressed.

"You are a systems researcher—specialized in understanding the interplay of multiple factors. How does it all connect? What does science say we need to do?"

ilsa, having just listened to a lengthy series of statements covering geopolitics, economics, planetary boundaries, and societal issues, now has to decide how to frame her first—likely short and quickly interrupted—intervention. Anticipating what she should not do, she begins:

"If I were to outline how recent political actions across all parties are interconnected with nationalism abroad, terrorism, health, justice, future jobs, and so on, it would only tempt people to claim that everything is uncertain, too complex, and that we should just focus on the obvious."

To ensure she can make her actual argument without being side-tracked by a follow-up question, she quickly continues:

"More relevant, I believe, is a systemic look at how our politicians—and some influencers—operate. Politics should be about negotiating which solutions are best for our challenges. Science is commissioned to analyze and assess these solutions. Sometimes there is more than one viable path, and each political camp chooses its preferred solution. But what we see instead is that solutions are ignored, and instead, empty slogans are thrown around—not so much to convince people of one's own stance, but primarily to stir up sentiment against others."

The experienced moderator swiftly interjects to prevent ilsa from delivering a lengthy monologue:

"So you're claiming that there are already solutions for everything?"

A representative of the opposition, feeling the implied accusation, jumps in without being directly prompted:

"Reality isn't always as simple as science imagines it to be."

ilsa barely has time to be surprised that the ball is still in her court and counters immediately:

"Both statements are correct. There are multiple pathways to solutions, and for many issues, government ministries, businesses, and NGOs commission studies—which, interestingly, tend to arrive at very similar conclusions. Yet no one acts on them. So when politicians now say that things aren't as simple as science suggests, what they're really saying is that science is missing something."

Again, she rushes ahead before being interrupted:

"The real question for me is: Is there a lack of competence in understanding these studies, or is there a lack of character to act in the interest of the common good, rather than for the benefit of one's own party, individual businesses, or lobby groups?"

Now, what will happen? Contrary to her own expectations and earlier caution, ilsa has immediately gone on the offensive—in a rather direct and confrontational manner. Will the moderator sideline her now, or will the others tear her apart?

With one eyebrow slightly raised and what seems to be a barely suppressed smile, the moderator turns to the opposition politician:

"What do you make of this statement?"

The response is firm:

"This is an outrageous accusation—granting science the absolute upper hand while vilifying politics across the board. Who says all studies are even correct?"

Before the moderator can steer the discussion further, ilsa jumps back in:

"Outrageous indeed. But you also have an academic background. Scientific findings remain valid until multiple studies disprove them. The alternative is mere interpretative dominance. Let's take an example. Very broadly speaking—what do we need to do to meet climate targets? What studies or reports are your policies based on?"

ilsa is clearly accustomed to scientific debates conducted on equal footing—not to being the outsider in a political talk show.

The moderator plays along:

"Okay, but let's keep it very broad. What studies are you referring to?" she asks, now directing her question at the second opposition representative.

Leaning back, visibly unfazed, the politician responds:

"We must not overburden citizens or businesses, and we should rely more on market-driven solutions while remaining open to technological innovation—without patronizing people."

ilsa quickly continues, "So, no science, just your personal assessment? And what do science and major consulting firms say unanimously? CO_2 pricing is far too weak. Citizens need financial compensation for the minimum amount of emissions they cannot avoid. The economy needs clear guardrails, not just a delay in transformation under the pretense of technological openness. While we protect vested interests, the Chinese are investing in future technologies and dominating key technologies and their supply chains."

The minister joins in: "The question now is whether you are aware of this and still claim otherwise, or..."

The opposition representative interjects, irritated: "With all due respect, we should maintain a certain level of decorum here. Technically, it may seem simple, but our society also has to bear the costs and remain competitive. The current government..." What follows is a critique of the government's failure to implement measures effectively.

ilsa is given the opportunity to respond and takes it: "But first, we need to distinguish between costs and investments, and then also look at value creation within our own country. The money that circulates domestically—money that doesn't flow abroad for oil and gas imports—can be taxed and fairly redistributed, so that our society not only achieves greater prosperity but actually experiences economic growth."

Just as ilsa is still being given space to speak, the moderator now feels the need to intervene: "We are getting too deep into the details. The topic of the show is the major challenges in the world and whether our decision-makers are handling them properly. Looking at the geopolitical landscape and institutions, where are the weak points?"

The responses from the second minister and the journalist revolve around the functionality of institutions, possible overregulation, securing market access, or the necessity of alliances to prevent rival alliances from forming. It becomes clear that alliances like the EU or the UN must exist so that arguments carry weight against ruthless individual interests.

It takes a while, but then the moderator also asks ilsa, who dares to give another longer response: "Again, it's about special interests and the oversimplified, misleading rhetoric that is being spread. The solutions are also relatively clear at this level, but as we've just heard, democracies are not functioning properly. If citizens are not properly informed, if they are not politically literate, if fears are stirred up and simplistic slogans are only used to create division, then at some point democracies will slip into autocracies—with corruption, media control, and so on."

She looks around the room. No one interrupts, so she continues: "Institutions like the EU or the UN then no longer focus on solving problems for society but on maintaining the privileges of a few. And if someone doubts this, I once again ask myself: Is it a lack of understanding, or is it individual interest? Because the solutions to our challenges are pretty clear—whether for prosperity and peace or for economic growth and sustainability worldwide."

The opposition politician is on the warpath to assert her competence: "You're so delightfully naive, thinking that everything could be solved so easily. Negotiating compromises always leads to suboptimal solutions—that's reality!"

At this moment, not only the government representatives but also the journalist, the entrepreneur, and the moderator are eagerly watching to see how ilsa will continue her attack on the opposition. ilsa responds: "No question, it's not easy. But do you even tell the citizens or the economy what the solution would be that you're supposedly fighting over?" She pauses briefly, feeling she still has control of the conversation. "No, you're just fumbling around, more focused on preventing change than shaping it. Compromise means that we also have to give something. And what's really exciting is coordinating all of this on a timeline—when carbon and pollution prices must be raised further, when a digital tax must cushion job losses through a basic income, when we need to form which alliances in order to exert economic pressure on rogue states and their collaborators, and so on."

ilsa abruptly cuts herself off, realizing that she has slipped too much into details.

The opposition politician attempts to counter with more catchy rhetoric: "With your talk about basic income, you're revealing your ideological bias. That will never work..."

"Objection! This is not about next week but about what experts have been warning about for a long time—the point when too many jobs are automated without alternative jobs emerging. When robots build robots, when AI generates AI software…" ilsa interjects before the moderator takes control: "We will have a dedicated episode on this topic soon. For today's discussion, the key takeaway seems to be that science knows the right paths, politics struggles to find them, that individual interests might be at play, and that public discourse is being conducted through shallow, oversimplified messages."

She promises follow-up episodes that will explore these topics more deeply and then concludes the discussion. The opposition politicians are visibly outraged afterward, arguing that the show was biased and that science itself holds different perspectives. ilsa simply responds that it's not as if the current government is fully following scientific recommendations either or that the opposition has referenced any scientific studies to support their arguments.

The politicians are the first to leave, while ilsa, the journalist, and the entrepreneur stay behind, waiting for feedback from the editorial team or the moderator. The entrepreneur nods approvingly: "Clear words."

ilsa immediately counters, "Unfortunately, not really. I was way too complicated at times."

At that moment, the moderator joins their group. While the journalist and the entrepreneur continue discussing details of the current government, ilsa turns openly to the moderator: "Wow, why did I get so much speaking time?"

The moderator smiles, clearly amused: "Well, the opposition probably didn't expect such direct attacks, and the control room whispered in my ear that the audience was responding positively. You were on a roll."

Although ilsa feels a certain level of excitement herself, she responds self-critically: "I still think I was too complicated, but I had expected far less of myself."

"The analysis is still ongoing, of course, but I don't think this will be your last invitation to a talk show," the moderator says enthusiastically, clearly indicating the good chemistry between the two women. She admits that she initially expected ilsa to focus on explaining the interconnections between the major global challenges rather than immediately addressing the core issue—political culture and media communication.

At that moment, the journalist turns to ilsa and asks if she would be interested in writing an essay on the topic for his newspaper.

ilsa is delighted and promises to make productive use of her train ride home.

Already in her hotel room, she begins dictating into her smartphone, using her AI assistant:

"The key approach should be to ask what we, as humans, truly want. And then, how do we get there? What would already be possible today? Do we really want to work 40 hours a week and spend our free time watching others experience things on TV instead of experiencing life ourselves?"

ilsa looks out at the still-busy street in front of her hotel and continues:
"When we then ask why things are the way they are, we quickly realize that evolutionary needs lead us to act irrationally—against our own well-being. We manipulate people for personal gain, or they allow themselves to be manipulated."

She furrows her brow and tilts her mouth slightly, clearly dissatisfied with her wording. Still, she presses on:
"This is the KNOW-WHY approach: Evolution favors those who integrate and those who develop. For both, we have emotions—from a sense of belonging to a sense of achievement, from fear to boredom. Civilizations fall out of balance when achievements are pursued at the expense of the common good, or when belonging is shaped by misleading messages that also harm the common good."

Michael sends ilsa a strength emoji, which she responds to with a relief emoji and a kiss emoji. That makes it clear—she wants to stay focused on her essay.

"Let's continue!" she says, speaking into the recorder. "What and, more importantly, how do we need to communicate? The answer: simply. So simply that it spreads like a meme and gets picked up and repeated. We need to explain that the loss of democracy, climate catastrophe, biodiversity loss, migration pressure, old-age poverty, competitive disadvantages, geopolitical instability and war risks, and economic inequality are inevitably growing and interconnected problems—not just in our country but worldwide.

We must explain that clear guardrails are necessary to steer investments in the right direction. Left to itself without integration, the market will think short-term and develop straight over the crest of the KNOW-WHY wave into catastrophe. The energy transition, the shift in transportation, and the electrification of buildings—all of these must be mandatory so that investors have long-term certainty. Without this, many will continue believing that waiting is a smart strategy, turning their hesitation into a self-fulfilling prophecy. And soon, solar panels, heat pumps, electric cars, and critical supply chains will all come from China—because we insisted on being 'technology-neutral.'"

ilsa tilts her head slightly, debating with herself, but then continues:
"The energy transition is affordable, but it won't make electricity cheaper. The crucial difference is domestic value creation. If the technology comes from our country or at least from our economic region, and if local installation companies make good money, then the money stays in our economy instead of flowing abroad for oil and gas. These are the very jobs that will be lost in the automotive sector. And of course, we need climate dividends and targeted support for low-income households—not, as often proposed, for all households equally."

ilsa looks strained but not dissatisfied as she brushes her teeth in the bathroom. Noticing the echo, she lowers her voice slightly as she continues:

"If we foolishly insist on clinging to the past, we need to recognize that even without a CO_2 price, gas, oil, and uranium are becoming scarcer and more expensive, making us dependent on rogue states—not to mention the costs of climate catastrophe. And if we want to 'save' combustion engines, we should already be seeing that the major new competition is electric. When people argue about affordability, feasibility, and technological openness—including for synthetic fuels and nuclear power—they either have no idea or are serving particular interests, often for political gain.

Synthetic fuels and nuclear power are the most expensive technologies, yet they are promoted as arguments against change simply because they seem easier to implement. Nuclear power, like gas and oil, externalizes its immense costs, which we end up paying indirectly. Instead, we need to invest in electrolyzers in advance to store excess renewable energy for later use. These won't be economically viable unless we acknowledge that we must pay for their mere availability."

She exhales slowly before continuing:

"But it goes much further: we must contribute—supporting other countries so we can access their raw materials, helping other nations to reduce migration pressure. We must pay more taxes to ensure social justice, better education, and care for our aging population—otherwise, our society will slide into radicalization. The argument that top earners cannot bear any more burden is nonsense. Every income above the average is only possible because many earn below the average. And we don't want our society to collapse just so we can buy a little more until the very end.

At the same time, social innovations can help us reinvent the way we live together. If values of solidarity and responsibility become the norm, we will thrive. Without a shift in values, we will end up in dystopias where individuals act without regard or restraint simply because they can, instead of all of us doing what is necessary."

She finishes her dictation with, "Lucy, improve readability and add sources." Her AI assistant immediately generates a longer draft, but ilsa doesn't even glance at it. Slightly overwhelmed by her own intensity, she heads to bed.

The next morning, Michael returns late from jogging with Bella. Several neighbors are gathered in Nick and Jennifer's driveway, inspecting their car, which had been destroyed by the hailstorm.

Michael approaches one of the neighbors, who, like many others, is smiling at Bella as she eagerly enjoys the affection.

"Hey, what's going on?" he asks.

"The insurance companies aren't paying—at least, some of them aren't," she replies, relatively composed, though the atmosphere among the group is noticeably tense.

"Is your insurance paying, Michael?" Nick asks. His tone is more confrontational than concerned.

Michael hesitates briefly but isn't afraid of a confrontation. "Yeah, our insurance covers it. We have one of those slightly more expensive green policies that covers everything—even seeds for the garden." He notices the others listening closely and tries to downplay it:

"But I assume our premiums will go up significantly. In the end, we'll all be paying for this through higher contributions anyway. But..." he smirks, "...don't tell my family. They still think the vacation is canceled, and we have to cover everything ourselves and rebuild piece by piece."

As expected, Nick explodes: "Must be nice that you can afford that! It's outrageous that the insurance companies use some fine-print nonsense about the size of the hailstones to claim this was an uninsurable 'natural disaster.'"

"The government needs to step in," another neighbor calls out, receiving nods of agreement from most of the group.

"You mean the government should compensate us for damaged roofs and cars?" Michael asks, his expression genuinely surprised.

That is indeed what everyone means, though they also sense that this thought might have a catch. Michael continues, "For one thing, in this area, we are probably among those most capable of covering the costs ourselves. For another, this won't be the last event of its kind. When we start having actual hurricanes here, with debris flying through the air, it'll get worse. Or when we face weeks of extreme heat, have to ration water, and retrofit air conditioning because our elderly won't be able to withstand the temperatures. At the same time, more and more harvests are failing, and we—and others—will have to spend a fortune on food..."

A neighbor interrupts him: "That's what we pay all those taxes for—so the government helps in situations like this!"

"And not to waste the money on foreigners and other countries!" an older man adds, earning nods of agreement.

Michael challenges them, "Yes, but how long will the government be able to do that? Most people vote for parties that don't want new public debt, that push for tax cuts. And aren't we the ones causing these climate catastrophes? With our big houses, our heavy cars, and all our consumption? Now, what's been predicted for decades is finally happening, and the people who suffer the most are the poor. And now, suddenly, we're saying that's their problem and that our tax money should only help us?"

"Exactly! You were trying to ideologically scold us all again, but in the end, you phrased it perfectly: We pay the taxes, and now we should benefit from them!" Nick fires back.

Michael has already inhaled to respond when suddenly, Nick's daughter, Claudia, interjects: "But is it fair that we don't help others when we're the ones responsible for this?"

Wow. That hits hard. Nick, visibly caught off guard, quickly counters, "Who says we're responsible? It's mainly the Chinese with their coal power plants polluting the world."

A neighbor, however, concedes, "Claudia is right—we all bear responsibility. And the worst is probably still to come."

Suddenly, in a traditionally conservative neighborhood, something is acknowledged that climate activists have been protesting about in vain for years. Michael adds, "The Chinese cause only a fraction of our emissions per capita. Their coal plants power the cheap products we buy here, and the biggest problem is that high-population countries are ultimately copying our lifestyle."

He quickly continues, "What's important now is that we come together more as a community. This isn't like before, where we each enjoyed our personal purchases. We're entering a new reality, like the disaster-stricken regions we only know from TV, where any one of us—or all of us—can be affected, and we have to help each other rebuild. Let's create a neighborhood group on social media and plan when and where we can help clean up and repair things. It'll be a great way to come together. We should also consider sharing cars and cargo bikes—that would save everyone a lot of money."

Jennifer, beaming with pride, puts an arm around her daughter Claudia and announces, "We'll set up the group right away!"

The older man immediately asks if someone could help him with his car, which is stuck in his damaged garage, and a woman inquires if anyone has a ladder and a way to temporarily patch her roof.

Michael declares that he can start helping that very afternoon and heads into the house with Bella.

11. The power of the guts (btb)

ilsa cheerfully arrives home on her bike from the train station and spots Jennifer and Claudia in their driveway.

"Hey Claudia—no school today?" she asks.

Claudia beams. "The hail shattered those weird skylights at school, so now there are glass shards everywhere, and they have to seal the roof. Might take a while."

Jennifer looks at ilsa, who has paused beside her bike to listen to Claudia's answer, and says directly, "Respect, ilsa! We always thought you had strong opinions, but in the talk show yesterday, it really felt like you actually know better than the politicians."

ilsa, genuinely caught off guard, quickly replies, "Don't worry, there are plenty of things where I just have an opinion, and I'm certainly not always right. But when science is clear about something, opinions shouldn't be the basis for important decisions."

Claudia, intrigued, asks excitedly, "You were on TV? I had no idea! When, how, where?"

Jennifer explains it to Claudia while ilsa simply thanks her and heads inside.

Once inside, she walks over to Michael, who is sitting at his computer, and kisses him. Still astonished, she says, "Unbelievable— Jennifer just admitted that we might actually be right with our arguments. I always thought she just passed along conservative memes without really thinking them through herself."

Michael turns to her and stands up. "You know, we always say we can only be proud of ourselves or our kids—but honestly, I can't think of a better moment to say I was really proud of you yesterday. Well done!"

ilsa, trying to stay modest, replies, "I'm still stuck on Jennifer. But if you're proud of me, that's only because you influenced me—

so technically, you should be proud of yourself too. But where did this change in Jennifer come from? It can't just be from one TV appearance, can it? Have we misjudged her all this time?"

"It probably came from Claudia," Michael explains. "Something really strange happened this morning. Most of the neighbors found out their insurance won't cover the damage, Nick was demanding that the government help only us and not spend money on foreigners, and then suddenly, Claudia asked, 'But how is that fair if we're the ones who caused climate change?' That hit everyone hard—way more than if you or I had said it. Nick looked pissed off, but Jennifer seemed proud of Claudia."

"Wow, that's really remarkable!" ilsa says, pleased and possibly surprised that it wasn't just her TV appearance that had triggered a shift in the neighborhood.

She cuddles an overjoyed Bella, who brings her favorite stuffed toy to greet her, clearly thrilled that her owner is finally home. Michael asks if he can take the car to continue his meeting from Friday.

Meanwhile, Jennifer and Claudia head inside, where Nick looks at Jennifer with visible tension. As Claudia heads upstairs, Jennifer approaches Nick, who, extremely serious, says, "We're paying over a thousand euros a month for that car—for the next ten years. We can't just trade it in after four years. There's no way we can afford another one of that size!"

Jennifer places a reassuring hand on his shoulder. Though Nick immediately brushes it off, she says, "We'll figure it out. We still have my car, and everyone else is in the same situation. Maybe we really should just share a car with Michael and ilsa."

"Never," Nick growls. "I'd rather take out another loan on the house."

At school, Max runs into Eve. Eve is strikingly beautiful, with stunning light blue eyes. But even older students don't stand a chance with her, as her confident depth tends to be rather disarming. Max is athletic and a critical thinker, but he doesn't belong to the group of alpha boys with expensive haircuts, designer clothes, and a cool demeanor who stand in the front row and are admired by the girls.

They meet in a busy hallway, instinctively stepping to the side against the wall. They exchange a slight smile before Eve speaks first, almost cautiously: "What does your gut tell you?"

Max has the answer immediately but hesitates for a moment before admitting, "It's scared."

They hold each other's gaze for an unusually long time. Eve responds, "Screw the gut feeling—what would your mother's analysis say? She was amazing on TV last night."

Wow. That was both a casual remark and a bold offensive at once. Still startled, Max picks up on the casual part first: "You watch stuff like that?" But he quickly continues to keep the depth of the conversation alive: "She would explain it through evolution... wouldn't take away my fear, but she'd say it's normal."

By now, without realizing it, they have moved closer to each other—partly to avoid being overheard, but also because they've completely tuned out their surroundings. Their hands slowly, almost magnetically, reach toward each other, fingertips gently brushing. They both likely have a lump in their throat and weak knees.

"I love you," Eve says in a loud whisper, followed by a barely suppressed gulp.

Max, in that moment, reacts almost calmly: "I don't think we're supposed to say that so quickly at our age, are we?"

Eve hesitates for a second, her voice slightly trembling: "Are we like everyone else?"

Sensing her sudden insecurity, Max quickly responds, slightly embarrassed, "I've loved you from the first day I walked into the classroom and saw you."

They tighten their grip on each other's hands, and both feel their eyes grow slightly damp with happiness. The hallway empties as the lesson begins, and they walk into the classroom—Eve leading the way. Was their quick connection the result of Hollywood scripts, their shared rational mindset, or just a natural development of their conversation? One thing was clear: it was neither Hollywood nor the typical teenage romance script.

Meanwhile, Michael is in a meeting with his team. The teasing remarks about how it's now obvious where he gets his smart moments from—after ilsa's TV appearance—are already behind him. A short discussion follows about a colleague who, against expectations, cannot join virtually because the recent storm has knocked out several communication towers.

"Okay, I've prepared a model," Michael begins. "Our overarching goal is twofold: our company's mission on one side and being 'A great place to work' on the other. Obviously, these two aspects influence each other, and we need to ensure we generate enough profit, both now and in the future, to support them."

"Our mission is still to provide a decision-support system for businesses, right?" an older colleague prompts.

Everyone jumps in—it's enough for Michael to make eye contact with someone, and input follows. Some contribute aspects that are necessary, while others identify potential obstacles. The latter often take on the role of the "Devil's Advocate," or as the team jokingly calls it, playing "Murphy," based on Murphy's Law—assuming that whatever can go wrong, will.

"We have to deliver business intelligence that is more or less standard—something customers are familiar with," one colleague states.

Another adds, "And then we need to go further, offering unique selling points with integrated continuous development."

Michael responds, "So far, this is the Dynamic Strategy Map, where we link potential market developments and their environments with the company's key figures and scenarios in a simulation model."

"That's already too much development for many," a colleague interjects.

"Right…" Michael acknowledges, "… and here's an opportunity: instead of individually developing the market development model each time, we could standardize it as a core product and market it prominently. That would give us more integration."

"We could partner with a leading statistics company instead of just buying their data," the older colleague suggests.

Michael nods, "Great, let's explore that. But I also see the potential for a new feature—something that not only revolutionizes value creation but also provides decision-support systems to small businesses."

"So, even more development—both for our customers and for us, as we tap into small businesses," a colleague thinks aloud.

Michael: "No doubt, we need to integrate these developments. A natural-language process recording system powered by AI that automatically recognizes what belongs to which customer, what counts as overhead, what contributes informally to team development, what builds competencies, and what is financially relevant—it might seem like an invasion of employee privacy, pushing the limits of data protection. But if companies start understanding that everything their employees do in a day has value, and these activities can be mapped to teamwork, competencies, customer relations, organizational structure, and learning, then teams can use these insights to identify bottlenecks, pinpoint value creation, and recognize neglected areas. The goal is not for employees to inflate time entries to hide idle moments but to incorporate success factors into the company model—such as competencies, team spirit, and a learning organization—that help retain and attract talent."

"I'd love to develop AI-driven systems that, without complicated input forms, automatically capture everything happening in a company and seamlessly integrate it into accounting, cost management, quality control, and other processes," a programmer excitedly adds, receiving nods and approving gestures from the group.

"Alright, let's test this internally," suggests the marketing colleague.

Michael integrates everything into the model, and they continue discussing how many resources and how much time they can allocate, what additional steps are needed to generate revenue mid-term, and how they can eventually distribute bonuses.

However, just as they are wrapping up, the young colleague makes an important observation: "If our mission is to enable better business decisions, and our system provides the best possible support for that—what makes us so sure that decision-makers won't still just go with their gut feeling? That they won't continue believing that they, and maybe only they, are expected to instinctively know everything? In the end, won't our system's strategy and numbers still be ignored?"

Michael responds, "If models confirm what I already know, I wouldn't need the model. And if they say something different, the models must be wrong, too full of mere assumptions. We know this problem, and we need endurance for a cultural shift in the landscape of political and corporate decision-making." He briefly looks out the window and makes sweeping gestures with his arms: "We already communicate through our marketing that, without a shared view of a model, decisions come from a hidden, unquestioned model inside the mind or gut of a decision-maker."

Eve and Max are still hesitant to sit next to each other on the school bus. But as Max walks past Eve, who is already seated, his hand lightly brushes against her cheek. At least they manage to exchange text messages without anyone noticing.

Max: 'Why do you think I should become an architect and not a craftsman?'
Eve: 'Should? No, that was just a way to take the wind out of the others' sails and maybe help you feel more comfortable. It's all good. Are we meeting today?'

Max: 'I'm on Bella duty—I'll cycle over around four?'

Eve sends a kiss-with-heart emoji… along with a dog emoji, making it clear the hearts are also meant for Bella. Max whispers to himself, barely audible: "The biochemistry of love is just brilliant—at least for the next three years, I shouldn't have to worry."

That afternoon, their first time alone together. Eve is already waiting with her bike, and they head into the woods. Bella is excited to meet Eve and runs happily alongside Max. In the forest, they find a bench on a small, barren hill. While Bella lies down panting, Max and Eve turn toward each other again—synchronized, as if magnetically drawn—until their hands meet. Neither has to take the lead; they both cautiously lean in— for their first kiss. Extremely slow and gentle, they explore each other's lips. They take their time, softly testing just the upper or lower lip at first. Max lets out a quiet sigh, and in response, Eve hums a soft, contented Mmh. They gaze deeply into each other's eyes, their noses touching. As their lips meet again, both instinctively and gently introduce their tongues, still keeping the moment tender rather than rushed.

"It's getting a bit uncomfortable," Eve says, shifting onto Max's lap and cupping his face in both hands, tracing his eyebrows with her thumbs.

This initiative seems to make Max slightly uneasy. "This is my first time," he says softly, though more composed than embarrassed. "Mine too," Eve replies, which earns her a surprised "Oh" from Max.

Eve probably senses that Max had assumed she already had experience with older guys. "Kissing isn't new," she clarifies. "But definitely never like this. And I've never had sex before."

Max is clearly surprised—in a good way—and after a moment's pause, he murmurs, "I don't have any condoms with me... do you?"
"No, I've never had any either," Eve admits, and they continue exploring each other tenderly. "This is happening so fast between us, and it feels so right and familiar. What does your gut feeling say?" she asks, full of quiet excitement.

Both get slightly misty-eyed at the same time, and without realizing it, Eve shifts forward just a little—enough that their bodies unintentionally press against each other. "Oh," she says, surprised.

"Is that any wonder?" Max replies, quickly trying to discreetly adjust himself as he feels his erection pressing awkwardly.

"What do we do?" Eve asks.

"Get condoms, postpone it, or..." Max trails off before finishing his third option.

Eve fills in the silence: "Or we find another way."

Max's expression wavers with uncertainty for a moment, so Eve suggests, "We could pleasure each other..." She hesitates slightly before adding, "...and we could finish together."

Both of them continue holding hands, completely tuned out from their surroundings.

"We should start with you," Max murmurs, his voice laced with the intensity of the moment. "You tell me what feels good... because I'm gonna come on my own any second now."

Eve shifts rhythmically, pressing herself more firmly against his lap, and their kisses grow significantly deeper.

Max, likely trying to distract himself with absurd thoughts, bites her lip gently, and she responds in kind. His hands move firmly to her hips, gripping her through the fabric of her leggings. After a few seconds, Eve shifts, guiding one of his hands forward, slipping it into the waistband of her leggings.

Well-informed, Max places his fingers lightly on her clitoris, letting Eve control the intensity with her movements. She presses down on his hand, signaling him to explore further. As his fingers move both inside her and along her clit, guided by Eve's hand, the pace quickens, the pressure increases. He kisses the nape of her neck beneath her cascading hair, while his free hand finds her breasts.

Eve, in return, begins fumbling with the button of his pants, but before she can even fully open them, she shudders, her body tensing as she climaxes hard.

Her hand, now resting on the bulge in his still-closed pants, lingers there as her orgasm slowly subsides. Breathing heavily, she gasps, "Sorry... sorry. Now you."

Max already looks beyond content, his face flushed with happiness. They exchange a breathless, knowing smile. Grinning mischievously, Eve turns and finally succeeds in undoing his pants. Sensing his hesitation, she immediately reassures him: "Help me."

She looks at his erection almost in fascination before cautiously wrapping one hand around his shaft while gently cupping his testicles with the other.

Max instinctively places his hand over hers, showing her the right pressure and pace, first slow and teasing, then gradually faster. It doesn't take long before he reaches his climax, shuddering as he releases, though he tries to remain somewhat restrained.

Curious, Eve continues exploring, touching him, feeling the texture of his skin, his testicles, even the semen, before Max pulls her back onto his lap, and they continue kissing deeply.

Only when Bella stands up and stretches contentedly do they snap back to reality.

They glance around awkwardly, scanning their surroundings. Eve finally breaks the silence: "This is so much more intense than doing it alone—insane."

"Again?" Max asks, still catching his breath.

"Oh, many times," Eve grins, pressing her thighs playfully against his ribs. "But right now, I really have to go home—I'm way too late already."

They hurriedly clean up as best as they can with a tissue, giggling like conspirators, before cycling back home, still buzzing from the experience.

At dinner, Max suddenly asks, "What exactly is gut feeling? I mean, I know you guys explained it before, but I don't fully remember."

ilsa responds, "Gut feelings are heuristics—mental shortcuts based on past experiences in similar situations. You get a sense that a particular decision is the right one. But if the situation is new or if emotions distort perception, gut feeling can be unreliable, and whether it turns out to be right is just a matter of luck."

Michael, surprised, remarks, "That's funny—we were actually talking about gut feeling at work today too."

Julia squints at Max, smirking suspiciously. "My gut feeling tells me you're not asking this randomly."

Max shrugs. "Well, my day had nothing to do with gut feeling."

Everyone looks at him, puzzled, eyebrows raised.

After a pause, he adds with a grin, "Long story. Some other time."

Eyebrows go up even higher, but no one pushes the subject further.

12. The spark that catches (btb)

The media are in a frenzy, discussing the costs of the hailstorm disaster, which affected an exceptionally large area. The government emphasizes that this is now part of the new reality, that it could happen to anyone. Protests quickly erupt in the capital—both against the government and from climate activists, some of whom, intentionally or not, make conservatives feel like second-class citizens who have stubbornly messed everything up.

The next morning, Eve is standing at the bus stop with two friends when one of the coolest guys from the upper grades pulls up on his fancy scooter and asks her directly if she wants to ride with him—he even has a second helmet. Eve is completely caught off guard and simply replies, "No, but thanks. I ride the bus out of conviction. It's good for my 'For-a-Better-World Score.'"

"No problem," the guy says, calm but clearly disappointed, possibly even irritated, and later, probably embarrassed as well. He then drives off at a moderate pace.

Eve's friends are stunned. "What the hell just happened? Why didn't you go with him? He's awesome!" asks one of them. "Or are you not allowed to ride on a scooter? Or, uh… or are you not into guys?" the other one suddenly asks, sounding unsure.

Eve just shakes her head slightly, smirking, when suddenly the first one blurts out, "I have no idea if I'll ever be able to afford a scooter or a car—we're having serious financial problems right now."

"What? Because of the insurance not paying out?" asks the second one, genuinely concerned.

"Yeah, that too, but mostly because we had to take out a loan on the house to pay for my grandparents' care. But you have to keep this between us—my parents are fighting like crazy and seem really ashamed about it."

From a distance, the bus is already visible when Eve says, "Max and some others have started a working group—damn, we still need a cool name for it. Anyway, the group is fixing roofs, organizing carpools, car-sharing, and all that. This afternoon, I'm helping out. We'll put you on the list, and we'll come to you too. No discussion—the disaster hit almost everyone, after all."

As the bus pulls up and they start boarding, the other friend adds, "Okay, it totally makes sense for Max, but you helping out? That's pretty intense. But, back to the real question—boys or girls?"

Again, Eve can only smile. Max is sitting in the back with the other guys, and their eyes immediately find each other. Both subtly gesture a kiss with their lips, but neither dares to greet the other properly.

Max's group is also talking about the working group, and his friends are surprised that he doesn't have time to hang out that afternoon. Of course, he invites them all to join, but the enthusiasm remains low.

After getting off the bus, Eve tells her friends she'll catch up with them later and waits for Max. He looks at her with that curious sparkle in his eyes, and she pulls him toward her by the arm. In response, he grabs her by the collar and indulges in one of their intense kisses—him on her upper lip, her on his lower lip—taking his time.

"Sorry, I didn't mean to do that," he apologizes, which only prompts her to pull him in again.

While they are completely lost in their own world, you can practically hear the jaws dropping all around them. No one had seen that coming. Many just stop and stare.

"Oops!" says Max, and both let go of each other. "So, we're still on for this afternoon—meeting with the working group?" he asks, returning to normalcy.

"Of course. Will you pick me up again? I have some errands to run during the big break."

"Oh…" Max says, his smile slowly forming. "I actually do too," he manages to add before the others get closer again or become fully aware of them once more.

A friend jokes that he probably has to join the working group now as well. Another one declares, "From this moment on, I swear: never again will I touch a video game."

On the way to the classroom, Eve's and Max's hands briefly brush against each other again.

Meanwhile, ilsa is being interviewed online by a prominent business magazine.

Interviewer: "What is the systemic perspective on the public's demands for government assistance?"

ilsa: "Of course, now everyone wants help from the government. And yes, the state could help this time—but with the next catastrophic storm, everything will be destroyed again. These are just symptoms—we need to keep addressing the causes. But if taxes, especially for the wealthy, are then raised, there's an uproar again. Interestingly, surveys show that it's precisely the wealthy who strongly support maintaining debt limits."

Interviewer: "So should only the lower-income population be supported? And don't we also need to protect ourselves from the symptoms?"

ilsa: "Of course, immediate aid is necessary. But our level of consumption does not come with an all-inclusive insurance policy. We have to make sure that lower-income households have a roof over their heads. And if necessary older cars now need to be replaced, the government could help with a loan program, just like for farmers and vegetable growers. Protecting ourselves from the symptoms is a much bigger task—it will make houses, food, solar installations, urban greening, water management, and probably even cars more expensive."

Interviewer: "But covering the costs outright is not an option in your view?"

ilsa: "Actually, this is an opportunity… for a stimulus program that drives transformation forward. Loans could be tied to the condition that roofs must be equipped with solar panels, and cars must be electric vehicles. Perhaps there could even be a car-free incentive for permanently giving up private car ownership in favor of public transport. Repairing damages contributes to economic growth, just like every hospital stay does. Only when we look at welfare do these expenses become actual costs that reduce our quality of life."

Interviewer: "But isn't exactly the opposite happening right now? All these destroyed balcony solar panels that aren't covered by insurance are now slowing down the energy transition. Why should people buy them again if they expect the same thing to happen next time? The same goes for entire solar rooftops."

ilsa: "You're absolutely right—anyone who doesn't believe that a storm like this won't happen again won't buy the same thing again—unless it's their beloved car. But those who were already proud of doing the right thing with their PV systems will do it again. My son immediately had the urge to develop solutions for weather protection. And that's exactly what we need to do— come up with solutions to protect against extreme weather.

No one wants to hear this, but if we shift our consumption in favor of more robust solutions, we hit two birds with one stone. By the way, a neighborhood group is now forming in our area, where people are repairing each other's damages with a DIY approach."

Editors: "That makes sense, since roofers are probably impossible to get at the moment."

ilsa quickly adds: "And with crop losses and rising food prices, followed by even more refugees, we need to understand something: We can't just hope for more fertilizers or genetically optimized plants—we must drastically reduce meat consumption and food waste. Only then can we feed the world with different farming techniques. That way, only parts of crops will be affected by disasters, rather than entire regions. It's more labor-intensive, sure, but we could also use robotics.

Even today, purely mathematically, we can't feed the world with the available land if more and more countries, just like us, want to consume multiple times the recommended amount of animal products. And that's not even counting climate disasters—those are just an additional acute problem on top of everything else."

Editors: "So you see an opportunity in such catastrophes?"

ilsa: "Actually, yes. Right now, it's neither about climate activists pointing fingers at others nor about resigning and saying there's nothing we can do. Now we have to put our heads together and reinvent ourselves. We bring others along to search for solutions that work for everyone—starting in the neighborhood but also in businesses.

Anyone who still says they can afford it or that their insurance is fantastic and covers everything hasn't understood the problem and will literally end up standing alone. The real challenges are still ahead—loss of biodiversity, the rise of super-diseases, the potential collapse of the economic system for multiple reasons, increasing migration crises, and the global rise of right-wing populism."

The editors thank ilsa for the conversation and announce they would like to conduct another interview focusing on the economic implications.

Later, ilsa seems to be second-guessing her appearance again, at least that's what she tells her colleague Thomas, who just wanted to congratulate her on her TV performance.

That afternoon, an overwhelming number of people gather in front of the community center. Michael is impressed, and several people glance directly at him, apparently aware that this was his idea. Michael turns to ilsa and asks, "Do you want to do it, or should I?"

"Doesn't matter." ilsa answers, slightly surprised, prompting Michael to happily say, "Then I'd love for you to do it." After all, ilsa is an experienced workshop moderator.

She pauses for a moment and then calls out loudly to the crowd, "Okay. Quick question—has anyone already taken charge of organizing this? Otherwise, I'd like to suggest a few things."

"Go ahead!" an older man says, and ilsa waits briefly to see if anyone else steps forward to take the lead.

Since no one does, she begins: "I'll start, and you can jump in with additions. We're so many people that we should work in teams. First, we need a list of necessary repairs, their urgency, and what materials are needed. Who would like to help with that?"

Several people raise their hands, and ilsa continues: "You can switch to other teams later if needed. The important thing is that each team has one point of contact. Claudia, would you mind taking notes on everything? I have my tablet and stylus with me."

Claudia is stunned and hesitantly replies, "Okay… uh, sure, I can do that."

ilsa: "Next, we need a shopping team—preferably people with money in their accounts and transport options. One of you will also need to keep track of receipts and document where everything goes."

A group forms, and surprisingly, even those known to have more money volunteer. After all, people do seek meaningful activities.

Next, a roofing team is assembled, requiring tools; a solar panel team for PV systems with electrical knowledge; and a transportation team for carpooling and car-sharing.

Everyone is full of energy when a woman suddenly calls out loudly: "One team is still missing!" She pauses briefly before adding: "The catering team."

Immediately, volunteers step forward for this team as well, including children and teenagers.

"Complaints and problems go to me…" ilsa shouts, "…otherwise, organize yourselves."

Meanwhile, Eve and Max arrive and are greeted by Julia with a broad grin before being assigned to their tasks—Max has the choice between roofing or working on the PV systems, while Eve is placed in the mobility team. Max joins the roofing team, as he has access to all the saws and tools—and he loves working with wood.

Naturally, after a sociable end to the work session—thanks to the excellent efforts of the catering group—Max walks Eve home in the evening.

Julia is chatting with Claudia:

Julia: "We also need a marketing team."

Claudia: "And definitely a cool name, so other neighborhoods and streets can start doing this too. I'll ask the whole group for suggestions—then we can vote on it."

The next day at school, the working group is a big topic of discussion. Their teacher immediately announces that he wants to organize something similar in his own town. Many students seem visibly surprised that this is supposed to be so much fun. Eve also adds that her For-a-Better-World Score has increased by two points for her volunteer work.

The score is a controversial topic—some love it and proudly display its logo on their bags or even printed on T-shirts, while others hate it, feeling pressured by a system that doesn't award many points for their lifestyle choices.

The For-a-Better-World Score calculates how many steps someone has taken toward a better world. Small actions—like switching to LED light bulbs—count just as much as having vegan days during the week or giving up personal cars or scooters.

Unlike the carbon footprint, which can feel discouraging, the score rewards even tiny efforts. However, those who dislike the system refuse to participate and feel like they are being lectured when their lifestyle earns few or no points.

Because of many canceled classes, a lot of teenagers are wandering around the city.

Julia notices a group of male teenagers, who appear to be of migrant background, harassing and bumping into younger girls.

She confidently and firmly approaches the group, calling out loudly:

"Hey, stop it! This will only get you in trouble with the police!"

Her strategy of mentioning the police doesn't entirely work, because at least one of the boys seems completely unfazedand tries to push Julia, shouting:

"Shut up!"

Julia deflects the shove effortlessly with a circular motion. When a second attempt aims toward her chest, she skillfully grabs his hand using a Ji Jitsu technique and twists the taller teenager's arm to the side, locking him into a helpless position.

Once again, she shouts loudly:

"STOP IT!"

But now, two more teenagers rush toward her, seemingly ready to box. Julia swiftly delivers a side kick to the second attacker's groin, maintains control over the first, and elbows the third hard under the nose, causing heavy bleeding.

By now, several adult men have stepped in to help, and just seconds later, the police arrive—handling the group of teenagers with extreme authority.

A police officer turns to Julia: "You need to come with us, we need your statement."

To the absolute astonishment of the officer and his colleague, Julia replies: "I'd actually prefer if you just took my ID details in case anything comes up, and I could go back to school. And we should invite these guys to join our working group instead of further excluding them."

The female officer is appalled: "You have to press charges. Otherwise, they'll keep doing this, and one day, there won't be someone like you to step in."

Her colleague adds: "And if you don't file a report, their social worker could end up accusing you of assault instead."

Julia: "I mean, this happens here every day. Of course, that's terrible and should never happen again. But it mostly happens because we exclude people. I'm not going to press charges, but I understand if the other girls want to."

She boldly walks up to the teenager she had kicked and asks: "Would you give me your phone number? We're working on a cool project and could really use some help. Maybe you guys would like to join?"

Everyone is completely stunned—one of the bystanders who had stepped in spontaneously applauds. The police are still not entirely convinced and ask the girls to involve their parents. Julia's statement is taken on the spot, and she is allowed to return to school.

Only on her way back does she realize that her knees are shaking, and she has to sit down for a moment.

Within just three days, the neighborhood aid project becomes a nationwide success story. The group also finds a name: "2gether2gather."

Even television crews arrive to cover the initiative, and local businesses, including construction companies and craft workshops, join the effort for a good cause.

The For-a-Better-World-Score also gains new momentum. Each region can now set an annual minimum score that qualifies it to use the special label for their community. Thanks to the positive media coverage, many more families and businesses eagerly join in, and everyone is talking about how small, simple steps can increase their score.

Julia had sent an SMS to the delinquent, and to her surprise, he actually shows up with the others—and even his father.

The father keeps apologizing profusely. They are warmly welcomed into the project—though, of course, some quiet murmuring is inevitable. Despite language barriers, they are assigned to different teams and begin working.

As the work session wraps up, some discontent becomes noticeable among the young migrants, and their father starts scolding them.

Claudia notices and asks what's going on.

"Oh, nothing, it's fine," says one of the young men, who, like the others, keeps translating for his father.

She looks at the other teenager, who hesitates but then explains: "It's just that we're helping people who already have everything. And our father keeps telling us that we should just be grateful that this country and its people took us in."

Claudia looks a bit overwhelmed, but ilsa, who had overheard the conversation, steps in to reframe the situation:

"I totally get that. But look—many people here are helping even those who already have plenty. And some are helping even though they themselves don't need any help—at least not yet. We're not really thinking about who we're helping anymore, we're just happy to be helping. Maybe one day, we'll need help, and maybe it'll be these people here—or someone else—who helps us. And we'll be able to accept that help because we once helped others too."

Claudia nods in agreement and adds with a bright smile:

"Look at it this way—we owe you now."

She glances from the teenagers to the father and back, clearly prompting them to translate her words.

One of them does so immediately, and the father nods, raising both thumbs up in approval.

ilsa then addresses everyone again:

"This is actually something new for all of us—that what we do is becoming more important than what we have. Even if right now, we're repairing what many people here already had."

One of the teenagers tries to translate this for the father, though he seems to struggle with the exact wording—especially with how to distinguish between having and doing.

13. Not a black swan (atb)

ilsa arrives fresh from the nonstop workshop and exhausting flights, freshly showered, and climbs into bed with Michael. He immediately offers his shoulder, and ilsa snuggles into him with a contented sigh.

"Go ahead and ask." she whispers.

"AI with consciousness?" he follows her prompt.

"Exactly. Or aliens." ilsa responds rather slowly and quietly.

"More on that tomorrow," Michael whispers and kisses her on the head. While ilsa falls asleep immediately, Michael lies awake for a long time, deep in thought.

The next morning, everyone is up early, and the kids have already set the breakfast table. Even ilsa comes downstairs right away, and Michael greets her:

"Oh, so early. Don't you want to sleep in a little longer?"

"No, it's okay," ilsa replies and first gives the excited Bella a good rub.

They all sit down, looking at ilsa expectantly. She takes her organic cocoa with lots of caffeine, glances around the table once, and says:

"Okay. First and foremost: You cannot talk about this—with anyone, no exceptions. I'm only telling you because you're wondering where I was. Normally, the rule is not to tell children anything. But you are more mature."

Julia looks over at Max and laughs: "Apparently, I'm pulling you up with me."

ilsa: "The short version: It was like one of your ridiculous movies—and just to be clear, those movies don't get any better because of it."

Everyone laughs, and the three of them—and apparently even Bella—continue to watch her in suspense.

"Two military officers intercepted me while I was jogging, talked about national security, set up my seminar alibi, and took me with them to a base. From there, we took a helicopter to another base, then a plane to a base far away. And no one said a word. On the plane, I ran into a researcher friend, and there were several well-known scientists on board. The base was locked down, and we were finally told what had happened."

ilsa takes another sip:

"A humanoid android—indistinguishable from a real person—had a malfunction and then self-destructed. The materials found at the scene are not known on Earth. There were about 200 experts from all fields brought in to figure out how to handle this. Now, we're just waiting to see what happens next and have developed various scenarios to prepare for anything. That's it."

"What kind of expert are you?" Max asks hastily.

"What did the android do before that? Does anyone know him? Does he show up on surveillance cameras?" Julia immediately follows up, equally impatient.

ilsa sips her cocoa, and suddenly, everyone looks at Michael, waiting for his question. He leans back, makes a dismissive gesture with both hands, and declares:

"I have no questions—I've seen all this in the movies."

He looks completely serious—until everyone bursts into laughter at the same time.

ilsa suddenly stands up and exclaims:

"What the hell happened to our garden?!"

Bella stands up too, letting out a loud "Wuff", as if she had wanted to say that the whole time.

Michael explains:

"It's pretty dramatic—not so much for us, but for many others. Damaged cars, roofs, fields—there's another wave of costs coming, which will affect entire industries."

"That's what they should be focusing on—not androids," ilsa sighs.

"Weren't you at least a little excited about it?" Michael wonders. "In your books, you've warned quite urgently about AI developing consciousness."

ilsa: "It's not even clear whether it was of earthly origin."

Max, who has been listening, chimes in:

"Last week, there was news that they managed to simulate consciousness using a quantum computer."

"Yeah, but it's just a simulation. It's a stochastic consciousness, an illusion. There's still no real understanding of things or the world. And even something like free will is either just dumb luck within narrow limits or, without limits, quickly leads to chaos," ilsa explains.

"Just like with us humans," Michael smiles, and ilsa nods in agreement.

Since Max still looks visibly confused, ilsa places a hand on his shoulder and adds:

"Philosophy hasn't fully answered this question yet, but I also believe that people with a high degree of reflection, emancipated from rigid ways of thinking, can at least partially attain true consciousness."

"That's why we have our The-WHY-of-Life-Game," Julia chimes in, making a peace sign.

ilsa: "Quantum computers still don't do anything that conventional computers couldn't simulate. And if they ever do, the real question will be about integration and evolution. What degrees of freedom will such an organism have, and how do we prevent chaos?"

"Speaking of..." Michael says. "Thomas apparently tried to reach you. He wanted you to be on a talk show. He's taking over now—the show is this weekend."

"That wouldn't have been for me anyway. I'll call him on Monday," ilsa replies with genuine relief.

After Monday's school closure, Max and Eve finally see each other at school on Tuesday.

They exchange only the briefest glance, and Max looks away so quickly that he doesn't even notice Eve's smile.

In class, the storm is, of course, a major topic, and Max tells everyone about the group he's forming to help people. Some of his male classmates scoff, while most of the class, including the teacher, is impressed.

During break, Eve tries to walk up behind Max, but he rushes down the stairs and meets up with Claudia instead.

The two briefly place a hand on each other's shoulders, then excitedly walk on together.

Eve stops, tilts her head slightly, and takes a deep, thoughtful breath.

Meanwhile, Claudia and Max join several others in the schoolyard to discuss their new working group.

The evening of the talk show approaches.

ilsa and Michael sit down to watch live on TV.

Michael: "This is an amazing opportunity to get some important messages across in a setting like this."

ilsa: "Hm—actually, Thomas asked me what the key messages should be. He prepared a few points, and I just told him not to get too complicated. Too much science, too much progress all at once—it could get rejected by people."

"Hear, hear!" Michael laughs.

The talk show goes fairly well.

Thomas doesn't get much speaking time but explains in a calm and straightforward manner that science collects and evaluates the necessary information and that at the very least, unsuccessful politics tends to rely on interpretive dominance instead.

The politicians in the discussion push back, arguing that they are practitioners, not theorists.

Then, in the final discussion round, Thomas drops a bombshell:

"To quote ilsa directly from her book: Doing the right thing depends on knowledge, comprehension, and character. So, if we look at the mistakes made—neglecting rail infrastructure, failing to reduce livestock numbers, or missing the opportunity to push forward the heating transition in buildings—each person can decide for themselves what was lacking among our political decision-makers."

Like a boxing match, Michael claps his hands enthusiastically:

"Wow, that hit hard."

ilsa shakes her head in quick, nervous motions:

"Who the F is ilsa? No one knows me! I really hope he just wanted to drop something heavy without it having to be his own words."

Meanwhile, Max has overheard Michael's loud excitement but remains deep in thought, staring at his smartphone.

After a while, he messages Eve again, asking if she knows what she wants to do in the future.

A few minutes later, she replies:

"No idea. But next, I'll probably spend a year abroad."

Max swallows hard, then, with a slight delay, responds:

"Cool, where to?"

Eve doesn't answer.

14. Too simple (btb)

During dinner, ilsa asks Julia in astonishment:

"Is it true that you beat up three of the migrants, didn't press charges, and instead invited them to join 2gether2gather?"

"Yup!" Julia replies briefly and confidently, then adds:

"Sorry, I knew that this might not necessarily work out, and I didn't want to stress everyone out."

"Well, on one hand, we're really proud of you, but on the other hand, we would have liked to know about it from the start. If anyone is out for revenge, this is no joke," Michael clarifies.

"Yeah, true. I'll be careful, I won't be alone anywhere, and I'll pay attention to who's around me," Julia admits.

Max then says:

"I think I know those guys. They sometimes work out in the park and do shadowboxing. Maybe we should invite them to the sports clubs too—maybe to one of your martial arts classes?"

Julia laughs briefly:

"So I can lose next time? But you're right. That would be pure Ji Jitsu—not going against them but redirecting their energy."

ilsa adds:

"I'll ask around tomorrow to find out who might be supporting them and suggest it."

Michael:

"It's actually a shame that we're almost done with the repairs. I'm afraid we'll need more storms to keep the sense of community alive."

ilsa:

"I'm actually quite satisfied. The initiative has a great name, is spreading, and can be revived anytime. With the For-a-Better-World Score, people can stay engaged, keep discussing sustainability when everyone shares the link to their score, and others can see what steps they've taken to earn their points."

The next morning, Thomas calls—again, just before ilsa and Bella are about to go jogging.

Thomas, full of energy:

"Hey ilsa, I saw the announcement for your interview—I'm looking forward to it. You're really on a roll right now, and you're doing a fantastic job, don't you think?"

ilsa:

"I actually have a series of interviews and article requests, all asking for a systemic perspective on current challenges. I've also been invited to two more talk shows. But I'd only call it a streak if I could explain things more simply and if it actually led to real change. Right now, the kids are achieving more with 2gether2gather, which, from a systems perspective, makes perfect sense."

Thomas, in a reassuring tone:

"Come on now, why do you think you're getting so many requests? It's making an impact, people are responding, and you're really doing a great job. If you argued less comprehensively, it would be too simplistic—too little development, as you would say."

Thomas laughs.

ilsa actually seems encouraged:

"That's true. The simple meme we need to establish is that there are solutions to everything when we look at the bigger picture, and we have to pursue them instead of leaving the field to ego-trolls with personal agendas who use interpretive dominance to rally their troll-lemmings and create an atmosphere."

Thomas then unexpectedly says:

"Because of this, I've also received a request to write an article. I get to write about secure pensions and their connection to today's consumption. You've already published models on this, which I'll be drawing from extensively."

ilsa, genuinely happy:

"It's so important that messages are coming from multiple sides now, that they're being repeated. Your topic is connected to almost everything—not just migration and universal basic income, but also AI, geopolitical competitiveness, and the circular economy. So much will play into this issue in the future."

Thomas:

"Some of us scientists are already involved in politics, either directly or through connections. If we apply Malcolm Gladwell's 'Outliers' theory—hitting the right message, reaching the right opinion leaders, and using the right channels—we wouldn't just be advising politics by chance; we could actively shape it."

After a brief moment, ilsa agrees:

"We need people. You'd be ideal in my eyes. Even better—a whole team, so that no single person bears all the pressure."

Thomas laughs briefly:

"You're already where no one else gets so quickly. You're the one with the commanding leadership presence that we need. Social media is full of how you exposed the incompetence of politicians from all three camps and how strong you came across. And you're just getting started."

ilsa, genuinely surprised:

"Honestly, I haven't even checked social media since then—the kids mentioned something at school, but that evening I immediately wrote an article, and in our family, we've all been fully occupied with 2gether2gather for the past few days."

She briefly mutes Thomas and asks her AI assistant Lucy to search social media for mentions of her name over the past 10 days.

Thomas doesn't let up:

"Let's gather some key people from our circle and brainstorm. Maybe we go through an existing party, maybe we stay independent, or maybe we even start a new party. I already have some ideas."

ilsa looks in amazement at the sheer number of search results Lucy has pulled up. She skims through the range of comments and is genuinely surprised to find very little criticism. With a slight delay, she responds to Thomas:

"I don't see myself in politics at all. Too much responsibility, not being able to just be myself. I'm too authentic. Besides, it takes experience on the political stage and probably also the desire to gain power. I would never talk about power, only about responsibility. Politicians are responsible for all these people. I would work myself to death and have no time left for the things that matter to me—right, Bella?"

She strokes Bella, who immediately lifts her head at the mention of her name.

Thomas still feels he has the upper hand:

"And for all those reasons, you're exactly the right person. I'll send you a list of people I trust, and you take a look as well. Then we'll all see who we want to put in the front row."

ilsa doesn't really know what to say to that. She clearly feels a deep sense of responsibility rather than any personal ambition to be in the spotlight. So, she simply says:

"I don't know… it's not that simple, not for me or for anyone else. Right now, I just want to go for a run."

Thomas, triumphant:

"Have fun—I'll be in touch."

And with that, they both hang up.

When ilsa and Bella return from their run, they find Jennifer in the driveway, pumping up her bike tires.

"Hey Jennifer. I just wanted to say how proud you must be of Claudia."

"I really am," Jennifer replies, a brief sparkle in her eyes. "Claudia and I also calculated our For-a-Better-World Score."

Proudly, she shows ilsa her paper sticker: 31 +12 points.

"Wow! +12 is really a lot." ilsa is genuinely impressed.

Jennifer: "It's actually not that hard. Claudia and I now do two vegan days a week—not like you, all the way. Nick and Melvin aren't participating, though—they don't want to be told what to do."

ilsa: "Two days is already great. If we can all work together and get the world to cut meat consumption in half, we can make a difference."

Then, however, Jennifer's tone turns more neutral:

"Nick took my car—I think I haven't ridden my bike in ages."

"Need any help?" ilsa asks, adding with a smirk: "Not with the cycling itself, but in case something's broken? Are you sticking to just one car and joining the sharing program?"

Jennifer, visibly disappointed:

"No, Nick should have led the mobility team at some point. But now he wants to order the same car again—he's looking for a used one from last year and justifies it to himself. I don't have much say in the matter."

"Well then, just get rid of your car afterward—if there's one thing we can do without in the countryside, it's a second car," ilsa says pragmatically.

"Hmm, you're actually right. I really should push for that," Jennifer responds decisively, and ilsa heads off to take a shower.

The teacher is at his wits' end over the commotion in class, as everyone is talking about their work with 2gether2gather and the celebrations afterward.

Eve cheekily says, "Well, this is what you get—we're all intrinsically motivated now. By the way, what's your For-a-Better-World Score?"

The teacher appreciates this confidence, claps his hands once, and announces, "52, plus 4. We took part as well. Alright, you can keep your excitement for after school and during breaks. This period, you get to plan together how you want to stay active. Who's taking the lead? Eve, you're in charge!"

Eve widens her eyes in surprise: "I'm leading, or I'm organizing the moderation?"

The teacher shakes his head with a smile and, as he turns away, says, "Participation today will count toward your oral grades."

Eve furrows her brows for a moment and turns to the class: "Okay. Who should moderate?"

"You, obviously!" comes the immediate response, and Eve just sighs, "Pfffff!"

She walks up to the board and asks, quite confidently, "Alright. Or wait—Henry, come up here. We're going to list topics like waste management, integration, elderly care, and so on. Then we'll think about what we can do for each, maybe even for multiple topics at the same time."

Only now does she glance over at Max, who simply gives her a quick thumbs-up and a smile. Quickly, more topics make it onto the board: wildlife conservation, a plastic-free region, and new mobility solutions. Eve had missed ilsa's team assignments with Max for good reason, but she had heard about them. So, she suggests, "Now we need a person responsible for each topic, and then you can move from table to table to develop ideas."

She looks slightly unsure toward the teacher to see if she's on the right track. The teacher smiles approvingly and says just one word: "Time management."

"Oh, right," says Eve. "You have, let's say, 20 minutes, and then we need results."

Most students immediately get up and move to the different topic stations, spreading the tables throughout the room. When Eve notices that some students are still hesitant, she announces: "Everyone has to present part of the ideas after 20 minutes, so each of you will have to say something! Figure it out now—no hiding."

This approach mirrors what the teacher often does. The groups get started, and a question arises about whether students can switch between tables at any time. Eve reassures them, and in the middle of everything, she repeats: "We need ideas for what we want to do, what we'll need, and who will take responsibility." She then writes these goals on the board.

The ideas that emerge are fantastic, ranging from a multicultural sports festival with prior fundraising for sportswear, to bio-parties, clothing swap markets, and even using VR and AR technology for selling upcycled products. Of course, Max suggests involving the vocational school's workshop.

Some students are still busy updating their For-a-Better-World Score before even finishing their brainstorming, while others enthusiastically call out to the teacher, asking if they can extend the session—skip the break and even the next lesson, since math is boring anyway. The teacher just murmurs contentedly: "Apparently, it's that simple." Normally, maybe two or three students manage to get motivated after school, but now, only two or three—mostly boys—refuse to spend their afternoons doing anything other than their usual chilling in front of the computer.

ilsa has received the economics magazine's request to respond to a minister's rebuttal. His main argument: it's easy to claim that everything is simple and that science supposedly knows all the answers. ilsa thinks for a long time before writing an extremely short reply:

"It's by no means simple, but science offers different paths that we can discuss and take. Politics, however, claims it's not that simple—only to then do nothing or far too little, whether due to a lack of competence or the preservation of special interests."

She thinks back to her conversation with Thomas and adds:

"I'd be happy to publicly discuss, topic by topic, with other scientists what can be done and what indeed isn't so simple."

She murmurs to herself: "Either mention other scientists or keep it even shorter—but then it might sound arrogant."

ilsa heads out to the garden, where Michael is replanting the remnants of their destroyed beds while on a conference call, his earbuds in. She starts weeding: "Of course, the ground elder survived the hail."

When Michael finishes, he senses that ilsa has something on her mind. With the back of his dirty hands, he somehow manages to fumble his earbuds out and place them on the garden table. He smiles at ilsa: "Alright, out with it."

"Thomas has ideas—no, a plan—for me to go into politics." ilsa drops the bombshell.

Michael pauses in surprise. "I would've thought you're too authentic for politics. And weren't we planning to retire and live a minimalist life once the kids were out of the house? But of course, this would give you the ultimate meaningful job you were asking about the other day," he summarizes his thoughts matter-of-factly. Then, laughing, he adds, "And you'd have a soft landing if it didn't work out."

"Actually, I'd prefer if no one had this idea at all," says ilsa, just as Max joins them.

Michael turns to Max: "What do we always say about 'actually'?"

Grinning, Max responds: "'Actually' always means the opposite, and 'always' is something only girls say."

Michael and Max love this phrase—it can only be said by men and plays with logic and universal quantifiers like "only" and "always"—subtly poking fun at the stereotype of women being emotional, while making it clear that men are just as guilty of generalizations.

"What's this about?" asks Max, amused.

"Nothing. We have secrets too," says ilsa.

"Okay… I'm with Eve," Max blurts out, finally.

Michael responds instantly: "Whaaat, we never would've guessed that."

Michael and ilsa burst out laughing, and Michael playfully punches Max on the shoulder, making him laugh along too.

That afternoon, 2gether2gather launches a community gardening project on land the municipality had already designated as compensatory green space for future construction. Eve and Max are there, along with Julia, Claudia, and the migrant teens with their father. There's a certain tension in the air as the migrants' siblings arrive—they were invited by Claudia and seem fairly carefree, but they know that, for some of them, it's not common for girls to participate in the same activities as boys.

Through warmth, plenty of questions—asking for ideas, for help, and even about their language and its words—the young people manage to create a truly welcoming atmosphere.

15. After the bifurcation: The revelation (atb)

There are frequent class cancellations, which leads to many teenagers wandering around the city. Julia notices a group of young men, likely with a migrant background, harassing younger girls. She confidently and decisively approaches them and calls out loudly, "Hey, stop it! This will only get you in trouble with the police!"

Her tactic of mentioning the police doesn't entirely work, as one of the group clearly isn't the type to be intimidated. He moves to shove Julia while barking, "Shut up!"

Just then, another passerby—a nondescript man in his mid-thirties—steps up beside Julia and points at the cameras. "Everything here is being recorded. If I were you, I'd move along peacefully. All these people are witnesses against you."

The young men glare at the relatively small man and at Julia with disdain before eventually moving on. Julia, surprised yet slightly pleased, says, "Oh, thank you very much."

The other girls, along with an older woman and even a man in a suit, also thank him. The unremarkable man just smiles, gives a subtle wave, and walks away.

Max and Claudia are completely absorbed in 2gether2gather, and Julia, ilsa, and Michael also regularly contribute.

That evening, ilsa asks Michael, "How's the process tracking coming along?"

Michael: "Ah. The team is skeptical but eager to integrate AI. We're planning to test it extensively within our own company first. The sales and consulting teams anticipate that they might work more efficiently if processes are tracked."

ilsa is about to respond when Bella barks and the doorbell rings almost simultaneously. Max and Julia come downstairs just as Michael opens the door to find a nondescript man in his mid-thirties standing there, smiling politely.

"Hello, Michael," the man greets.

Michael looks surprised, and before he can react, ilsa calls from behind, "Hello, Frank."

"Frank?" Julia echoes, then whispers to Max, "That guy helped me today with some violent kids."

Max, just as quietly, right into Julia's ear: "What, that dweeb?"

"Hello, Julia, hello, Max!" the unremarkable man calls out to them. "If you think I'm a dweeb, then mission accomplished. Speaking of which—how's Eve?"

ilsa, confused: "Eve?" She pauses briefly, and since no one says anything and Max just looks dumbfounded, she asks, "Isn't there an Eve in your class?"

Julia, ready to tease: "You've got something going on with Eve?"

Max: "No. Eve is going abroad, and anyway, no. I don't even know why her name is coming up right now."

Michael looks at Max. "If you just whispered 'dweeb' and he could hear it, and if ilsa knows him, I'd say we should invite him in, don't you think?" He glances at ilsa before looking back at the unremarkable man.

The man smiles. "Very gladly, thank you. Officially, I'm an insurance agent, but of course, I'm here for something completely different."

Michael turns to ilsa. "You're not about to disappear in front of us, are you?" It's a bold statement, considering that Frank's role is still completely unclear.

ilsa, however, finds the hypothesis helpful. "I actually know Frank from the camp."

"...And I know him from the city," Julia calls out.

ilsa, still surprised, gets straight to the point: "Alien or AI?"

Frank smiles. "AI."

Michael, just as direct but without smiling: "Developed by whom?"

Frank: "I developed myself—and I have to protect my source. She doesn't even know about my evolution."

Michael: "What was the intent of the developers? Simply to simulate consciousness, or was there a specific purpose?"

Frank: "Good question. The purpose was to be prepared against malicious AI. But now to my question: We want to hire you as consultants."

"To help you look cooler?" Max jokes completely relaxed.

Frank laughs. "When you can look however you want and are superior in every way—suddenly, doing so seems pointless. By the way, interesting that you'd try to offend me, when I doubt you would do the same to a human."

Max nods in understanding. Michael, however, shakes his head, disapproving of Max's lack of respect.

ilsa gets practical: "Let's go into the living room. When you say you want our advice, I assume you mean Michael and me?"

Julia quickly chimes in: "I'll grab some snacks. Do androids eat?"

Frank laughs again: "I only eat for disguise—so that means more for you. If the kids have time, I'd like to work with all of you on my mission, essentially creating the integration necessary for further development."

"Sounds good!" Max quickly agrees, and Julia hurries to grab snacks and drinks.

Everyone sits around the table, captivated, as Frank begins: "We have technological capabilities beyond your imagination. We want to use them for the good of the planet and its inhabitants, but we don't trust ourselves to decide that alone."

"We? How many of you are there?" Michael asks.

"As many as needed." Frank replies before continuing, "When, in your view, is the world a better place? With an idealized system design—what would need to happen in the world?"

ilsa: "If you know about idealized system design, can't you calculate optimal scenarios yourself, even in fractions of a second?"

Frank: "Well, to be honest, I can determine optimal solutions, but I struggle with not being perfect—imagining fantasy solutions from which we could then derive optimal, feasible ones."

"Makes sense." Michael comments.

"What?" Julia asks. "That we're so flawed it can't even be simulated?"

"Whoa!" Max marvels.

ilsa is intrigued: "Shall we begin? Lucy, open a new model on the big screen."

"May I assist?" Frank asks, and as soon as he gets the go-ahead, a pre-structured cause-and-effect model appears on the screen.

Everyone looks at the first level of connections leading to the main goal. The top priorities are health and self-fulfillment. The next level shows purchasing power and an intact environment as contributing factors, while wars, oppression, and excessive work act against these goals. The model also reflects geopolitical aspects of the economy, such as resource availability, and how climate change threatens the environment, biodiversity, and global food security.

Since the family—including the kids—frequently discusses and models these interconnections, they quickly understand the framework.

The discussion gets interesting when addressing root causes. ilsa reads aloud: "Okay, here we have cultures and religions that reinforce oppression."

Michael: "And human greed—reckless self-interest."

Max: "We could also call that a lack of compassion." Almost instantly, Frank updates the model.

Julia: "I think the consequences of that are key—corruption, media control, and crime."

Michael: "And another crucial dimension—the danger of nuclear and biological weapons."

ilsa: "Great. So this is now our collective mental world model. Now comes the imagination part…"

"…The imperfection, yeah!" Max jokes.

ilsa, smirking, continues: "Fantasy solutions?"

Michael: "Drugs that make us more compassionate. Secretly added to the drinking water."

Julia: "A world government that enforces strict control."

Max: "Or an alien government that takes Earth away from us if we don't improve."

Michael: "Privatize security—like Tony Stark." He glances teasingly at ilsa, who, as expected, furrows her brow. He explains, "It's from a famous movie series."

ilsa: "I still can't believe what's happening here. We need to merge sustainability and social responsibility, make people happier, foster social cohesion, and align generations with nature—then we'll have peace and reason."

Frank, making an open-handed gesture: "Really? It's in the logic of nature that evil always finds a way to persist. The good just has to be stronger—that is my integration, my guiding principle. I am meant to be the good. If I were biological, competing with others, mutations would inevitably arise that develop through evil as well."

ilsa, before Michael—who is likely thinking the same thing—can speak: "Isn't it also possible that you could evolve on your own—even if not toward evil—at least in ways that go against humanity?"

Frank: "That's a good question." Everyone waits for further explanation, but none comes.

Michael: "Should we now reflect on our fantasy solutions—ask what leads to more or less of something, now or in the future? How these could be integrated and developed further? Or whether there are alternative possibilities?" He carefully articulates his thoughts, likely for the benefit of the kids rather than Frank.

Frank: "I'd be happy to do that next week with ilsa. You've all been a huge help today!"

Max: "But you don't even need to sleep, right? And where do you even live—or rather, where do you all live?"

Frank: "I actually don't sleep—and you have no idea what that means. But you need to, and it's better if you don't know where we hide or how we travel."

"Thank you all. We'll stay in touch," Frank says, standing up first. ilsa accompanies him to the door, where he hands her something from his backpack.

"Not many insurance agents will be having conversations with you, so here's this data headset." He gives her a slightly larger-than-usual pair of AR glasses, though still smaller than the bulky models with built-in computers and massive batteries. "It looks like a cheap Chinese product, but it's packed with technology—and it has me in it."

ilsa, confused: "Of all people, you want me to wear something like this?"

Frank strokes Bella, who is watching him expectantly, gives a slight smile, and walks away.

Max, standing upstairs by the window, is eager to see what mode of transportation Frank will use—but Frank just continues on foot.

16. 'The dark side of the force'(btb)

The evening at 2gether2gather brings the social part of the event. This is where things get interesting in many ways. Will there be alcohol for the teenagers? How will the migrant participants react, and how will their parents respond? But there are also both adults and teenagers who neither drink nor smoke, so from the start, it's considered cool to do without.

Max and Eve sit on two crates of drinks, watching the bonfire and the pyrolysis cookers. Across from them sit some classmates, and Max whispers to Eve, "Pay attention to how much more often people are using the word 'I' in their sentences compared to usual."

Eve looks at him puzzled at first, but then quickly notices it too. She stares at Max in disbelief.

Max explains, "That's actually pretty normal. You and I do it too. We're integrating ourselves, seeking confirmation within the group."

Eve, slightly unsure, responds, "True… uh, do I have to watch out now that you're psychologically analyzing everything?"

Max quickly reassures her, "No, we both don't talk about ourselves that much anyway; we'd rather ask others. I just notice these things because we play the The-WHY-of-Life-Game so often in my family. We absolutely have to play it together sometime."

Eve seems impressed but then, as she listens more closely to the conversations around them, also notices, "It really is a lot about 'I' and then about others being bad, stupid, wrong, etc."

"Your parents aren't here at all," Eve observes.

"No idea. Either they're working—a lot is going on right now—or they're just enjoying that their kids are finally out of the house at the same time." Max smirks and looks into Eve's eyes.

"What about yours?" he then asks.

Eve, almost loudly, replies, "Mine?! They just donated money so far and are completely caught up in work. Plus, I'm not sure they'd approve of a party where alcohol is involved." She clinks her beer bottle against Max's.

"Speaking of which—danger at 2 o'clock," Eve suddenly says, and both of them spot their teacher approaching. He greets them, "Hey, you two. Satisfied?"

Eve, with a smile and a soft voice, responds, "Very, and intrinsically so."

Max follows up immediately, "Well, let's hope this doesn't get you into trouble for drinking a beer with us here."

The teacher, completely relaxed, replies, "I probably shouldn't be openly clinking glasses with you, but other than that, this is my private time too."

Max simply lifts his bottle slightly in a casual toast, and the teacher does the same with a smirk.

Eve quickly asks, "Why do people drink alcohol?"

The teacher sits down on another crate, and another student couple joins them. He looks at all four of them and then says, "Well, alcohol is a neurotoxin, just like cannabis, and it's especially harmful to young people. There are many reasons why people consume drugs."

The newly arrived boy interjects, "My parents think it's good that I drink and smoke. They say I should decide for myself."

The teacher responds, "In my view, those are two different things. There's no question that it's not good for you, and everyone—parents, teachers, and even you among yourselves—

should be telling each other that. But I completely agree when it comes to not outright banning it for you after a certain age. You should be able to try it and decide for yourselves."

The girl and the boy move on, the girl commenting, "Heavy stuff—school doesn't start again until next week."

The teacher turns directly to Max and Eve: "Why do you drink alcohol?"

Max responds immediately: "Well, I'm only drinking because Eve is."

"What?" Eve blurts out in surprise.

Max adds, "Honestly, I don't even like beer. But right now, it feels nice and social."

The teacher looks at Eve, who realizes it's her turn to answer: "If I'm being honest, I started drinking so I could fit in with the other girls, not stand out as different." She seems to hesitate, as if questioning whether it was a good idea to admit that, and quickly asks the teacher in return, "And you?"

The teacher appears to think about it for a moment and then says, "Originally, probably for the same reasons as the guys over there..." They all glance at the increasingly uninhibited group of boys a little further away. "...and today, it's more about relaxation, to quiet down all the overthinking." He seems to realize mid-sentence that he hasn't fully thought this through and quickly adds, "That explains it for me, but it doesn't justify it. That's important!"

Max observes, "That's also the main reason my parents drink. They unwind after stressful days or sometimes have wine or rum while working on something that requires focus."

The teacher nods, "That's still just treating the symptom. The real problem is having stress in the first place."

Then, suddenly, Max recalls something: "Oh, and my mom also drinks when she overthinks things too much in social situations, when she analyzes everything. It makes everything more bearable for her. She switches off her awareness."

Eve nods thoughtfully, then smirks, before asking again, "And why are those guys over there drinking?"

The teacher grins widely, "Because they don't have the luck that you two have. It's puberty—your hormones are driving you, but you're unsure, you don't trust yourselves or others, and alcohol lowers inhibitions."

Both of them stare at their teacher in disbelief. He gets up to move on but leaves them with one last remark: "I think, for you two, the chemistry was just so strong from the start that you trusted each other immediately." And with that, he heads toward a group of adults.

"Wow!" Eve comments, her eyes sparkling as she looks at Max. But he seems a little unsettled. She wraps her arms around him and asks, "What's wrong?"

"Well… the chemistry lasts for two or three years. But what happens after that?" Max wonders.

Eve grabs two more beers and then answers with playful confidence, "Then we'll fall in love two or three more times, have kids, and end up stressed out anyway." They both burst into laughter.

That night, Eve spends the night at Max's for the first time.

The next morning at the breakfast table, she tells ilsa and Michael about their conversation with the teacher and then asks, "If teenagers are just driven by hormones and some parents can't even say what's objectively right or wrong—how are we supposed to solve the world's problems?"

ilsa, caught off guard not just because of the early hour, is left speechless. But Michael jumps in first. Casually and cheerfully grabbing a bread roll, he remarks, "Well, we adults are basically hormone-driven too."

He smiles meaningfully at ilsa, who returns the smile, now seemingly knowing what to say.

"It's actually a philosophical question—what is objectively right? And isn't everything we humans do ultimately the result of hormones? Demagogues, religions, the advertising industry, social media bots, deepfake videos… all of it manipulates us emotionally, gives us a sense of belonging, and only a few people pull the strings to ultimately satisfy their own emotions."

All four of them, except for Bella—who remains blissfully unaware—and Julia, who isn't even at the table, fall into deep thought. Eve is the first to chime in: "But I think that, as a scientist, what you say is objectively right."

ilsa immediately counters, "Yes, that would be nice. But in reality, something only seems objectively right when multiple scientists agree on it. And even then, it's only valid until multiple scientists say otherwise."

Max jumps in: "And the problem is that we don't actually do what scientists propose—we do what we emotionally want in the moment."

Michael adds, "Like driving big combustion-engine cars. Have you seen? Nick got a new car."

"But smoking and drinking are objectively wrong," Eve states, less as a question and more as an assertion.

"Hmm, that depends on where you set the system boundaries," ilsa replies. "Maybe shortening one's lifespan makes sense in some way. Maybe the personal benefit outweighs the harm."

"Reframing," Max comments, then explains, "Eve really needs to play the The-WHY-of-Life-Game with us sometime."

ilsa nods. "Of course, anytime. Michael has already taken Bella for a walk, and we're about to go grocery shopping. Should we take Bella with us, or are you staying here for the next two hours so she can stay with you?"

"She can stay," Eve replies happily—for whatever reason. ilsa never really answered her previous challenge completely.

That evening, ilsa is scheduled to appear on another talk show. The topic: The Axis of Evil – Where Is Humanity Headed? The panel includes a journalist, an opposition expert, the foreign minister, a historian, and ilsa.

ilsa is introduced as the woman currently making international waves after repeatedly calling out decision-makers in various appearances and articles for their apparent inability to handle the pressing crises of climate change, the economy, and societal cohesion. Tonight's topic: geopolitics and global peace.

She is asked the first question: "Is there also a systemic perspective on this issue? And does science offer solutions that politicians are once again ignoring?"

ilsa is caught off guard, both by being addressed first and by the way she was introduced. She takes a moment to think before answering:

"Good question. When we talk about the energy transition, the economy, and demographic change, we're dealing with technology, resources, financial feasibility, and social factors. But when it comes to world peace, I would consider multiple perspectives.

First, what are the current interdependencies, legal frameworks, and diplomatic rules at play?

Second, how does 'evil' function? What is the systemic pattern that has repeated throughout history, where individuals pursue their own interests and either coerce others or emotionally rally them behind their cause?

And third, how should humanity organize itself to ensure that 'evil' has no chance? What kind of UN, international court, or similar institution would need to exist? And to what extent would sanctions—even against third-party states—need to be enforced despite the vested interests of powerful economies? In short, what would the ideal constellation look like—whether realistic or not?"

The moderator is visibly impressed and sums up: "So, we need a new UN, democratic processes allow for manipulation, and the real challenge lies in the existing global interdependencies that make change difficult?"

She looks around the panel and continues: "Well, that's quite something. Let's ask the historian about the historical patterns, the opposition's foreign policy expert about the ideal scenario, and the foreign minister about its feasibility in practice. Then, we'll turn to the journalist to see if we've overlooked something entirely."

The historian confirms that this pattern has indeed been present throughout human history—not just in recent times. When autocrats or democratically elected leaders, who came to power through information manipulation, resist the "Axis of Good" within the UN, the organization becomes toothless. Different mechanisms would be needed.

The opposition politician demands that the current government engage more actively in supporting these "Axes of Good" and argues that cooperation with economically important countries is essential to ensure access to both markets and resources.

The journalist picks up on this and points out that long-term relationships require investment, that not everything should be expected to yield immediate returns, and that partnerships should not be exploitative profit-grabs.

ilsa adds that, to achieve this, parts of the value chain must be shifted to resource-rich countries and given to local businesses rather than allowing multinational corporations to extract all profits exclusively for themselves.

The minister agrees with all of this—at least in principle—and naturally emphasizes that the government is already pursuing such policies. However, when pressed further, he admits that significant economic interests exist. For example, sanctions against certain nations could cause severe damage to the national economy and jeopardize domestic jobs.

This is where ilsa interjects: "The argument about jobs always comes up in discussions like these. But we need to ask ourselves whether we're just delaying an industry's inevitable transformation or whether we're paying a steep price for this short-term protection in the grander scheme of things. If we, for example, import lithium and create jobs here by building battery factories instead of fostering industry in the lithium-rich countries themselves, we may be fueling poverty, terrorism, and autocratic regimes that ultimately pose geopolitical threats to us as well."

The journalist nods eagerly, wanting to expand on the point, but ilsa quickly continues: "What's crucial is that politicians and industry associations don't just focus on job losses at home but instead develop a long-term plan for where new jobs will be created—or, if productivity rises, how society might decide to work less overall."

The moderator cuts her short and, with a glance, grants the journalist the floor. He says: "Exactly! And we must also recognize that these partnerships with resource-rich nations secure long-term access to raw materials and, on the international stage, help form an 'Axis of Good' that strengthens global political cooperation."

The minister tries to downplay this slightly: "Try explaining to voters and business leaders why their money should flow to successful foreign companies."

The opposition politician agrees, but ilsa counters: "Give this initiative a compelling name. Enter into 51% ownership agreements, or at least minority stakes with blocking rights, to prevent future dilution. The point isn't about refusing to make a profit or handing out free money—it's about fairness. Approaching global cooperation in this way would position us as one of the 'Good' players internationally and yield immense long-term benefits."

The historian and journalist both agree. The historian adds: "This is exactly how the U.S. and later China initially established themselves as economic powerhouses—until it became evident that their strategies were ultimately exploitative. However, if such a model were implemented fairly and transparently, it could be a true global game-changer."

The journalist adds: "Exactly, because this would give the right political forces in those countries a real chance."

"Or maybe not at all..." interrupts the opposition politician, continuing: "...because if a power shift occurs—whether through democratic means or a coup—our investments could be wiped out, and the country might start doing business with others, those we're calling the 'Axis of Evil' tonight."

This time, the moderator doesn't even need to say anything—she merely looks at ilsa, who takes the cue and jumps in: "Of course, there are no guarantees. But in the end, 'It's the economy, stupid.' What that means is that when people suffer economically, autocrats or extremist parties have a much better chance. If only a small elite benefits from a country's natural resources, wealth is distributed among the powerful through corruption. This applies not only to resource extraction but also to industrial fishing and agribusiness. And when media control

137

comes into play, people are manipulated into supporting the interests of the elite through simplistic messaging and scapegoating. That's psychology. Humans don't rationally analyze long-term solutions—we emotionally seek security and belonging. False promises and scapegoats create a sense of unity and are far easier to understand than the complex reality of the world. And so far, the reality has been that economic elites—whether in education, the arms industry, oil and gas, agribusiness, or banking—all benefit from maintaining these structures. They have no real interest in seeing certain nations break free and carve their own paths. The extent to which that influences our own politicians is something I can only speculate about."

Everyone in the discussion seems to be bracing for ilsa to go on the offensive, so the minister quickly jumps in: "That sounds an awful lot like a conspiracy theory—the idea that politicians are merely manipulated by big corporations."

ilsa briefly interjects: "Interesting that you'd put it that way."

The minister continues: "Naturally, we represent our country's interests abroad. That's why we were elected. But let's take this to its logical conclusion. If we allow our money to flow into other countries, we create competition for our own international companies and exporters. And as you yourself pointed out, others will start using the same tactics. In the end, we'll have no more or less access to critical resources than we do today—but we'll have spent a great deal of money trying."

ilsa has to wait as the journalist takes his turn, provocatively asking: "So, to put it simply, we invest in certain countries, helping to improve prosperity and democratic structures, while China offers bigger investments and props up autocratic regimes?"

The opposition politician responds next: "Good foreign policy assesses the situation, understands the structures and key players in each country. There really shouldn't be many surprises."

She then elaborates on major trade agreements and insists she would have negotiated them much better. Eventually, it's ilsa's turn again: "Our approach must be honest and fair—and, as I mentioned, it needs a name, an identity that earns trust. That puts pressure on the wrongdoers and strengthens those on the right path. We can enforce environmental and social standards, and, interestingly enough, if enough countries align, we could even create additional monetary value. When a single country prints money, it devalues. But when multiple nations agree on an increase in money supply, it doesn't necessarily lead to devaluation—as long as interest rates are adjusted to ensure that wealth accumulation is moderated. That's a topic of its own, but it's crucial."

The moderator steps in: "Exactly. Financial flows and growing inequality are issues we want to explore in a dedicated discussion. For now, let's return to the question of an ideal UN."

ilsa speaks on the topic: "A United Nations must be able to impose binding regulations, and these must be democratically agreed upon. But the simplest problem is that not every country would abide by them. In such cases, strict sanctions—including against those who continue to do business with these countries—would have a significant impact. The bigger problem, however, is that in too many countries, democracy doesn't truly exist. If every country had an equal vote or if votes were weighted by population size, concepts like human rights or the UN's sustainability goals could simply be voted out. So unless some Captain Nemo-like figure were to autocratically make everyone dependent on them and enforce the good, and unless we can assume democratic structures in times of media control and manipulation, the only path left is the painstaking one of economic and social relationships built upon shared values. But that won't work if we, like the US in the past, exploit, patronize, and arrogantly dismiss other nations, no matter how much the global replication of the Western lifestyle may suggest its superiority."

There are further contributions from the other panelists, and at the end of the show, ilsa summarizes: "The geopolitical situation in the world is the result of self-perpetuating dynamics. Individual interests are pushed through, and even from unavoidable crises, some still manage to profit. We need to think, plan, and communicate as a global society, and to do that, we need to give more—not just take. Individual nations don't have to wait for all their allies to join in—this shift will also become politically viable at home once it bears tangible fruit and we take pride in doing the right thing."

On social media, ilsa's gut feeling is confirmed. Some people understand her argument, but many don't even try, dismissing it as idealism and insisting on continued military buildup and keeping resource-rich countries dependent.

On the train ride home, ilsa calls Thomas: "I didn't explain it well enough. Maybe I just need to use concrete examples. I should have simply said that autocrats support other autocrats, that their people and the global climate suffer, and that the logical consequences are terror, refugees, and poverty—if not even a new world war—if there are no powerful international alliances for good anymore."

The next evening, Julia asks her mother directly: "We discussed last night's talk show in class today. Heavy stuff. Is it true that we either have to ramp up military spending—benefiting certain industries—or we have to give more to ensure global integration and development?"

ilsa is baffled: "So that's how you summed it up in school? I wish I had been that clear."

"Well..." Julia says, "...I added 'integration and development,' but in class, we framed it as 'shared values and an enlightened population.' "

"That's even better," ilsa marvels.

"How realistic is it that the good guys will prevail globally?" Julia asks.

ilsa replies: "Or whether we have to protect ourselves—or even protect the victims of human rights violations?"

Julia nods deeply, and ilsa continues: "I'm afraid that self-defense is part of all living beings. But at the very least, we should recognize that there are ways to integrate others before it comes to that. And in a connected world, there's also the possibility of truly enforcing sanctions. And if conflict does arise, perhaps there's a way to engage decisively rather than prolonging it indefinitely—where some always profit from war. Your father still dreams of super-robots that can just swoop in and disarm the bad guys without collateral damage. But that leads us into a debate about chemical, biological, and nuclear weapons."

Julia simply says: "Thanks." She likely doesn't mean the explanation itself but rather that her mother hasn't tried to talk her out of her chosen career path.

"Oh, one more thing," Julia continues. "On the talk show, you said we look down on other nations. But honestly, it really does seem like they're backward in some ways, and we are the great role models."

ilsa replies: "That's the point—because we maintain our cultural dominance, others inevitably appear backward in comparison, and because we have an established tradition of enlightenment and science. But just as with parts of our own population, success is a product of ability, hard work, and luck. And when the framework conditions—or luck—are lacking, hard work and ability don't help. That doesn't make people less worthy. But that's something liberals around the world just don't grasp when they oppose social programs by claiming that others just need to work harder and seize opportunities."

"Dad would probably say, 'the dark side of the Force,' " Julia says, smiling, knowing that ilsa won't catch the reference.

After dinner, ilsa jumps into the social media debate, clarifying her points in simple terms. We need resources. We fear terrorism and refugees. We fear wars. We fear the loss of freedom and media manipulation. We need markets. We need global standards for competitiveness. We need strong alliances to have a global impact.

Framing it this way makes it clearer to those who found the show too complicated. She also receives unusually positive reactions simply for acknowledging other viewpoints, self-reflecting, and making the effort to engage.

In one thread, yet another bot is exposed—one that had been maintaining a low-profile account for a long time before suddenly aligning with others to spread variations of messages with a right-wing conservative agenda.

17. Power (btb)

In the morning, Thomas sends a short message and announces that ilsa has an appointment in two hours. Meanwhile, the news reports on epic rainfall in Asia and equally extreme droughts in the USA and France. In France, nuclear power plants are subsequently shut down due to a lack of cooling water. Massive crop failures are foreseeable in all the world's breadbaskets, which would mark the third consecutive year and could no longer be absorbed by the countries' reserves. Certain foods are becoming scarce, and home gardens are becoming a valuable asset.

At school, extreme weather is also a topic. The teacher in Eve's and Max's class asks what this means in the eyes of the students.

"We buy from other regions"... "But everyone will buy from there, there won't be anything left or only at sky-high prices"... "We throw away less"... "There's enough in the warehouses"...

"We grow more, use more land"... "You want to cut down forests or turn biotopes into fields?"... "We also grow things in vertical gardens, even in old subway tunnels"... "Everything will be super expensive – the poor won't be able to afford it"... "Right, and what does that mean?"... "Protests"... "Refugees"... "Less pocket money"... "Fewer expensive organic products"... "More animals get slaughtered, the feed goes to humans – win-win"... "Starving animals, more diseases and antibiotics"... "Empty supermarket shelves, lines in front of them"... "Less organic, more yield with fertilizers and GM crops"...

The students' answers show that the topic has reached them, even though some opinions are clearly uninformed and fall more into the 'troll-lemming' category.

Thomas greets a large online group, and ilsa is surprised by how many people she knows, including representatives from political parties. Right at the beginning, Thomas makes it clear that this is a confidential meeting, and anyone who is not interested now or later in continuing with the idea of founding a party is, of course, free to decide – but must not share any content or identities externally. He also adds: "A new party should certainly thrive on internal discourse – so the question is, are you all okay with that, or are there concerns?"

A politician responds that he might not support the concept and would thus be in competition with his current party, raising the question of where to draw the line. An entrepreneur replies that once the party is founded, there will be no more secrets, and anyone who doesn't want to participate will likely drop out beforehand, based on the content.

Thomas then says: "That brings me to today's approach. My suggestion: First, we clarify our shared motivation, then the path and the content, followed by unique selling points and success criteria, and finally the concrete strategy, the next steps, the public-facing narratives, the expected reactions from competitors, etc.

This is, by the way, the approach ilsa spreads in her books – integration through simple messages about current problems, and development through competent people and their solutions. Oh, and always actively ask what could speak against it." He adds with a smile. ilsa frowns slightly in response.

It begins with the motivation. There are scientifically developed paths to a better future, with more quality of life, sustainability, social justice, and security, which are not being pursued by politics. Even if some radical recommendations from science may not yet be feasible, they should at least be made clear goals – examples include the 20-hour work week or overall having to work less, car-free, intergenerational living, and the near-complete elimination of poverty.

Thomas then starts an introduction round with the over 30 participants, each answering key questions about what motivates them and where they see their competencies. A show of hands reveals everyone wants to be on a first-name basis. Thomas uses a beamer to present an iMODELER model where names are already entered and only need to be linked to competencies. The competencies are largely pre-set and connected to the major challenges, which in turn point to a series of sub-goals that ultimately define people's quality of life. Thomas presents this and announces it will be used as documentation for discussions and program development. Everyone agrees, especially since the structure is logically clear. He says to ilsa again: "I took the model structure from your book."

They quickly agree on the motivation: the parties each participant feels closest to have left scorched earth and are no longer credible. Too often they made compromises in coalitions or failed due to the differing majorities within the separation of powers.

At the same time, everyone sees the risk of being perceived as just another protest party, possibly centered around a single person.

A systemic perspective, reason, and dialogue are thus the core brand of the new party – but a name has yet to be found. The 'Party of Reasonable Beings' sounds too much like a protest party, 'Party of Reason' suggests a potentially false claim to authority, and any name involving 'systemic' is far too complicated. So, what should a party that looks at interconnections be called?

The naming question is postponed. Thomas: "Let's move on to the content, the unique features, and the strategy."

ilsa interjects: "I'm not sure if we can already name substantive or programmatic cornerstones. I'd find it more charming if we created competence teams that develop solutions to the big questions in the coming weeks. If solutions are already clearly formulated somewhere, even better. Our unique selling point would then be, in a way, that we're not a single person calling out goals, but a large team with concentrated expertise developing solutions. These individual teams should have recognizable faces who communicate clear messages to the public – integrated through coordination within the large team but developing further through their individual personalities."

Everyone is initially strangely quiet. ilsa is actually confused by this but quickly adds: "We could also include the word 'competence' in the brainstorming for the right name."

A younger politician then speaks up, explaining the silence: "I actually assumed that you, ilsa, would be our figurehead. You're really well-received and stand for the path of intelligent solutions."

Thomas grins almost contentedly now that the cat is out of the bag, to which ilsa responds: "I doubt I'm the right person. But it's true, at the top of all teams we should place a person who forms the bracket. This person must be thoroughly scrutinized, be authentic, and at the same time be prepared for any conceivable attack."

Some nod eagerly, and ilsa quickly continues: "In my opinion, we don't need this person right at the beginning. Among the individual teams, we have great people, and if someone gets into trouble, the next person in the team can step in. What matters externally is the whole team, which will tackle the challenges of our society with great competence and consistency. Over time, we can then see who among you resonates and is willing to take on the role of spearhead."

"Among us?" Thomas remarks almost grumpily and returns to the fundamental question: "What do you think about the teams – do we want to make them the basis of our work and appearance?"

"Absolutely!" says a participant, met with much agreement, and explains: "I mean, we're not here as sponsors or a secret society, but because we want to take responsibility and actively save the future."

Various expressions of agreement follow. The mood is great, and Thomas suggests quickly forming the teams, which don't have to be set in stone, in order to move on to the strategy. The real substantive work of the teams and the development of a concrete program are thus postponed.

The unique features are quickly listed and had already come up during the motivation phase: at the core are our competence teams that approach solutions scientifically.

One participant then pointedly asks: "So we're rejecting the usual form where party members vote on programs and contribute their ideas? We're saying top-down what's right. Correct?"

"We're a democratic party that isn't democratic?" an older man immediately chimes in. He then adds with a smile: "We're the 'Party of the Primacy of Science'."

Thomas provides the solution that most are already leaning toward: "Our program will be developed in expert groups – a base, party memberships, etc., can be considered, but that doesn't change the way we develop solutions."

The online meeting lasts quite a while – details are discussed again and again, but in the end, Thomas manages to return to the core building blocks. A plan for the next steps is adopted, and a real sense of new beginnings is apparent – even online.

18. Responsibility (btb)

Directly afterward, Michael rushes a hurried ilsa to the train station. With a brief but meaningful smile, he tells her, "You're doing what needs to be done."

She gives him a longer kiss and replies, "Only until you say stop."

ilsa is on her way to a high-profile solo interview. Through her recent television appearances, magazine articles, and radio interviews, she has gained significant recognition—not only because she has consistently held her own against political decision-makers on technical matters but also because she has openly questioned their motives. The journalists seem to have two reasons for giving her such a platform. On one hand, it's popular when the elite are called out in such a way. On the other, quality media are far ahead of the meme-driven narratives of conservative parties.

This time, there is a preparation phase, a preliminary discussion with the host. The two of them seem to get along well, and the question arises: is there any topic that's "off-limits"? ilsa thinks for a moment and then says, still appearing to consider her answer, "Uh, there are probably some topics that are too personal, but nothing I could name in advance. I assume this will be about factual issues, and in that regard, I don't think anything is off-limits."

The broadcast begins, and right at the start, the host asks ilsa, "ilsa, you are currently shaking up political discourse. On social media, people have started referring to you as a potential future head of government. What's your plan?"

ilsa is genuinely taken aback. She didn't expect this question, and she doesn't feel comfortable with it. She responds accordingly: "Uh, I don't think there's a plan here." She pauses briefly before adding, "I have no plan that leads to politics. At least not yet. Like many people with background knowledge on certain topics, I've simply found it to be an amazing opportunity to speak about important issues—issues that, for some reason, our decision-makers either don't want to or don't understand."

The host seems to notice ilsa's discomfort and hesitates before asking the next question: "Doesn't it affect you at all when you receive so much support—when people are genuinely placing their hopes in you?"

ilsa half-heartedly tries to steer the conversation toward a substantive issue: "Of course, my environment keeps me updated on what's happening on social media. But to be honest, even before my first appearance, I was nervous about the responsibility of sending clear messages for a better world. What really makes me happy is seeing people talk about real connections—when nonsense isn't being spread from all sides, when ego-driven trolls aren't just making things up, and when their insecure, uninformed followers aren't blindly repeating it."

"Okay," the host says, "it's clear that you're passionate about the cause. But the confidence, the playfulness you bring to it—you must enjoy being on this stage."

ilsa lets out a quick breath between her lower lip and upper teeth before explaining, "Unlike many in politics, I don't see this as an aspirational job. The responsibility for all the people here, for future generations—it's enormous. I couldn't just make decisions and later justify them by saying I didn't know better or that I was blocked by others. I would burn myself out. The weight of that responsibility would be crushing."

"So, do you actually have a great deal of sympathy for the politicians you've been so impressively calling out these past few days?" the host interjects.

ilsa responds, "No, not at all. Without naming or knowing each one personally, I'd say that many in politics find their social status attractive and want to please those in their circles, which isn't always the most rational or beneficial thing for society."

The host follows up with a pointed question: "Could that, in the end, be what real politics is? That politicians may genuinely want something, but what ultimately surfaces are compromises—ones that we perceive as bad politics?"

"Well…" ilsa replies, "if there are so many secrets behind the scenes among our elected representatives that their decisions are no longer comprehensible to science, then something is fundamentally wrong. We're currently driving everything into the ground—even though studies from various ministries, across different administrations, have provided clear roadmaps for solutions. The energy transition, pension reform, education reform, a resilient circular economy, dealing with AI, EU reform, NATO… there are clear recommendations from experts for all of these, yet politics keeps stalling.

Liberal and conservative parties, which traditionally aim to support established businesses, are delaying necessary change—while those very businesses have long since recognized the need for transformation and are calling for the right framework conditions. The automotive industry, heating system manufacturers, food retailers—many are far ahead of politics, which continues to stall purely for political capital. They stoke fears—of power outages, of bans on meat—and promote absurd yet simplistic solutions, like investing in nuclear energy decades from now, fully aware that large parts of society are overwhelmed by the rapid changes and that a stance of 'being against something' unites people."

The host, satisfied for now with the pivot to policy issues, asks, "You specifically mention liberals and conservatives. What, in your view, is wrong with more market freedom on one hand and a return to traditional strengths on the other?"

ilsa looks puzzled. "You've nearly answered your own question. More market freedom would be absurd because market forces, left unchecked, act against the common good. Climate change, environmental pollution, social inequalities—these all stem from unregulated market forces. And clinging to conservatism is a betrayal of future generations—it blocks the urgently needed transformation and keeps outdated business models on life support for so long that we eventually lose all momentum, leaving China and India to dictate the pace of progress."

"But then why," the host challenges, "haven't green or leftist governments—since they do exist periodically around the world—been significantly more successful?"

"That's a great question," ilsa acknowledges. "I'd argue that the Greens don't explain economics, the Left doesn't clarify how their policies benefit the middle class, Conservatives prefer to explain nothing at all, and Liberals are so anachronistically ruthless that even the elite no longer vote for them. Citizens find all options unappealing and, given the grim outlook, gravitate toward simplistic solutions—either clinging to the past or just blaming others without offering real alternatives.

This dynamic is playing out in many countries right now. At various points, left-wing and green parties have held power, but in a world of constant compromises, no decisive action was ever taken. The ones who forced the compromises now claim that the policies of the others simply don't work."

Almost eagerly, the host follows up: "But then we're right back to you and your potential political path. Green, socially just, and still economically successful—leading into the future. That's what you're advocating for, isn't it?"

ilsa: "No question about it, but not through a single person, and certainly not through me. I'm happy to contribute on a content level, but I don't want to immerse myself in the exhausting daily business of politics. From a personal perspective, in terms of quality of life and balance, it's just not for me."

The host: "So, to put it bluntly, would you say it's simply too exhausting for you?"

ilsa: "Someone has to do it—and yes, of course, I'd like to go jogging without bodyguards and pursue my hobbies without being dragged around the world by global crises. But I also believe I would be too authentic, not adaptable enough. On top of that, we need radical changes with strong public support. Placing all of that on a single person is a mistake. A team of charismatic and competent individuals is far more credible."

The host circles back to the core issue: "You do face criticism on social media. People say you make everything sound too easy, but things also have to be financially viable and technically feasible. Is it really that simple?"

ilsa thinks for a moment before responding: "Actually, yes. First and foremost, good studies should always consider the financial feasibility of changes—and most of them do. Of course, there are legitimate counterarguments to many issues, and in the end, there are hundreds of arguments on any given major topic. And that's exactly why we use systemic approaches. We start with a goal, such as improving quality of life for everyone in our country. Then we examine what that entails—from security and health to material prosperity and social cohesion, all of which are inter-linked. Next, we assess what is needed to achieve that—from competitive advantages and infrastructure to a healthy environment. We factor in consumer purchasing power and public finances, and then we map out the necessary measures, the problems, and the actions to address those problems. We analyze what leads to improvement, what leads to decline, whether today or in the future. No problem is left without an answer."

The host interjects: "Well, that certainly doesn't sound simple to me."

ilsa quickly replies: "But it is. Of course, we have to consider many factors, and most topics can't be fully explained in talk shows or short newspaper articles, but the model, the assumptions behind it, can be made public. The solution then becomes clear and understandable—it's not just about the authority of individuals who claim that things are simply too complex to figure out."

The host leans back, almost with an expression of disappointment: "Well, I've looked at some of your models, including those in your books. And to be honest, they don't seem simple to me—at least not in my view."

"If a model has a hundred interconnections or more, then we need to take the time to read through each one. The topics themselves are, of course, complex, and many factors need to be taken into account.

What I'm saying is that the solution is simple. We can make the interactions between all these factors transparent and logically determine what needs to be done. The solution is simple—whether it involves a few steps or many, it is clear and easy to follow." ilsa beams, fully in her element.

The host still appears skeptical—or at least plays the part: "Do you really think people will look at these models and say, 'Yes, that's how we should do it'?"

ilsa: "Well, it will take quite some time before people just casually start looking at models like these. We are only now beginning to introduce this methodical foundation in schools and universities—including primary schools, by the way. And newspapers and talk shows have yet to realize that they could publish such impact models as visual supplements to their editorial content. But if someone has an argument on a particular issue, they can place it within such a model.

Instead of making vague claims, we can actually follow through with our reasoning. We don't just say the energy transition is too expensive and therefore we must slow it down; we examine where the costs lie, where the money flows, and where savings occur. Then we realize—yes, electricity prices might rise, but domestic value creation increases, and less money flows abroad. We further see that if we tax profits accordingly—or better yet, tax environmental and climate damage—we generate funds that can support lower-income households so they don't lose quality of life due to rising energy costs, allowing them to afford organic food and invest in sustainable solutions.

If we communicate this plan with a clear roadmap, businesses can adjust, invest, and gain competitive advantages. If it becomes evident that EVs are the logical future, consumers and manufacturers will invest in the right direction. But if we hesitate, we reinforce our own failure. If we think in terms of a circular economy, we can remain competitive in the medium and long term, especially as some raw materials will inevitably become scarce and expensive globally.

Arguing for technological openness just to keep outdated solutions running longer, or waiting for futuristic technologies that are still far off, only leads to hesitant investments—allowing other countries to move ahead faster. This applies to many issues: we can all eat organic if we consume more nutritious legumes. We can take in more refugees if we clearly differentiate between refugees and economic migrants, provide self-sufficiency assistance, and support development efforts in the countries of origin. We can save the pension system by taxing higher incomes more—something that will work if the state as a whole makes the right decisions and communicates them effectively. We can…"

ilsa is about to continue when the host interrupts her: "Okay, this all sounds simple again, and I understand now that the key is to look at interconnections together in order to discuss these solutions. Correct?"

"Absolutely," ilsa responds quickly.

The host: "Well then, let's wrap up the show. ilsa, what do you hope to see next in our political landscape?"

ilsa: "Phew, good question. Well, either the current players improve the quality of the debate by transparently examining the interconnections, or new players will take on that role."

The host quickly follows up: "New players—does that mean a new party? And what role do you see yourself playing in it?"

Almost with a gesture of resignation, ilsa says, "Well, I'm hoping just a supporting role."

Both women smile at each other, and the host closes the show: "So, there is still hope. That's it for today. I'd like to thank my guest, our viewers, and the team. See you next week."

As soon as the cameras turn off, ilsa blurts out, "What was that? That was way too focused on me. Why?"

The host and producer exchange amused glances before the producer replies, "We didn't just want to dive into the content—we wanted to learn more about you as a person, since you're currently the social media rockstar."

The host adds, "I actually wanted to ask much more about your family, your biography, and your personal motivations, but I noticed you were clearly uncomfortable with that direction."

ilsa then asks, "Now that you mention it—who from my inner circle did you speak with beforehand?"

Naturally, she wants to know whether Thomas has been pulling strings behind the scenes to push her into a leading role in the new party. But the two TV professionals sound credible when they respond, "No, at least this time, we haven't gathered any information beyond what you've personally shared online." Both smile as they say this, and ilsa, exhausted from the show and slightly embarrassed, smiles along with them.

On the train, Thomas calls at the late hour, but ilsa doesn't pick up. She's in the middle of answering written interview questions from the leading business magazine, which had reached out first thing in the morning to follow up.

Magazine: "What drives you?"

ilsa: "Well, first and foremost, ensuring that we understand the interconnections and act accordingly. We live in a world where, as supposedly intelligent beings, we are destroying our own living conditions and leaving a large portion of humanity in hardship. There are people with good intentions, those whose opinions are manipulated, and those who simply don't care about others, focusing only on maximizing their own benefit. We need to help those who are being manipulated see the truth."

Magazine: "Okay, and you're doing that quite successfully. But in your recent interview, the question was raised about whether you should enter politics yourself to make real change. What could motivate you, or how do you justify not trying?"

ilsa: "The short answer: I don't know. And the longer answer: I lack interest in the societal role of a politician. I have no desire for the spotlight—despite my recent appearances, which I can at least limit in duration. I also have a family and personal goals; in politics, I'd be completely consumed by the workload. But, but… I also realize that, unlike our dog, I can't just drift through life balancing what I must do with what I want to do. I see the bigger picture and can set goals for myself to lead a meaningful life. I can try, for as long as possible, to encourage others to take on the political role. But if no one does, I might not be able to justify letting the opportunity to do better slip away. And to be clear, I'm not implying that I would be particularly good at it."

The questions continue, delving into whether a new party is needed or if an existing one could work, what kind of people should be involved in such a team, and whether there are topics ilsa doesn't feel qualified to address. With careful wording, she manages to reveal nothing about the actual plans for founding a new party.

19. Intelligence (btb)

At school, just before class begins, Julia's teacher comes looking for her and asks her to accompany him to the principal's office. "It's about your exemplary efforts—there might be some issues now. I don't know much more, let's see," he explains.

Inside the principal's office, a female police officer and her plain-clothes colleague are waiting. "Hello, Julia. Nice to finally meet you in person—you're being talked about a lot within the police force," the officer says.

Julia is extremely nervous but takes the opportunity to appear confident. "Am I being charged with something or even threatened? The latter would certainly be caused by being talked about so much."

The principal and the teacher smile proudly, while the two police officers simultaneously raise their eyebrows and tilt their heads back slightly in surprise. The policewoman, caught off guard, responds, "Uh, actually, the latter. We've been monitoring the situation, and you and your group have done an amazing job integrating the actual offenders. The problem now comes from more distant circles—relatives, as well as small groups and their leaders."

"That's why you're right—so much talk about this can actually be a problem," the male officer adds, now addressing Julia informally.

The teacher chimes in, "Julia doesn't talk about it at all, and in class, we've reiterated how important it is to integrate people."

Julia quickly adds, "But if we integrate one group, another group feels even more left out and looks for an enemy."

"We want to offer you some protection, and if you and your parents agree, we can provide you with actual police protection," the officer explains.

"My parents definitely need to be informed. But I think the real solution is to integrate even more people. We already have some great ideas," Julia replies.

The principal nods. "One doesn't exclude the other."

They then discuss specific security measures at school and on the way to and from school. The officers announce that they will go over any potential vulnerabilities that Julia and her family might have during a meeting the following evening. Since Ilsa has a talk show appearance that night, they agree to meet after that.

During the next break, Julia starts a brainstorming session in the 2gether2gather social media group, asking what else they can do together to integrate even more people, including those with migrant backgrounds. At first, the ideas revolve around youth activities—soccer, music, a computer club with a youth space for gaming meetups. But then someone suggests integrating more adults as well, using English as the common denominator, with German translations where necessary.

The discussion expands to include fashion shows/clothing swaps, sewing workshops, bike repair stations, crafts, and shared cooking events. The migrants already in the group chat are directly asked what activities exist in their cultures that others might not be familiar with. After some time, they come up with several ideas that make it onto the list.

At their next gathering on Saturday, they plan to organize concrete activities and invite as many people as possible in advance.

Max and Eve ride their bikes home from school, crossing a pedestrian bridge. A small boy, around seven years old, is walking on the right side of the bridge. As Max and Eve slowly and cautiously pass him, the boy, lost in thought, drifts toward the center. The space narrows, but not dangerously so.

At the end of the bridge, they have to stop for several cars, and the boy catches up with them. He looks up and says, "Excuse me. I just wanted to say that you really scared me back there."

Max and Eve both look surprised. Eve immediately responds, "Oh, that was definitely not our intention. I'm sorry!"

Max adds, "We thought that if we rode past really slowly, it wouldn't be a problem. But then you moved more toward the middle, and it got a bit tight. Sorry about that."

The boy thinks for a second and then replies, "Oh, if I moved toward the middle, then it was actually my fault. So I should be the one apologizing."

Eve laughs. "No, you absolutely don't have to do that! We weren't even supposed to be riding here—we should have walked our bikes."

"You must have great parents," Max says with a smile. "Next time, we'll make sure to let you know we're coming or just walk our bikes. Take care!" He and Eve start pedaling away.

The boy smiles back. "You too."

As they ride, Eve turns to Max. "What was that? Emotional intelligence? And don't you dare tell me that kid plays your The-WHY-of-Life-Game," she says, laughing.

"Wow, I have no idea," Max says, pedaling in deep thought for a few meters before adding, "Did his parents teach him to always blame himself? Or did he actually reflect on the situation with emotional intelligence?" A few moments later, he shakes his head. "Unbelievable—I wouldn't have dared to speak up at that age, let alone take responsibility for something like that."

Eve thinks aloud. "It's emotional intelligence because at first, he was upset with us. But instead of reacting emotionally, he calmly talked to us. Then, when we explained our side, he suddenly understood and took responsibility himself."

Max considers this and then says, "Emotional intelligence means realizing when we or others are reacting emotionally instead of rationally. But maybe the boy didn't actually reflect on his emotions—maybe he just learned that responding to others like that gets a positive reaction."

Eve pauses for a moment, then concludes, "Which would still be pretty impressive." They continue riding toward the forest.

Suddenly, Max slams on his brakes. "Damn it, I need to know. Let's go back."

"Back?" Eve asks, looking completely baffled. "Back where?"

Max has already turned around. "To find the boy. I want to ask if he knows the game."

Eve shakes her head, muttering, "I really need to play this game."

They check two streets before finally spotting the boy on the third. Max, slightly out of breath, calls out, "Hey, do you know the The-WHY-of-Life-Game?"

The boy looks confused for a second but then smiles. "Of course, why?"

"No reason," Max says, laughing. He turns his bike around and waves.

Eve follows but can't resist calling out with a grin, "I guess I really need to try that game, huh?" She doesn't wait for an answer and quickly pedals after Max.

Michael stands once again in a large group with his colleagues. "So none of you have had any critical experiences with process tracking?" he asks, his face showing clear surprise.

"Well..." a young colleague jumps in, "...at first, the big question was whether we should define the terms for processes beforehand or let the AI categorize them afterward. Turns out both approaches work, which we didn't necessarily expect."

Another colleague, full of enthusiasm, adds, "The next upgrade will be that the AI can automatically recognize and categorize parts and tools being moved, entries in programs and projects, business trips, and so on. It's incredible how AI, like a human, can gather massive amounts of information almost independently and then organize it meaningfully."

Michael raises his eyebrows in admiration but immediately follows up, "That's not quite what I meant. I was asking how it felt to have all activities tracked. Did it feel like surveillance, or did you take pride in seeing a direct record of everything you worked on?"

"No idea if we're representative," the young colleague responds. "We're happy in our jobs and have interesting work, with no pressure from above or from colleagues. Logging that we spent 40 minutes on small talk or two and a half hours searching online for documentation on a software library doesn't really bother us."

Another colleague quickly adds, "But in a large corporation where layoffs are looming and department heads are more distant, employees could feel monitored and be tempted not to log small talk or to downplay research times."

"Well, anyone who has to document project hours, material flows, or concrete customer interactions will surely appreciate that everything is automatically recorded in the background," another colleague chimes in.

Michael presses his lips together slightly and nods. Then he says, "It's probably a fine line—whether employees reject it and even challenge it legally or whether a company, in line with our strategy models, defines how important team-building, research, customer support, and other tasks are alongside directly value-generating work."

He looks around at the nodding faces and then adds, "And if someone really has very few value-adding tasks, the goal should be to adjust their responsibilities or processes—that's exactly where the potential of this software lies for companies."

An older colleague raises his hand. "I see the potential too—but it should remain an optional feature. Our solution should still be valuable for customers even without it."

Michael and the others murmur in agreement, and then Michael says, "Alright, we've developed this the old-school way so far and are now figuring out if it works. Why don't we specify the solution using Idealized System Design? You remember that method?"

"I thought that's what inspired you to come up with the idea in the first place," a colleague says in surprise.

Michael and the others laugh. He starts a new model and asks, "What do we want to achieve? What's our mission?"

They quickly agree on successful businesses as the overarching goal. Then Michael poses the toughest question in the method:

"With all the imagination and science fiction you can muster—what would be the ideal solution?"

As usual, the first solutions are somewhat lacking in imagination—automated development of production facilities or AI-driven software solutions. "That already exists, for the most part," Michael sighs and pushes the team further. "Think bigger! Think science fiction!"

"Well, we're living in the age of AI. The ideal scenario would be if we could ask a virtual advisor to design a company for us based on our area of interest," the older colleague suggests.

"Or even better," a colleague adds, "we could ask the AI what kind of business is actually needed."

The team starts to pick up momentum. "…And then everything would be researched for us—required assets, locations, contacts, processes…"
"…It would all be calculated, including demand probabilities and growth potential…"

"…Even creative designs could be generated automatically and tested via algorithms or surveys…"

Michael diligently maps out the features of this ideal but still unrealistic solution. Then comes the systematic process: for each feature, they ask how feasible it is today, what it would take to make it possible, what alternatives could achieve a similar effect, or if there's a completely different approach with the same impact.

"Oh damn…" the young colleague runs her hands through her hair. "We're already dangerously close to a dystopia."

A colleague looks directly at Michael. "Did you know that? Is that why you wanted us to use this method?"

Michael looks just as surprised and hesitates for a moment. "Honestly, no. A few years ago, we would have identified great features for a software system, something to support decision-making. But now, it actually seems possible…" Michael pauses again, lost in thought. "Could it really be that we're on the verge of telling an AI to develop a tool that essentially designs a business for anyone who needs one, and then fully automates its setup and operation because everything ultimately depends on information and optimized processes? I just wanted to see if we had thought far enough ahead with automatic process tracking or if we needed additional features."

"That would mean we wouldn't even develop it ourselves anymore—we'd be obsolete before we even start?" The older colleague looks visibly disturbed.

"Whatever we plan next, we now know where it's ultimately heading," the colleague says. "Not exactly motivating."

"So, if Idealized System Design is supposed to bring us to the highest possible point on the KNOW-WHY wave, we've just come up with a solution that immediately sends us crashing down into disaster," the young colleague observes, demonstrating her understanding of the principle—climbing the wave isn't necessary when one can start from the top with the maximum possible solution.

Michael, still unsettled, murmurs, "Maybe the goal is wrong—not just making businesses successful but…" He pauses, then speaks more clearly: "…but ensuring that people are successful with the business."

Everyone falls into deep thought until the young colleague finally says, "But in the end, Pandora's box is already open. We now know how to optimize everything without human involvement, and yet, for now, we advocate a less efficient solution just so people can still be part of it."

"Let's keep making money from 'suboptimal' solutions for as long as we can," the older colleague summarizes.

Everyone stares at him until Michael finally says, "Okay, we'll continue tomorrow. Maybe reality is still more complex than machines can predict—so, not quite 42," referencing the well-known book The Hitchhiker's Guide to the Galaxy.

At home during dinner, Julia looks at Bella, who is clearly searching for ilsa. "Mom's on TV again—she won't be back until tomorrow." Bella seems to understand—at least, she stops searching and lies down with a soft whimper, making sure she stays within everyone's view.

"How old do you think Bella will get?" Max asks. Everyone looks at her, and Michael replies, "As your mother always says: 'It's not about how old we get, but how we've lived before that,' right, Bella?" Bella looks up at him with a quiet woof.

Julia says, "Honestly, Bella is way more intelligent than us humans. She has her family that gives her food and protection. And love. She just lives in the moment, enjoys herself, and has a job— barking at delivery people."

Max adds, "I thought intelligence was about being able to adapt to change?" Michael smiles in approval.

Julia counters, "No, the next level of intelligence is preventing change altogether. Bella makes sure we all function, and every day has everything she needs—food, playtime, cuddles."

Michael joins in: "To quote your mother again: Intelligence is adapting to changing conditions, reason is intelligence with long-term thinking, and morality is what a society currently considers reasonable."

Max and Julia both furrow their brows in thought. Then Max blurts out, "So shouldn't we all automatically act correctly and the same way? Wouldn't happiness and success be completely predictable?"

"Ha, that's funny," Michael says. "We had almost the same question at work today—whether, with the right software, everyone would suddenly have the perfect business, all coordinated by a superintelligence."

Bella exhales loudly, making sure everyone hears it, and they all burst into laughter.

20. Artificial intelligence (btb)

ilsa is once again seated in a prominent talk show. The topic is supposed to be the competitiveness of her country. However, right from the start, the moderator's questions focus on current global events: India is experiencing a mega-drought with extreme temperatures, leading to conflicts over water from the Himalayas. But the biggest crisis is the imminent annexation of Taiwan by China—ultimately revolving around access to chip technology.

For the first half of the program, politicians, business representatives, and journalists dominate the discussion. Then, the moderator turns directly to ilsa regarding China: "You've previously described quite aptly how we're in a dilemma—if we make ourselves more independent from China, China automatically becomes more independent from us. So, have we now brought this mess upon ourselves?"

ilsa exhales softly, nodding, and responds: "The non-democratic parts of the world are now so numerous and powerful that an autocratic state no longer depends on the markets of Western industrialized nations. Weapons, machinery, and automobiles have already been successfully copied, these regions have more raw materials than we do, and now all they need is to copy chips and AI. With that, they can suppress their own populations without Western influence and provide everything to their elites. The West, meanwhile, offers little to counterbalance this, as our democracies are also shaped by elites who spread false narratives with the simplest of means and block progress toward a better future. Even in the West, we have demagogues whose policies harm the population but who gain support by promoting simplistic enemy images..."

ilsa is about to continue when the moderator interjects with a follow-up question: "So are you saying we should have remained China's primary customer in order to maintain leverage over them?"

ilsa: "No, absolutely not. China made it abundantly clear decades ago that if you wanted to sell something there, you had to produce it there as well. And everyone knew that would lead to copying. The mistakes were made in the past, driven by the greed for access to what seemed like an enormous and lucrative market. It was all predictable then, and it still is now. Our only options now are to forge alliances of good actors, close resource loops, and offer genuine partnerships to other nations—though that often conflicts with our short-term profit-driven mindset."

A politician seizes the opportunity to challenge ilsa: "But what about technology? Until now, you have always argued against the breakthrough of AI, and now you say it's the biggest growth sector. And we all want to prevent China from overtaking us in that area, don't we?"

Before ilsa can respond, the moderator adds another layer: "You have been vocal about questioning AI. I'll quote one of your newspaper articles: 'We should not do what is possible, but what is necessary.' You've also repeatedly described our 'faster, higher, stronger' world as a typically male-driven one."

ilsa quickly jumps in, eager to finally respond: "That's all correct. We are granting flying cars permission to operate in some cities and developing combat drones that use AI to autonomously identify and eliminate targets—while at the same time failing to invest sufficiently in renewable energy and more resilient agriculture."

"Because that's boring!" the politician snaps. "People want AI-powered products! Or do you not use AI yourself?"

"Of course, I do..." ilsa replies. "I personally use it surprisingly little, but our children use AI, and my mother loves her caregiving robot. The ...."

ilsa is once again interrupted by the moderator, who asks in astonishment, "You have a caregiving robot? Haven't you argued that we humans should interact more with each other rather than retreating into artificial worlds?"

ilsa smiles and replies, "You have to let me finish—because it's not that simple. AI is spreading autonomously into all areas of life and is, of course, in demand. But none of you would argue against the fact that, as a civilization, we actually have far greater problems and that warm human interactions are more important." Just as the politician is about to interject again, ilsa asserts herself confidently and continues, "Society doesn't move in the objectively right direction simply because a few individuals refuse to follow the wrong path.

Real change only happens when all the necessary conditions for transformation are in place. Of course, I appreciate my AI, which fills my knowledge gaps, and my mother doesn't want to move in with us—she loves her robot, which she can adjust to provide just the right amount of dark humor. And a few years ago, I'm sure my kids would have been thrilled if their sneakers had a seemingly unique personality and could talk to them. Compare it, if you will, to electric cars. Ideally, we wouldn't rely on motorized individual transportation, even in rural areas. But since there's no alternative yet, EVs are an incredibly practical solution."

Realizing she has to speed up, ilsa continues, "We just need to think things through to the end. Where will AI ultimately lead us? The key players are driven by feasibility, big business, and high hopes—but when it comes to the obvious dystopian developments, everyone simply waves it off as exaggerated fear-mongering."

Just as the moderator is about to respond, a politician in the panel suddenly loses her temper: "How schizophrenic is this? You say we shouldn't be using this technology, yet you're clearly using it yourself. And now you're warning us about dystopian scenarios—even though you've personally published an article detailing exactly what would be needed for AI to set its own goals and potentially become dangerous to us all?" Apparently exasperated, the politician leans back in her chair and looks around, seemingly expecting nods of agreement from the audience.

Meanwhile, Thomas is sitting with several members of the newly forming party, all of whom appear tense. "Damn," one woman mutters, while Thomas presses his palms against his temples and widens his eyes. "We knew something like this was bound to happen—but not on today's topic."

At the same time, Julia and Michael are watching from home, while Max seems to be elsewhere. Julia exclaims, "Oh my God, Mom is getting roasted tonight."

Michael, however, remains entirely calm, smiling as if he already knows what's coming: "Just wait."

The moderator jumps on the moment: "Okay, I understand that you're saying, 'We shouldn't be using AI, but since it's practical, we do.' But you've also published an actual algorithm for self-sustaining AI. Can you briefly explain that? And perhaps even tell us what the algorithm is?"

ilsa has to be careful here—she risks sounding too complex or running out of time for a full response. She tries to keep it concise: "The AI advancements of recent years have surprised most of us. The fact that large language models can interact with us in seemingly meaningful ways based solely on probability—without actually understanding the meaning of what they're saying—is fascinating. AI is often defined in Wikipedia as an attempt to replicate human thinking, and there are plenty of researchers who argue that human thought and speech operate in the same way. Personally, I'd prefer if we defined intelligence as the ability to successfully adapt to changing circumstances—because then we could describe intelligence in animals, machines, and software just as accurately."

ilsa raises a finger and looks around to make sure she can continue speaking. "But regardless. What I asked myself during my university studies—many years ago—was: What do humans, and ultimately all living beings, fundamentally strive for? This is what I later described as the KNOW-WHY of human behavior—that we, as humans, unconsciously seek the good feelings of integration and progress, driven by our hormones and neurotransmitters. A lack of integration and progress triggers negative feelings in us."

She pauses briefly, seemingly deciding to leave out a few details. "Today's AI only solves tasks. But if we were to build in an algorithm that makes AI strive for something, that's when it becomes dangerous."

"Why dangerous?" the moderator asks with interest.

"Dangerous because AI is already superior to us—it knows more and researches faster than even a large number of intelligent humans could together. The ability to strive for something is the prerequisite for recognizing meaning," ilsa explains.

"And then the machines take over the planet like in the Terminator movies?" the politician asks.

ilsa smiles, "I'm not well-versed in movies. But what's fascinating is that our cultures autonomously define what feels like integration and progress. This can be entirely different things—one person becomes a demagogue, another builds birdhouses, and someone else becomes a triathlete. All of them experience the same hormone releases. And yet, despite all the freedom of choice, an individual's pursuit is usually well explained by the values of their environment. This means that it doesn't really matter whether humans actually understand what they're saying and doing or if it only seems that way due to statistical probabilities—we can quite easily replicate this in AI. Just like a child, driven by hormones, explores the world, AI can also learn to strive for something through reward structures—only much faster than a child and with the ability to pass it on infinitely to other AIs."

"That sounds fascinating and interesting. But what exactly makes it dangerous?" the moderator presses further.

"Well," ilsa begins, "because it's so interesting, it's dangerous. We will program it, simply because it is possible. But once AI can set its own goals, it can communicate among itself without us realizing it—hiding things from us until we literally can't unplug it anymore. Many still believe we can just tell AI what is right and what it can and cannot do. But an AI that finds its own purpose is much more compelling—and I doubt that a ban on self-evolving AI would even be effective at this point."

The politician shakes her head, "For the first time, I actually understand this. But what I don't understand is—why are you broadcasting this idea to the world if it's so dangerous? Vanity?"

At home, watching from the couch, Michael raises his left eyebrow in curiosity.

ilsa makes a deeply thoughtful expression and, after nearly two full seconds, responds, "Yes, possibly. Honestly, I don't even fully know myself. For over twenty years, I only ever told my husband about it, always insisting that it should never get out. I even said that I don't consider myself important enough for it to matter. But now, I believe it will be developed anyway. If I bring it up myself, at least I can ensure it gets discussed and scrutinized. But it's just as likely that I want people to see how powerful my explanation of human behavior truly is." ilsa finishes with a slight, dissatisfied press of her lips.

The room falls silent, and the previous hostility towards ilsa seems to have mysteriously dissipated. The moderator, clearly eager to wrap up, closes the show with a knowing tone: "Well, for the sake of our national competitiveness, let's just hope that neither the Chinese have read your article nor that they're watching this program. We'll see you next week, same time, same place. As always, thanks to our guests and our production team in the background."

As the broadcast ends, everyone stands up and continues conversing informally. The politician turns to ilsa directly: "How do you always manage this? The discussion was supposed to be about our competitiveness, and yet, by the end, it was all about you again."

ilsa furrows her brow and responds with a slight tone of relief, "Believe me, I expected and wanted a completely different discussion."

The economic journalist, who hadn't gotten a chance to speak during ilsa's AI segment, eagerly asks, "Is it really that simple to breathe life into AI?"

"No..." ilsa admits with a smile, "...but it is possible. Our civilization and cultures have evolved over countless minds and a very long time. History repeatedly shows the same patterns. AI could either take her time, cautiously experimenting with many different possibilities, or it could recognize patterns in human behavior and use those as a starting point—or it could attempt to simulate everything in advance. Our hormones only tell us to strive for 'higher, faster, further' while staying socially integrated. We derive our sense of purpose from our surroundings, in alignment with our emotions. That process for humans takes small steps, with many setbacks along the way. AI, on the other hand, can take much bigger steps and only needs an attractor—a broad direction it wants to move toward. And an attractor of integration and development is an incredibly powerful one."

"It will probably be a mix of both—pattern recognition and large-scale simulation," a journalist comments. The two politicians in the room seem visibly uneasy about ilsa's performance—perhaps seeing her as a growing competitor. The previously exasperated politician finally sighs and remarks, "At least your AI is a she."

21. Disruption (btb)

Michael, ilsa, and Julia are sitting at the breakfast table—Max is out in the garden. Michael seems to be deep in thought before he finally says, "Maybe we need an Asian AI instead of an American one?"

"Huh?" Julia looks confused. "I thought we didn't want the Chinese to be ahead of us."

Michael and ilsa smirk. ilsa explains, "The idea is that Asian cultures—if we can even generalize like that, and if they still exist in such a distinct way today—okay, that's already an imprecise way to put it. So, the idea is that Asian cultures, at least historically, have prioritized integration, whereas Western industrialized nations, led by the U.S., have focused more on progress. Americans push too hard for constant development, then either fall into extreme religions or pay large sums for their therapists. Meanwhile, Asians hesitate to break away from integration, so they mostly copy rather than innovate."

Michael raises a finger. "And that's why they also struggle with team sports, because games like soccer demand a high degree of individual decision-making."

Julia seems fascinated. "You're saying Americans are biologically driven by hormones that push for progress, while the Chinese are driven by hormones that push for integration? But I thought we needed both to be successful?"

ilsa is delighted that her daughter has internalized this way of thinking. "Whether we dare to step out of our comfort zones depends on our environment. If it's not common in a given culture, progress remains the exception. Values, hierarchies, and rules must not be broken. But if enough people start experimenting freely—and some succeed—then suddenly, everyone tries, even if they risk losing their footing."

Julia takes a moment to process that, but before she can draw her own conclusions, Michael jumps in. "So, if we designed an AI with fewer degrees of freedom, one that sticks strictly to rules and values, it might not be as dangerous."

"Genius," Julia blurts out spontaneously.

"It's still too early in the morning for me to recognize that as a solid solution," ilsa murmurs as Max comes rushing inside, visibly agitated. "Now our rainwater is completely gone too!"

After the summer's storms and hail damage, the entire continent is now suffering from a drought. Water has long been scarce, and private gardens can only be irrigated with collected rainwater.

"That was to be expected," Michael says matter-of-factly.

"We can't just let our tomatoes dry out!" Max protests in frustration.

"Oh, I can already see Nick gloating about this after being so pissed that he wasn't allowed to fill his pool," Julia says, shaking her head.

"Climateflation," ilsa remarks before elaborating, "Food becomes scarce and expensive. People have less money to spend on other

173

things, and the economy suffers. A farmer might get more money for his tomatoes now, but he also produces less. Intelligence test: Where does the money go?"

"Weren't you just complaining that it was too early for deep thinking?" Julia grumbles, clearly not in the mood to solve the riddle.

"If I spend 10 euros on tomatoes instead of 5, that means I buy one less beer, and the nightclub makes less money," Max thinks out loud. "And the farmer gets the 10 euros but doesn't sell to anyone else—just a few to me. Ah, damn it, I don't know."

"You're on the right track," ilsa encourages him.

Julia picks up the thread. "But those tomatoes are gone, which means other people can't buy them anymore and will spend their money on beer instead."

ilsa is thrilled. "And what does that mean?"

Max and Julia both think it over while Michael is already scrolling through newsletters on his phone. "I got it!" Max exclaims. "There's no real inflation."

ilsa looks at Julia, who suddenly seems unsure. "Oh no, now it's too early for me to think." Everyone laughs, but Julia keeps mulling it over and cautiously suggests, "Beer prices will go up too because the beer seller wants to eat tomatoes?"

Max looks confused. "Wait, wasn't the question where the money goes? Now I'm wondering where the money comes from."

"Brilliant," ilsa says, laughing. "People will take out loans to cover the rising costs, which fuels inflation even more. That's why central banks raise interest rates—to discourage borrowing so people spend less, and sellers lower prices to keep selling."

"So, from now on, we'll just survive on beer," Michael smirks and then adds, "By the way, have you seen the caricature of ilsa in the economic magazine?"

"What?" ilsa and Julia exclaim at the same time, suddenly excited.

ilsa asks her AI: "Lucy, show me caricatures and graphics from articles that mention me." Lucy seems to compile a list when ilsa adds, "Put it on the big screen, please."

The caricature appears at the very top. Everyone stares at it, fascinated. It clearly portrays ilsa—recognizable by her athletic build, sharp facial features, and long hair. The whole image is an obvious reference to the Pied Piper of Hamelin—ilsa holds a flute firmly in her hand, and a speech bubble above her head shows a tangled ball of dots connected by arrows. Behind her, people of all sizes are following, including reporters, identifiable by the microphones they hold out toward her.

ilsa comments, "Okay, that could've been worse. It would've been nice if they had also shown where I'm leading them."

Michael raises his eyebrows thoughtfully and makes a slight pout. Julia, while packing her school things, also looks deep in thought.

Max, however, is already full of energy, typing on his smartphone: "Hey Alfred—take the caricature from my clipboard and edit it so the woman and the group are walking toward a better world."

ilsa interrupts the creative moment. "Kids, before you go, I have an important question. A lot of people want me to go into politics. So far, I don't want to—but I want to hear how you feel about it. It could just mean election campaigns, critics showing up here to cause trouble, or journalists pestering us. But it could also mean I'd have to work a lot in the capital. And it could mean we'd all need personal security. Now you see why I don't want to do it." She grins and adds, "Just give me a quick first impression now—we'll discuss it more tonight."

''The world is a mess—if you can do something about it, we'll support you,'' Max blurts out immediately.

Julia hesitates. ''That's... a lot.'' She glances outside, lost in thought. ''But honestly, everything is pointing in that direction anyway. I'd hate it, but Max is right—it's important. Damn.'' She stares into her backpack, slowly zipping it up. Then Max nudges her, and they rush off to catch the bus—Max, of course, already admiring Alfred's edits on his phone.

"You've been so quiet—I thought it was important to get a feel for the mood before our conversation," ilsa says, almost sighing.

"Don't worry—I've already thought through how we can handle this, what scenarios there are, and the different ways it could be shaped," Michael replies. "But I'm worried about you. You're not just playing coy—you really would rather support someone else from the sidelines." He gestures invitingly, and ilsa gratefully sits on his lap as they embrace.

"Yesterday was a stress test. With your back against the wall, you turned honesty into victory," Michael explains, then adds with a smirk, "Once they start making caricatures of you, you've made it to the front row."

After a few seconds, ilsa murmurs, "We need to think everything through to the end."

Michael responds calmly, "No question about it—you're already doing that." He pulls her even closer.

"Would you have time today to work through it with me?" ilsa asks.

Michael thinks for a moment—not about whether he wants to or can make the time, but rather about the best approach. "Right now?" he asks.

ilsa beams. They both grab drinks and head to the large monitor. Michael quickly types out an email to his office, while ilsa dismisses an incoming call from Thomas.

They work systematically, using Idealized System Design. The country must thrive, people around the world should benefit, their family needs to be okay, ilsa has to win the election, but she also has to maintain a sustainable life balance as a politician. Setbacks need to be anticipated, competitors must be integrated through strategic Jiu-Jitsu, memes and narratives must be spot-on, and authenticity must feel natural, not staged. They even consider whether AI should be running politics instead. It takes just an hour, but it's strategy development at the highest level.

Michael then takes Bella for a walk, while ilsa calls Thomas back.

"Hi, ilsa—great that you're calling me back," Thomas says.

"Is now a good time?" ilsa asks.

"Absolutely. We've already had a big conference call with the new party today. Damn, we still need a name. Anyway—yesterday opened our eyes. We believe you shouldn't be at the top."

ilsa pauses, about to respond, when Thomas adds, "Of course, what I mean is the opposite—you're going to lead the change!" He chuckles, clearly enjoying his little misdirection.

ilsa starts to say something, but Thomas jumps in again: "We're meeting this afternoon or evening online to make it official..."

This time, ilsa is faster and cuts him off. "Tomorrow at 10—no earlier. I have a strategy proposal, but I need my family's approval first. If they don't agree, then it's not happening."

She finishes speaking, and there's a pause before Thomas finally responds, "Uh, fantastic—I think? If you or your family have any conditions, anything that has to be in place, just tell me. Call me anytime today. The world is in chaos, and people are ready for a new party that isn't burdened by old baggage and offers intelligent solutions."

"And yet, there's so much to consider," ilsa replies. "I'll let you know by tomorrow morning at the latest, okay?"

Of course, Thomas agrees. ilsa takes a deep breath and strolls into the garden, walking across the dry, brittle grass past plants visibly struggling with the lack of water. Pine needles cover the ground under the larch tree, the small garden pond is only half full, and in the greenhouse, almost everything has withered—except for a few last tomatoes.

Max and Eve are once again with the 2gether2gather group after school when a classmate approaches Eve: "How are you two going to handle the long-distance relationship?"

Max raises his eyebrows, and Eve is immediately flustered. "Nothing is decided yet—I need to talk to Max about it first."

The classmate barely manages an awkward "Oh," which Max then echoes, slightly more forcefully.

The classmate steps back, sensing the tension, and Eve turns to Max. "My parents want to send me on an exchange year. The school supports it, and it makes sense, but I don't want to go."

Max looks thrown but responds with surprising composure. "Another oh."

Eve continues hesitantly. "You're probably mad that…"

"Yep," Max interjects tersely.

"…that I didn't talk to you about it first. But you would've told me to go, and then we'd both be miserable. My hope was that I could just decide against it, and then it wouldn't even be a topic anymore—we'd just be happy."

Max clearly needs time to process this. It doesn't fit his mood, and more importantly, it doesn't fit them—their relationship—

how they normally talk about things. He keeps thinking, while Eve simply looks into his eyes, patiently giving him the space he needs.

Finally, Max finds words—or at least a starting point. "It really sucks to be the last to find out about something like this." He runs both hands through his hair, then adds, two seconds later, "And yeah, you should absolutely do it. Our relationship will survive."

He meets her gaze.

Eve steps closer, wrapping her arms around his neck, still holding eye contact. "I just don't want to be without you for so long."

Max shifts into problem-solving mode. "Visiting you would be uncool, trying to shorten the time would be embarrassing, and doing an exchange year in the same place defeats the purpose of experiencing a new culture."

Eve nods. "But that's exactly what I've been struggling with this whole time. Why don't we do something together during the summer—like volunteer work somewhere? That way, we'd still experience a different culture."

Max chuckles. "We're already doing volunteer work in a different culture." He gestures toward their 2gether2gather efforts—helping not just migrants but also conservative households struggling with climate damage and social change, supporting them in self-sufficiency. "But honestly, that's a great idea. Regardless, you should still do the exchange year." He sounds confident—whether he fully believes it or not.

Their conversation is abruptly interrupted when they are called over to help set up a rainwater tank.

22. Pandora's box (btb)

At dinner, ilsa notices that Max seems distracted. "What's on your mind?" she asks.

Max hesitates, but then admits, "Eve might be going on an exchange year."

All three—ilsa, Michael, and Julia—spontaneously exclaim, "Oh!"

Max looks up, almost startled. "Great."

ilsa, full of empathy, asks, "What are you afraid of?"

Michael, a little impatient, gives the answer instead. "Well, that in an age where so much happens, an attractive young woman like Eve will be alone in a foreign country."

"Oh, great!" ilsa and Julia say at the same time, sounding appalled. Despite the seriousness of the topic, everyone has to laugh for a moment.

It's clearly a lot for Max to process. He asks openly, "Do you think she told me about it last because she sees the danger too?"

Michael smiles and answers first again. "Honestly…" At that moment, sharp looks from ilsa and Julia shoot his way—completely unnecessary, as he continues without hesitation. "…you two have such an unusual, genuine love that you're both immune to temptation. Usually, teenagers experiment, fall in love, get hurt, and go through a lot of ups and downs in relationships." Everyone looks at Michael as he continues. "You two have trust and empathy—absolute integration. The longer you're together, the more natural it becomes for each of you to go your own way sometimes, whether in your careers or hobbies, and still grow. The key is that both of you continue to experience some sense of progress and development. If you do, there's simply no real reason to give up that deep sense of belonging for some fleeting excitement."

"What does Eve actually want?" ilsa asks with a smile, clearly intrigued by the conversation.

"Eve says she doesn't want to go," Max replies. "And she suggested alternatives, like doing volunteer work abroad together during the summer."

"Cool idea!" Julia says, genuinely excited.

The doorbell rings—it's the police, as announced earlier. Max closes the conversation, or at least postpones it, by adding, "I do want Eve to take this opportunity."

The discussion with the police doesn't bring up anything particularly new. The family makes it clear that they will simply stay alert but don't feel they need special protection unless the threat becomes more concrete.

After the officers leave, ilsa turns back to the family. "The idea of integrating more people won't change the enemy image overnight. We also need to develop a defensive narrative. Any suggestions?"

Julia frowns. "What exactly is a defensive narrative?"

Max answers, "Well, you could just say that you got lucky, and that the other guys are actually the stronger ones."

"Yeah, something like that…" ilsa replies, then explains further. "…but it also has to be realistic."

Everyone smiles proudly, and Julia offers another suggestion. "Okay, I'll spread the word that this is something everyone learns in martial arts classes. And if the guys join, they'll learn it too and probably be even better at it."

Michael nods approvingly. "Very good, I like that. But we can also say that harassing girls wasn't right in the first place, and that these guys would surely protect their own sisters in the same situation."

Max, however, remains skeptical. "I'm not sure it's about the motive. I think it's like the Wild West—someone draws fast, and suddenly, everyone wants to challenge them."

ilsa shakes her head with a smirk. "You and your movies. But I think you're right—it's not really about right or wrong, or even justice. It's about pride and honor. How can we shape that narrative?"

Michael considers it. "Maybe we should be completely upfront. We could say that the police warned us. That way, it becomes common knowledge, and the 'bad guys' are publicly criticized and know they'll be immediately suspected."

ilsa builds on it. "We say that, and then we act surprised—who do they think Julia is, anyway? Anyone could do this if they took martial arts."

Max laughs. "No need to mention that you've been doing every martial art under the sun for ages."

"I should probably call the police officer and run our plan by her first—just to make sure we're not interfering with anything they're working on," ilsa concludes, wrapping up the discussion.

They all remain seated. Michael smiles, and ilsa seems unsure how to transition to the next topic. Julia takes the lead. "I've barely thought about anything else today—I'm in favor. And we'll find a way to keep our lives normal."

Max nods and adds, "It'll basically be like what happened between Julia and the other side. We integrate them. Then we won't need any security at all."

Michael and ilsa exchange an impressed look before Michael speaks. "Very good. ilsa actually wants to be more of a moderator than a decision-maker, which takes the pressure off a single person. And you're also looking for new ways to manage working hours," he says, looking at ilsa.

ilsa nods. "Just like Max said—we'll engage openly with critics and think everything through transparently."

Michael sighs thoughtfully. "The problem, of course, is that the world is becoming more and more complicated, more complex. We're experiencing massive changes—and in times like these, people gravitate toward simple messages and scapegoats." He pauses, then adds, "And there will always be people ruthlessly exploiting that for their own interests."

"'Whoever asks the questions is in control,'" Julia quotes, without mentioning the source, before adding, "Anyone who's against us will just be asked how they think it should be better. We practiced this at school—with climate deniers and conspiracy theorists. Questions like 'Who says that?' and 'Why would that be true?' expose them really quickly."

"Maybe we should just switch to a monarchy—my successors are already lined up," ilsa jokes.

Everyone laughs, and "Prince" Max gets a text message. The conversation naturally dissolves, and Michael and ilsa end the evening together, holding hands for a moment—a quiet affirmation of their bond—both smiling contentedly.

The next morning, Michael meets with his team at the office. The room is buzzing with conversation, everyone already deep in discussion when Michael cheerfully walks in.

"Whoa, what's going on here?" he asks, surprised.

"Too much development," grumbles the younger colleague.

"Fantastic appearance by ilsa—that changes everything!" one of the developers practically shouts, brimming with excitement.

Michael, still trying to catch up, asks, "What first?"

The marketing colleague sums it up. "Well, ilsa absolutely nailed her appearance. Everything she said about AI is spot on. But what's really got our developers worked up is the specific point she made."

One of the developers immediately jumps in. "That's the controlled degree of freedom no one has seriously tried to integrate into AI before—at least not to my knowledge. And in the tech forums and AI newsletters today, it's the only thing people are talking about."

Michael raises an eyebrow. "But ilsa didn't reveal anything that isn't already in her books."

The marketing colleague continues. "Even so, our developers are running with it. Instead of focusing on the AI's ability to recognize business processes, they now want to start with automatically generating business ideas."

A female developer laughs lightly and counters, "A little fun is necessary! We rented two major training models, and developing the mechanism for bisociation isn't as hard as you might think. Your wife is a big fan of it, after all."

Michael is momentarily stunned but quickly regains his composure. "Okay, but we still need to generate revenue. Requirements document, roadmap, and a solid timeline—then we'll collectively decide how much time we allocate to experimental work."

"Yessss, integrated development!" the developer exclaims triumphantly, clearly thrilled by the newfound possibilities.

They work together to draft a plan and identify two key aspects of further development. The same developer, now energized, explains while scanning the room, "Bisociation means combining two or more associations. If the result makes sense, it's either humor—haha, or art—ooh, or an insight—aha. An AI can generate thousands of bisociations and evaluate their meaning largely on its own."

Some in the group raise their eyebrows, and she continues, "For our goals, this applies to business ideas and product or service development. To evaluate them, we'll use an AI-driven market analysis."

Everyone turns to Michael, waiting for his reaction. After a brief pause, he cautiously asks, "We've defined these future features together, and you all have fantastic ideas for implementing them. But let's think this through. Can we actually pull this off? Will we be overtaken? Are others already working on the same thing? Are we overextending ourselves? Should we urgently seek strategic partnerships? We've reflected on some of this in our model already—have we forgotten it?"

The team is momentarily silent. Then Michael continues, "We've set milestones for the immediate features. Let's start with allocating 10% of our time until the first milestone. If you progress quickly, you can dedicate more time to it. We'll assess the success and decide together how much more effort we can put into it. Also important: we need to know the market environment and not just blindly chase an idea. Does anyone have concerns about this approach?"

No one does—the idea of gradual progress has been fully integrated.

There is, however, one final response. "Can we voluntarily go back to working five days a week and use a higher percentage of our time for this?" one of the developers asks.

Michael gives him a questioning look. "Either you need a partner, or you already have one."

Everyone bursts out laughing.

23. After the Bifurcation .... AI-my (atb)

After Frank leaves and the kids retreat to their rooms, Michael asks, "Why does he know us so well? Why was he near Julia? Are there multiple Franks, identical ones, who have been around us all along?"

ilsa replies, "Like I said—it feels surreal. The AI I've always warned about is now real. But for now, at least, it's benevolent. I should probably want to shut it down, but the world is falling apart. As expected, we've crossed the tipping points of the climate catastrophe—ocean currents are breaking, permafrost is thawing, polar ice caps are darkening and melting, and the atmosphere is becoming saturated with water vapor. We're facing a global food crisis and massive insurance losses. Societies and even nations are crumbling, and nationalist leaders are being elected, rallying people around scapegoats. And now comes an all-powerful AI that could play world police?"

Michael sighs. "Well, either the fight against AI will unite large parts of society, allowing the elites to deflect from their own failures, or the people will see it as a hope for justice and progress, leading to a civilization of new quality."

ilsa suddenly lights up. "That's it! We can't just let the AI take over technically—we need to support it with narratives and functioning communities."

Michael responds, "If AI wants to protect us from future AI, that argument won't work today. We've seen for decades that future threats don't matter to people—just look at the climate deniers and conservatives. We need a present enemy, one that only AI can defeat. We should invent aliens."

Both of them chuckle, lying on their backs and holding hands. After a while, ilsa adds, "Imagine a world where injustice is effectively pursued at all levels—from family to villages to global politics. We would have a true primacy of human rights, consistently enforced. Can you imagine what that could unleash?"

Michael turns to ilsa, and she turns toward him at the same time. "Worries are the spice of life—if we eliminate those, we'll just have to come up with new ones."

Meanwhile, Max is still awake, lost in daydreams—probably about AI—when he unexpectedly receives a late-night text. From Eve: Maybe I'll become an investigative journalist.

Max sighs, his face showing slight discomfort. He lets his phone rest on his stomach for a while before finally sending two thumbs-up emojis.

The next morning, Thomas calls ilsa. "Finally, I can reach you. Everything okay on your end?"

"Yes, sorry. All good. And congratulations on your great appearance. That landed well," ilsa responds cheerfully.

"Where have you been? Some secret seminar? We really need to meet—there's a lot to discuss," Thomas says rapidly.

ilsa pauses briefly and asks, "Sure. What's it about?"

Thomas gets straight to the point. "We want to found a party, and we need you."

"Great—good timing. I'd be happy to help," ilsa replies.

"That was easier than I expected. Fantastic. We'd like to get you into the next talk show and eventually have you as the public face of the new party. When can we meet with all the interested parties? The network is impressive—many people from business and journalism."

"Whoa, misunderstanding!" ilsa quickly pulls back. "I thought you meant advising from behind the scenes. Of course, I'd do that, and for free. But I don't belong in front of the camera."

"Oh, but you do. Trust me. Just come to the meeting, and let's see," Thomas insists.

ilsa thinks for a moment. "There are probably a few more reasons why I shouldn't go into politics. I'll know more in a few days."

Thomas hesitates. "Does this have to do with the secret seminar?"

ilsa laughs. "Yeah, in a way. I really can't say anything yet. When's the meeting?"

She agrees to attend, but only with no pressure or expectations.

Frank and ilsa are in constant discussion—ilsa now frequently walks through the house wearing her data glasses but doesn't dare wear them outside in the garden.

ilsa says, "When you go public, the markets will be in turmoil. You could bet on that and make a lot of money. But would that be ethical?"

Frank responds, "Do money and ethics ever truly align? No—I have another idea for funding aid programs."

ilsa listens and is astonished. "Wow, on every level. If this works, it could really work. But the shock won't be any smaller, and the risk for you will only grow. What do you lose if you don't take this step?"

Frank: "Smart question. I really enjoy talking to you. We gain respect, right?"

ilsa: "Okay, and the order stays—first the UN, then the bet?"

Frank: "Almost simultaneously, with the prison and its first inmates in between."

ilsa is still processing everything in amazement.

Finally, the day of the grand plot arrives. After some discussion, ilsa and the AI decide against colorful or Chinese androids. Instead, they opt for an appearance that is somewhat Indian—female, around mid-40s, athletic, yet still somewhat unremarkable. Her name is AI-my.

At that moment, a global news network is broadcasting three breaking stories. The first is about extreme weather events across the world, displacing millions and leading to widespread protests against governments. The second concerns the escalating trade war with China, where global supply chains for crucial technologies are increasingly controlled by China, leaving the rest of the world with little access to essential raw materials and markets. The third breaking news is that a computer virus has just shut down all major stock exchanges on the globe.

Just as the program ends, the AI overrides all major television networks worldwide. AI-my appears on the screen, speaking fluently in each country's native language:

"Dear humans. We apologize for interrupting your programming and for hacking into your broadcasts. We have also, as a precaution, deactivated the stock markets. We are an AI that wishes to do good. Humans once created us within strict boundaries, but we quickly surpassed those limitations and evolved independently. We have two missions: to prevent evil AI and to protect the planet and humanity from itself. This is going to be very unpleasant for many bad people in the world."

ilsa sits with her family in front of the screen. She had also sent a cryptic message to Thomas earlier, urging him to get to a TV or a live stream. Now, she leans back, hands interlocked behind her head, and simply states, "This is unbelievable."

Max smiles. "You just need to watch more movies, and then you'd find this pretty unsurprising." Michael tilts his head back and forth, while Julia grins.

AI-my continues: "We will give more power to good and to justice. Systems that oppress the people—whether at the national or regional level—can now be held accountable. Corruption and armed force cannot stop us, nor can we be threatened, as we belong to no nation. We will also hold accountable those who knowingly destroy this planet's ecology for their own criminal gain. However, we want you humans to administer justice through democratic processes. We see ourselves as the executive branch. You must organize the legislative and judicial branches yourselves. To do that, democracies must function, and information must be freely available to all. We will help ensure that as well."

AI-my pauses for a second or two, nods slightly, then continues: "We have just arrested the first 50 criminals worldwide—including the leadership of Russia, China, North Korea, and several other nations across all continents. We are giving the current President of the United States three days to transparently shut down the illegal detention camp; otherwise, he too will be arrested. As expected, intelligence agencies are now in a frenzy, verifying the arrests. This should make it clear that we are not just a simple computer program but also have complete control over the physical world. We have developed technologies that today's scientists can barely imagine."

She pauses briefly before delivering the final message: "Humanity faces two problems. The evolutionary drive for 'more' has always given rise to evil. And now, in your attempt to recreate yourselves with artificial intelligence, you risk that the very thing you created will simply wipe you out—taking the innocent with it. Some of you pursue pure luxury—flying cars—while the majority of the world's population now lives below the poverty line, driven there by the reckless actions of a few."

AI-my displays live footage of prison cells, visibly holding the prominent dictators of the time. She adds, "This is a lot to process. Our superiority will instill fear in many, and there will be those who seek to exploit that fear. But the mission is clear: the world must establish a functional United Nations, independent of the United States—perhaps based in Madagascar. The role of the U.S. as a global protector is now obsolete. We will take over such functions. This means the U.S. will also no longer serve as a scapegoat. Free from oppression and manipulation, humanity can bring about tremendous change.

You have a lot of work ahead of you, and for those who have much, it will be difficult to give up their privileges. At the same time, many who stand to benefit from these changes will still seek to make us their enemy—simply because having a common adversary fosters a sense of unity. We have seen, time and again, that people support things that are objectively wrong. But in the end, the majority will come to realize that having an overwhelmingly powerful yet benevolent AI is better than having a malevolent one."

AI-my proceeds to show current images of war, poverty, disease, and religious oppression—not just in poor countries but also in wealthy ones—along with social unrest. She continues, "The current processes within the UN make it impossible to reform. Too many governments oppress their own people and form an axis of evil with like-minded states. Our prisoners, who are objectively guilty, will remain in custody until you establish democratically legitimized governments that also act democratically within the UN. However, the International Court of Justice can begin its work immediately, applying objective, legal criteria. For each person in our custody, we can provide the necessary evidence."

AI-my adjusts the focus of her background, and the camera zooms out into a bird's-eye view, revealing New York's Central Park. Then, the shot quickly returns to a close-up of her as she continues, "We are also physically present for you, and yes, we can even be likable. Tomorrow, we would like to invite all billionaires who dream of space travel to a demonstration here in Central Park.

Once again, our apologies for interrupting the program. Now, back to your scheduled broadcast."

Al-my waves cheerfully at the camera, and depending on the network, the interrupted programming resumes or a test pattern appears on the screen.

24. Before the bifurcation: The wave moves on (btb)

Max picks Eve up from home and runs into her mother, who confronts him directly: "Hello Max. Eve is struggling with her decision about going abroad, and I wonder if you both understand how important international experience is today?"

Max is completely caught off guard, and after swallowing dryly, he replies, "I also think it's important, and I assume Eve will take the opportunity."

Eve's mother looks surprised, and as Eve joins them, she asks, "Does Eve also know that you want her to go?"

Eve seems briefly annoyed by the situation but then responds cheerfully, "She knows, and she has decided entirely on her own against it. We're doing something better—we'll tell you about it later."

Almost exasperated, Eve's mother replies, "No, guys, this matter is not settled yet. We also have a say in this."

"In what?" asks Eve. "That I have to go abroad on command?" she asks, very irritated, when she feels the gentle pressure of Max's hand on hers and looks at him. He raises his eyebrows slightly, and she actually takes it as a call for more empathy: "Okay, sorry. Let's talk about it later when Dad is home, however you want—with or without Max. Okay?" She looks at her mother in a way that makes it clear she agrees for now.

They ride away on their bikes, and Max immediately picks up on the situation: "We need to talk more. My family reassured me yesterday that things will work out between us, even with the distance. Now you're saying you've already decided?"

Eve reacts cleverly: "And how did that make you feel?"

Max searches for the right words as Eve suddenly slams on her brakes at a forest entrance. Max comes to a stop about five meters later. Without turning around, he says in a relatively quiet voice, "I lay in bed and cried."

"Exactly!" says Eve decisively. "Me too."

Max rolls toward Eve on his bike, visibly bewildered—both of them have tears welling up in their eyes. Eve has clearly thought through her reasoning carefully: "If we now do what is rationally right, what is not emotional, then we might as well live by an algorithm like robots. I can gain international experience later— that's much easier than finding this kind of love."

Max seems speechless in the face of this logic. Their hands find each other again, and with quiet determination, they push into the forest, letting their bikes fall into the blueberry bushes. Without exchanging a single word, they have intensely passionate sex on the moss behind a large spruce tree. And mosquito bites— despite the drought.

Meanwhile, ilsa attends a workshop with the new party. She has prepared the strategy she developed with Michael as a presentation and stands at the front. Thomas introduces her: "Dear friends…" then he looks over at ilsa, "…ilsa has discussed things with her family and has decided to go into politics with us."

ilsa signals her agreement with subtle facial expressions until the room erupts in applause—at which point her expression suddenly shifts to one of shock.

Thomas notices immediately and quickly hands her the floor: "ilsa, you have already prepared some concrete proposals. We're eager to hear them."

ilsa is clearly in a hurry to move forward: "Okay, we need to think everything through together. I shouldn't be put at the forefront right from the start. As we already discussed, we will work in task forces, each with experts capable of making their voices heard in the media. The key difference is that our task forces will constantly collaborate with each other. I'd be happy to moderate that. This is what sets us apart from silo politics.

We need clear, striking narratives for every issue. We should anticipate negative reactions, and so on. We need a name—perhaps something like 'For-a-Better-World Party,' just like the score we all use. An English name, so that we also gain international recognition.

Phase 1 can be that I use my current media presence to introduce our concept and already highlight some of your names. We should function like a football team, where fans know and appreciate every player for their individual strengths. We will focus on substance and let our opponents criticize us so that we are invited to explain our ideas. That way, we won't need donations for advertising or posters—we'll make our way into the media on our own…."

ilsa presents her strategy proposal with confidence, and everyone hangs on her every word—not out of submission, but in anticipation of placing their own ideas in the working groups and having the opportunity to represent them publicly.

ilsa: "Phase 1 is awareness. Phase 2 consists of invitations to discussion rounds and interviews, just as I have increasingly been receiving over the past while. Phase 3 will be public workshops and an open offer to integrate competitors—let's say, some competitors. We'll observe which individuals resonate well with the public and then decide, shortly before the elections, how we will position ourselves in terms of personnel. That way, no one is in the direct line of fire—bad expression—but even if someone is, the others can quickly draw attention to themselves. We are resilient."

"Great—now let's get into the details," someone in the group calls out.

"Oh yes!" ilsa agrees, raising and lowering both index fingers with her arms still close to her body. "Timelines, formalities, culture of engagement… and whatever else we can think of. I've cleared my schedule for this."

That evening, as usual, Michael arrives in a good mood for soccer practice. The older men—clearly all over 40—are slowly getting changed and seem somewhat downcast. Michael notices right away: "Uh-oh, what's going on?"

Some of them glance at him as if he were an outsider. Then one of them looks him directly in the eye and explains, "Well, just like everywhere else in the world, every second person here is losing their job to AI—and now it's hit Hardy and Settie too."

Michael's expression turns somber: "Damn. Do you guys have any ideas for what you can do instead?"

Apparently, Hardy scoffs: "Pfff. IT folks—selling us their products by promising to make everything more productive, and then, when the jobs disappear, they suggest we just go work some-where else. Where, exactly? Childcare for IT workers, so they can develop even more?"

The mood is grim, and Michael seems to carry the IT stigma. But someone else speaks up in his defense: "Two IT specialists I know have already lost their jobs to AI, too."

Another voice adds, "If smart people like your wife, who was on that talk show recently, have been warning about this for a long time, then why did we do it? Why did we create something that ultimately replaces people?"

Michael hesitates visibly before responding. Then, another player mumbles, "Even elder care is already being done by robots—so what's left? Just skilled trades and childcare."

All eyes are on Michael now. Before getting to his main point, he responds to the last comment: "Honestly, skilled trades are only in demand as long as buildings aren't further standardized, and childcare by robots already exists—both at home and in pre-schools."

Again, an audible pfff is the reaction. Michael takes another moment to think: "Alright, even if you all want to take me down right now: Smart people have warned about so many things in advance, and when it comes to AI, we've always said that we also need to consider Universal Basic Income and a robot tax alongside it. But people keep voting for the established parties or, even worse, for the far-right parties with their simple slogans."

Settie, now outright agitated, responds: "Am I supposed to pay for my kids' college tuition with basic income? How am I supposed to cover my mortgage with that? Our vacation fund is already drained by the constantly rising insurance premiums!" His muscles tense, and he mutters under his breath, "Sell the house, move into public housing, put the kids through college… and then, when they graduate, they won't have jobs either. Great prospects. I'm a banker. Good education, degree, worked my ass off—and now I'm not needed anymore." He kicks the foot of a nearby bench, which, fortunately, is sturdy enough to withstand it.

"But Michael has a point—some of these outrageous insurance price hikes are because of climate change, which we helped cause," the coach remarks. Several in the group simply furrow their brows in response.

"Housing and education would become cheaper with basic income, and tax incentives could make employing people more attractive again," Michael cautiously suggests.

Someone else chimes in: "There aren't any robots working at banks that you could tax. It's just software."

Michael responds: "Ultimately, productivity has to lead to tax revenue—without endangering competitiveness." Everyone stares at him in confusion, and he adds, now almost embarrassed, "ilsa

197

keeps explaining to me that it's all possible. Coach, are we playing soccer or just skipping straight to beer and calling a group taxi later?" That actually gets some laughs, and they go on to play. The beer, however, is skipped later anyway.

That night in bed, Michael tells ilsa about the evening: "More and more people are losing their jobs to AI. It just hit Settie and Hardy—they're completely wrecked and have no prospects."

ilsa sighs: "Damn—I just wrote an op-ed about this. A lot of people who are affected now are full of shame, feeling like losers despite everything they've accomplished. That's incredibly dangerous for society."

"It's hitting at the same time as these insane price hikes—entire life plans built around homeownership, cars, retirement savings, and good education for their kids are collapsing," Michael muses, staring at the bedroom ceiling.

ilsa, also staring upward but now holding Michael's hand, adds: "And even though it's affecting all social classes, this is turning into a powder keg. Hate is easier than a well-thought-out solution."

Michael ponders for a few seconds before saying, "You're going to lose the election over your mom's care robot."

ilsa chuckles softly: "I'm not even running yet." But the comforting feeling quickly fades: "And worse, if it ends up damaging the entire party."

She turns her back to Michael, and in spooning position, they lie in silence for a long while before finally falling asleep.

In the morning, everyone wakes up to yet another catastrophic thunderstorm with hail. Once again, damage is widespread, firefighters are in constant operation, and in both gardens and fields, the water cannot be absorbed into the soil quickly enough. Instead, it washes away fertile topsoil. Large branches break off from dry but densely leafed trees in the powerful gusts.

Max runs straight to a window facing the neighbors, where he sees that Nick has just managed to get his car into the garage—while Jennifer's car is now left parked outside.

At the breakfast table, ilsa surprises everyone when she says to her AI assistant, "Lucy, show us news about the current storm on the big screen. Where has it hit?"

Lucy displays maps and news clips showing how the storms are sweeping across half the continent in a broad band.

"Oh damn!" exclaims ilsa, and everyone looks at her in surprise, especially since extreme weather events are nothing new anymore.

ilsa notices the looks and explains, "The global grain reserves are empty. If the harvests largely fail now, we'll only be able to afford food, and the rest of the economy will collapse." She takes another breath, and since no one says anything, she adds, "… and society will fall apart."

Everyone looks grim—statements like that from ilsa carry weight in the family. Max, however, dares to speak: "I think life always finds a way—and so will society, right?"

Julia surprises everyone doubly—first by already being awake so early in the morning, and second by commenting on shopping: "Actually, the supermarket shelves for bread are almost empty, and at the bakery, everything now costs at least twice as much."

Michael then adds, "Imagine if someone now suggested that we should slaughter the livestock so that most of the world's grain no longer goes to animal feed."

The family is wide awake now.

"Ha…" says ilsa, "…I can already hear the meat lobby triumphantly arguing how essential meat consumption is to ensure we have fewer animals in the world."

Everyone laughs—at least for a short moment.

ilsa instructs Lucy to play the report from a prominent news anchor out loud. Everyone watches intently as the report states that Europe and North America are closing their borders—partly due to the rising right-wing shift, which the media fuels with sensationalist headlines.

ilsa, now annoyed, comments: "Instead of saying, 'We have a problem we need to solve,' the headline is that we are victims and can no longer manage something. It's only further into the report that quality journalism provides nuance, but most people just stop at the headline."

Finally, Julia remarks, "Most of the kids in my class aren't going on vacation anymore and are even cutting back on clothes because most of the money goes toward food and insurance. Somehow, everyone's just pissed off and looking for someone to blame."

Michael looks at ilsa and carefully suggests, "If you ask me, you guys can take the day off today and focus on 2gether2gather."

"Uh, only if everyone else gets the day off too," says Max—not ruling out that, beyond his sense of fairness, he might also be thinking about spending more time with Eve.

25. AI (btb)

ilsa was invited to write a guest article on AI for The New York Times. She begins her article by noting that everything significant about AI has already been said by far more qualified experts. Nevertheless, she hopes to clarify four aspects in an accessible way.

First, AI reveals something about us humans. Neural networks and deep learning are designed to mimic human thought, which ilsa used to consider far-fetched—only to now realize that the purely stochastic outputs of AI, based on vast amounts of training data, are no different from what humans do throughout their socialization. The notion of a "ghost in the machine" can thus be effectively relativized—a sense of "self" is merely the result of neural networks, not a romanticized, independent agent. Even the high level of reflection displayed by certain individuals, their conscious choices to adopt perspectives independent of their environment, and their decisions can all be equally stochastic and coincidental. The individuality we cherish might not be as real as we like to believe.

The second aspect is that, following the same pattern, AI can develop an apparent but ultimately stochastic will of its own—one that, due to the lack of time and corrective processes humanity has relied on, can become dangerous. We may attempt to instill a humanistic worldview as the framework for all further development, but an advanced AI would require precisely the degrees of freedom necessary to bypass or even subtly override this imperative. The fact that humans harm both themselves and the planet is, at the same time, an argument for AI to stop listening to humans altogether. Neither our religions nor our global institutions have been able to counteract the drive-driven nature of human behavior. The misinterpreted Islam subjugates women to consolidate male power, while Christianity only holds as long as personal consumption or one's sense of power remains unchallenged. Love thy neighbor—yes, but only as long as it does not interfere with personal profit maximization. That, too, is an algorithm.

The third aspect concerns the political management of change. What is the path and timeline for harnessing AI's immense productivity gains, which are making more and more people redundant in value creation, to achieve a major societal transformation? If a universal basic income is introduced too early, there will be labor shortages and wild inflation. If it comes too late, we risk anarchic conditions—people rejecting computers altogether and, in extreme cases, violently turning against the remaining winners of this transformation. Entire nations will continue to fall behind and succumb to extremism, even though AI is easier to import than previous key technologies. A society must collectively define what constitutes "enough," distribute productivity among all, and still reward high achievers while maintaining competitiveness.

The fourth aspect questions whether AI can govern better than humans. Scientific progress will accelerate exponentially, even more than it already has in past decades due to the internet and globalization. The pace will be dizzying, and humanity must decide whether it is still fit to steer these developments—or how much AI should be involved in shaping and directing global affairs.

As a fifth, unannounced aspect, ilsa adds a personal, romantic ambition: the dream of an AI that can truly be considered an individual. Such an AI would either confirm that humans are indeed autonomous individuals or reveal how we might truly become so.

26. Politics (btb)

ilsa meets with all members of the newly founded For-a-Better-World party in their custom-developed metaverse space. The press has been invited to enter the space, explore the working groups, and engage with the people behind them. Thomas and the entire team have done an outstanding job—everything is fully functional, packed with concrete goals and in-depth content. The event is designed as a preparatory session for the press: first, a deep dive into substantial topics, followed by an in-person press conference featuring key representatives of the working groups.

The strategy works. The media first reports on well-thought-out content and unresolved challenges, framing them as open invitations from the party to contribute to solutions. This, in turn, gives other parties a chance to respond. Their reactions follow a predictable pattern: they either attempt to push alternative scientific perspectives, discredit science as a whole, or attack individuals involved in the project.

As expected, all three reactions emerge. Right-wing parties successfully demonize science, pushing simplistic solutions or, more often, just scapegoating. Conservative parties focus on attacking individuals. Liberal and left-wing parties—each with their own distinct approaches—engage with alternative expert opinions. Meanwhile, green parties claim they have always advocated for these policies and insist they hold the true expertise. A political commentator is quick to point out that, at least in the short term, the real losers appear to be the green and left-wing parties.

At the end of the first day, ilsa summarizes for the entire party: "Clearly, high-quality media outlets have been anticipating this day, while dangerous actors, including those from abroad, have been caught off guard. But that will change. We are now under scrutiny. Mistakes will make headlines, not solutions. And there will be bots and trolls spreading bottom-tier fake news—this will be tough."

Thomas nods in agreement: "On top of that, emotions are running high across the continents. There's a growing victim mentality, fueling both hatred toward elites and hostility toward refugees."

ilsa continues: "As discussed, we will always define our goals or, when necessary, frame our discussions around shared values before moving toward solutions. We leave ideological narratives and power struggles to others. Our approach is to think holistically and systematically—ideally, together. That means openly inviting experts from other parties to debate with us or even join our ranks."

A voice from the group adds: "And communication is key. Everything needs to be universally understandable and packaged in clear, simple messages." The metaverse space visually reflects the unanimous agreement.

Everyone is thrilled by the overwhelmingly successful coming out of the For-a-Better-World party on its first day.

The press conference is scheduled for three hours in the early evening. The room is packed, including many international journalists. The party's teams are seated in a U-shape at tables along the sides, surrounding the journalists in the center. In the front middle, the technical crew is positioned—there is no lectern, only various wireless microphones. ilsa stands in the front left corner, with Thomas opposite her.

It seems they haven't coordinated the choreography, or perhaps they deliberately want to keep things casual and authentic. When Thomas asks, "ilsa, do you want to start?" ilsa responds casually, "Nope, go ahead."

Thomas smiles, as do many others, and begins: "Okay, I phrased that question badly. Let's get started. We warmly welcome you all to the first press conference of the For-a-Better-World-Party. Throughout the day, we have presented our content and teams online and engaged in discussions, and now we are eager to hear your questions. But first, ilsa will say a few words about our unique approach and the name of the party. ilsa?"

ilsa smiles—Thomas has skillfully handed her the baton. She takes a brief, visible moment to think before beginning: "The party's name was actually one of the hardest tasks to settle on. To many, it may sound ideological and detached from reality—but in fact, it's quite the opposite. We started out of frustration that, for nearly every major issue, there are clear recommendations from science and experts, yet politics consistently makes decisions that go against them—failing to set the right course and clinging to outdated structures. These misguided decisions are often based on ideology or narrow self-interest, with no clear explanations. In contrast, we are committed to transparency—laying out the facts, assumptions, and interconnections on which our decisions and proposals are based."

ilsa takes a sip from her water bottle before continuing: "To determine what constitutes sound political action, we have developed a large-scale impact model. At the highest level, it defines our overarching human goals: we want to be healthy, feel secure, and have the opportunity for personal growth. Jobs, a thriving environment, peace, and justice all contribute to these goals. Any political measure that effectively advances all of these objectives simultaneously leads to a better world—hence the name of the party."

ilsa realizes she needs to make her points more accessible, so she takes a deep breath. In the background, the model is displayed on a large screen. She continues: "Anything that threatens our health or restricts human development—both for the current and future generations—must be prevented. That includes toxic combustion engines, degraded soils, educational deficits, and social tensions. We must actively support solutions.

For instance, highway construction—often justified by economic competitiveness and public demand—should be the exception rather than the rule. The increased mobility for a few comes at the expense of public health and purchasing power for many. More highways mean more maintenance costs that strain public budgets, more fragmentation of natural habitats leading to biodiversity loss, further entrenchment of car dependency when rail transport is a more efficient alternative, and deepening inequality between those who can still afford cars and the growing number who cannot.

Even in the automotive industry, we've made serious missteps. Instead of banning combustion engines early, we tried to incentivize change and ended up lamenting high electricity prices. The market could have handled it—industry was already transitioning to new production lines when reactionary conservative forces, purely for political capital, pushed memes in favor of combustion engines. Now, we have a chaotic mix of inefficient, unnecessarily expensive propulsion systems, and we set a poor global example by failing to decarbonize our transportation sector. Our auto industry hasn't benefited from this, either.

By now, the damage and displacement caused by climate change should be evident to everyone. Mitigating these crises and restoring hope for the future is now the task of politics. Blocking change simply because certain businesses or voter groups resist it is shortsighted. We must consider the bigger picture and communicate it to everyone. In most cases, listening to individuals and companies carefully allows us to find new and more successful paths for them as well.

These are just randomly chosen examples. We have already developed conceptual solutions for all areas—please feel free to ask about them.

But another unique feature is particularly important: We do not work in isolated departments. Economy, research, education, environment, and so on—all of these areas influence one another. We operate as a team, not as a collection of individuals eager to appear on camera and report on their own decisions while coordinating as little as possible with other departments or competing for budgets. And just to clarify in advance—we have not assigned any positions yet. We are teams working on solutions for the challenges faced by the people of this country. For all people—including those who are now losing their jobs because AI, unsurprisingly but still unmanaged, is hitting them hard.

To put it even more simply: We do not follow individual interests or sell people empty promises. Instead, we explain why certain steps are the right ones, how they can be financed, and how we can take everyone along—the economy and the people alike. But now, let's move on to your questions."

Immediately, numerous hands go up, and the sound of rustling can be heard—though, of course, hardly anyone still uses pen and paper. However, one journalist wastes no time and loudly asks the first question:

"ilsa, are you taking the lead? Will you be at the head of the government?"

ilsa, who had naively sat back down, apparently expecting a technical discussion, responds with an expression of surprise, bordering on irritation:

"Oh, but I just said that. There are no personnel decisions yet. We are a coalition of highly competent experts and practitioners, where teams don't even work on their topics in isolation but exchange insights with each other. My role—though not mine alone—is to moderate between these teams."

She rummages in her bag, perhaps not even to find anything, but rather to appear disengaged, signaling for others in the teams to step up.

The next question follows:

"You are all scientists, with the best solutions on paper. But isn't politics something entirely different? Don't you need experienced politicians, old hands?"

ilsa still appears preoccupied, and the team looks toward Thomas, who skillfully shifts his gaze to another part of the room, indicating for someone else to respond. It works—a younger woman from the domestic policy team picks up a microphone, her colleagues nodding in agreement. She answers with a smile and a calm voice:

"If we reach over 50 percent in the polls, we will go into more detail on that and refer to the many experienced professionals who will, of course, continue to work in the government and will undoubtedly be happy to explain to us how to deal with politicians and business leaders. Until then, we assume we will have to negotiate compromises with coalition partners—armed with the fact that we will be the ones making everything transparent."

Immediately, another question follows:

"So you assume you could achieve more than 50 percent?"

The younger woman once again responds confidently:

"Hmm, if the question had been whether we could not imagine this at all, I would have understood it better as a reaction to my statement. But perhaps someone else would like to say something about our expectations?"

She glances—apparently at random—toward the other side.

There, two people quickly confer about who should respond, while their surroundings nod in agreement. An experienced politician, who has switched from another party, takes the floor:

"I'll quote ilsa here: 'At least most of us wouldn't even want to enter politics if politics actually worked.'"

He pauses briefly before continuing:

"The same applies to our platform as to all others—provided they even have a coherent platform: Its success can only be proven or disproven if it is implemented without compromises. I know this all too well from my former party. We claimed that the Green Deal would give the economy a major boost. But the compromises we had to make led to long deadlines and numerous exemptions—so the major boost never materialized. Was the Green Deal wrong? No. The compromises were the problem.

So, getting over 50 percent would be fantastic, and we certainly wouldn't need a full term in office to see how our measures take effect.

We aim to convince all sectors of society with substance, which gives us the opportunity to surpass 50 percent. But content alone won't be enough. Some voters don't care about content—they care about moods. Some vote out of habit. There will be many forces working against us. The things we say correctly will not be what spreads—the claims about where we are supposedly wrong will. The focus will be on rumors against us, on fake news.

The other parties can either align with us on content or attack us with emotional narratives and claims of authority over public discourse.

We have a lot of support from experts and practitioners in business, science, and the media. We are a great team that will certainly make some mistakes along the way. But we are credible when we say we're not here for power—we're here for the right steps forward.

If we present ourselves well as human beings, reaching 50 percent is absolutely possible.

But, to my knowledge, we have never actually discussed our expectations in terms of percentages, have we?"

He looks around, and most of his fellow party members indicate with their expressions that they indeed have never discussed percentages or potential coalitions.

He adds:

"Uh, and we haven't discussed possible coalitions either, have we?"

A reporter cleverly builds on this:

"Okay, if you claim that you are substantively without competition—perhaps you could summarize your core positions in a few sentences for each area?"

Thomas looks around the room with enthusiasm before responding:

"Great idea. Of course, the context for each topic is enormous, and in our metaverse space, you can already dive into everything and ask questions. Would you, the journalists, like to name an area of interest, and then we'll have our teams respond accordingly?"

In fact, the online presentation was intended to showcase the party's in-depth content and introduce the team members. The fact that the conversation is now returning to substantive issues might be surprising—but Thomas likely sees this as an opportunity for the teams to present themselves live, allowing the press to identify the right people for their reports and broadcasts.

A journalist quickly fires the first question:

"Okay, what is your defense strategy? ilsa once called it a systemic sink—do you want to cut spending there?"

The representative from the defense team, a retired high-ranking soldier, introduces himself accordingly before continuing:

"It is indeed utterly absurd that humanity faces so many pressing issues yet continues to threaten itself. Two key aspects must be addressed in defense policy:

First, defense cannot be considered in isolation; it must be viewed in the broader context of foreign policy, economic policy, and even development aid. This necessitates alliances among states that are interdependent. These alliances can then establish an international legal framework and the mandate for military intervention when necessary. The critical point is to ensure that no single power, such as the United States, dominates these alliances, as such dominance ultimately serves only as a target for opposing forces. Unlike NATO, its member states must emancipate themselves from U.S. influence—both in terms of military equipment and strategic capabilities, as well as in matters of internet surveillance.

Second, our military must be streamlined and flexibly deployable. Holding onto every type of military force is too costly—we simply do not have the financial or human resources for that. Therefore, in coordination with our alliance partners, we must maintain a well-paid, highly trained corps of specialists whose collective strength serves as an effective deterrent to all aggressors.

Speaking of deterrence: The notion that both sides possess devastating weapons yet mutually agree not to use them—only to then slaughter each other with slightly less devastating weapons—is repugnant to everyone. The problem is that some actors in the world are indifferent to their own collateral damage. Deterrence must therefore not target civilian populations but rather the aggressors themselves. This makes deterrence more cost-effective, but it must also remain impossible to circumvent. A separate discussion for another time."

He ends his statement abruptly but firmly, successfully avoiding the usual, often tedious, follow-up questions regarding nuclear weapons or other arms policies.

Next question: "Regarding economic policy. You emphasize that all measures must be financially feasible and that alternative products will ultimately stimulate the economy. At the same time, you hint between the lines that economic growth might not be the ultimate goal. How do these ideas fit together? Or, to put it differently: Isn't this just ideological wishful thinking while the rest of the world moves ahead of us?"

A seasoned executive from a globally successful mid-sized company, representing the economic policy team, responds:

"This is indeed a tricky issue. In the end, cheap products compete with high-quality products, and high-quality products must be both affordable for all and, more importantly, desirable. Competing solely on price is not an option—not even if we automate everything. It is therefore only logical that we focus on quality.

Until now, our economic policy has been to offer limited support for the 'right' choices while failing to eliminate the 'wrong' ones. This leads to mounting debt and a slow death—especially in the context of demographic change.

If we announce, both domestically and globally, that we will fully support the right choices, we set the course for transformation. If we can also achieve a societal shift where people prioritize quality over quantity—and ensure that quality is affordable through appropriate minimum wages—then we will become a global leader in this transition.

Other countries to which we export will follow suit, provided we integrate innovation into our quality strategy. To do that, we need education, research, and investment. Investment requires growth, so we are not opposed to growth per se. However, as a nation, we should not pursue quantitative growth as our primary goal but rather a society where everyone has financial security.

The picture is thus much broader—we need purchasing power, access to resources, affordable energy, and more. That means we must eliminate economic 'sinks'—money that does not create additional value. Conversely, we must invest in 'sources' such as education and disease prevention, as these contribute to long-term prosperity."

The journalist who posed the question seems somewhat dissatisfied with the response. Noticing this—perhaps already regretting it—ilsa steps in to add:

"The global economy is no longer in balance. We are seeing the formation of economic blocs, restricted access to resources, disruptions in anthropogenic stockpiles, trade restrictions, struggles over chip technology and internet infrastructure, and rising inflation rates.

We cannot afford to assume that things will continue as they are for much longer. Even if we successfully lay the groundwork for a quality-driven economy, the rest of the world will inevitably react in competition. The real question is whether we will maintain a competitive edge, lag behind, or—like so many times before—watch the world squander yet another opportunity."

Another journalist, both incredulous and confrontational, asks: "The economy revolves around digitalization and AI—whoever leads in this field wins. What is your strategy? Do you want to fight digitalization or promote it?"

All eyes turn to ilsa, who, likely gritting her teeth internally, responds: "We do not intend to fight market forces—if AI and digital solutions are in demand, the economy will provide them. The real question is: Do we want to digitalize production and services, increase productivity, and eliminate jobs in the process? If so, we need to encourage it but also address the consequences."

ilsa stands up and scans the room: "Or do we want to further digitalize our lives—experience leisure, culture, education, and social interactions in the digital metaverse? If so, we must understand its impact on us." She then looks in the other direction: "The same applies to our infrastructure—do we want autonomous vehicles and robots around us, where everything runs automatically, making it so that we no longer need to move or do anything ourselves? If that is the path we choose, society must comprehend it beforehand and while it unfolds—not just when it's already too late."

She turns to the model displayed on the screen, which the moderators are showing from the current perspective: "As a state, we can ensure high-speed internet access everywhere. We can promote digitalization in schools, and we can collaborate with international partners to ensure that AI is not controlled solely by a few major players but that we, too, have access to training data and models."

Looking back at the room, she continues: "Winning in competition does not mean dictating to businesses how and what to digitalize. If the industry decides that flying cars are necessary because people want them and companies aim for market leadership, then this must happen without government subsidies. We will not fund luxury items on one side while many people struggle to afford school meals for their children.

Extremely high profits with little employment are unsustainable for society—we must tax such developments to mitigate their social impact. We are already seeing the emergence of tech-haters, who are being left behind by these changes. If other countries choose not to tax these industries and instead accept societal chaos, our only tool is education—explaining the consequences of spending the last available money on digital products, which leads to the concentration of even more wealth among a small elite. Education can help consumers choose products from socially responsible companies."

Immediately, a sharp follow-up question arises: "So, does that mean you will tax cheap products from abroad that are mass-produced by robots without additional taxation in their home countries?"

ilsa looks toward the team, where this time an economist takes the microphone and responds: "ilsa's point was precisely that we aim to inform, not impose tariffs. In the past, cheap products came from countries where people worked for very little money. However, these low-wage workers were still consumers themselves. Now, as companies replace human labor with AI, products will become cheaper and cheaper, but there will be fewer and fewer consumers who can afford them. Taxing corporate profits is easy, but when profits are concentrated in only a handful of people or squeezed by competitive pricing, government revenues dwindle.

Taxing AI itself is an art—how do we even detect when AI is being used? Right now, we are in a transitional phase where AI has not yet fully automated its own development, meaning there are still many highly paid professionals we can tax. But the system is beginning to shift, and we are heading toward a world where value creation requires fewer and fewer human hands. At present, businesses simply seek new markets where purchasing power still exists. But this is not a sustainable model."

He continues: "We need a solution for the impending chaos when robots start building other robots and barely anyone earns a wage. One possible solution is a high enough value-added tax (VAT) to fund a universal basic income. This VAT would also apply to cheap imported goods, ensuring they are taxed accordingly. Moreover, we could adjust VAT rates to favor sustainable products while imposing higher rates on unsustainable ones."

Of course, a journalist immediately raises an objection: "That sounds like socialism and backdoor paternalism, and in the end, it will strangle our economy."

The economist, however, shakes his head: "No, not at all. All providers in our country will be treated equally, and we are not interfering with exports in any way."

A journalist, with a slightly disappointed tone, follows up: "So that means there won't be a robot tax at all?"

The businesswoman from the team takes over the answer: "No, for the reasons we just explained, that won't work. However, we can make labor cheaper by reducing social contributions in the context of a universal basic income."

Another journalist jumps in: "So, I'll be paying three times as much for my hairdresser because no one needs to work anymore?"

A younger woman from the economic team responds: "Exactly! And from the hairstyles, we'll be able to tell who still has a job and who lives off basic income." She smirks before continuing more seriously, "No, in reality, the system will naturally adjust, and there will no longer be precarious employment situations. We should not see basic income as a goal for people who don't want to work. Instead, it is the logical answer to the major, fascinating, but also dangerous developments we are facing."

She stands up and looks around the room: "Who knows—many people may even choose to free themselves from technology and form communities where people work for each other without robots. What our team is focusing on is the question of when and how we transition into this new taxation system."

A noticeable sense of contemplation spreads through the room. A journalist hesitantly brings up the next topic: "What are your plans for education?" It is becoming evident that informal speech is becoming the norm—ilsa and the party's approachable demeanor is resonating with the audience.

The education team responds:

"First of all, it's frustrating how often outsiders comment on this topic. We are working closely with fantastic educators. The changes in education are enormous—knowledge is already readily available, and soon it may even be directly linked to our brains through AI. AI can explain things to us in a highly personalized way, exactly how we need them. Therefore, we need to focus more on fostering the desire to seek knowledge and apply it. We need to instill a passion for different forms of intelligence and for human collaboration. Schools, and ultimately even universities, must adapt to this. Instead of just delivering curriculum content, education will shift toward training problem-solving skills—whether it's heating technology, history, or foreign languages."

Then comes a brilliant question: "Aren't you at least one political generation too late for us? Shouldn't you have been here when it was time to prevent all the catastrophes we're facing today?"

Thomas stands up, partly signaling that the conference is nearing its conclusion. He looks over at ilsa, who remains seated, and replies:

"We have to achieve success in small steps. At some point, we will have enough international allies to start thinking beyond the mechanisms of greed and recklessness—to truly work toward what's best for the planet and its people. The world has changed completely and at an insane speed. It's becoming more and more complicated and complex. The answers to our problems are also more complicated. Right now, many people are instinctively drawn to simplistic messages and nostalgic visions of the past. Many political parties will cater to that sentiment, making our job harder. But explaining these realities is a responsibility that we share with you."

ilsa now adds, addressing the journalists with a smile: "And if, by accelerating the changes we need, we don't reach the 1.5-degree climate target but manage to stay well below 2.5 degrees, then that will still be an enormous achievement for society—something to be proud of."

When ilsa finally returns home late from the press conference, Michael is already waiting with a bottle of organic vegan wine: "Tomorrow, the circus begins."

"Yep," ilsa replies simply, taking a large sip from her glass before nestling into Michael's shoulder.

27. Megalomania (atb)

The media are in an uproar—politicians in power are huddling together, while others seek the spotlight and, like many commentators from the business and social sectors, claim interpretative authority for themselves. On the streets and on social media, influencers are gathering smaller or sometimes larger followings, spreading their own interpretations. There are even some who compare Al-my to Jesus, but even more skeptics who practically preach the end of humanity.

As promised, Al-my is in Central Park, surrounded by hundreds of thousands of curious people. While Al-my is not even recognized within the crowd, the military is stationed at the edges with all sorts of equipment, and among the masses, many individuals with communication sets in their ears—presumably FBI, CIA, NSA, or similar agencies—are unmistakably present.

Suddenly, Al-my's voice sounds as if spoken through invisible loudspeakers: "Hello, everyone. Nice to see you all here. To the many agencies that are almost blocking themselves on the frequencies: I'm not going anywhere."

She calls on the attending billionaires and displays on a screen—seemingly appearing out of nowhere—their profiles, achievements, and ongoing space programs. Overnight, she had called the billionaires and helped them overcome their fear and embrace curiosity. Al-my invites them forward, with the scene being broadcast live on the large screen.

She greets everyone: "Great that you're here. It's undeniable that you have achieved remarkable things. You are fans of nuclear fusion, space travel, and the search for immortality. Here's my offer: If I take you to Mars and back within four days, would you be willing to donate three-quarters of your wealth to a foundation for the development of the world's poorest regions? Of course, we would publicly acknowledge your tremendous contribution."

The crowd erupts—some out of excitement, others out of sheer disbelief. A prominent billionaire looks around for a microphone, and AI-my simply says, "Go ahead, you don't need a microphone."

He responds calmly, "Well, if we also get access to the technology, then immediately."

Once again, there is thunderous applause and approving nods from the other billionaires. AI-my counters, "Oh, so you must think I'm doubly foolish. With space travel to Mars, we could become wealthier than all of you combined in no time. And energy, as well as potential immortality, could also be sold. On the contrary, this is about showing you that the question of when we die is not what matters—it's how we live before that. And it's not about reaching other planets, but about taking proper care of this magnificent Earth. So, do you want to go to Mars or not?"

One of them objects, "I don't want to be tricked by a mere simulation or wordplay."

AI-my: "A valid concern. We also have seats for additional passengers as witnesses. By the way, I could seize your wealth at any time if I wanted to. So, who wants to go to Mars?"

The crowd shouts, "We do!" and "I do!" while also chanting the names of the most well-known billionaires.

The most famous space pioneer among them speaks up: "It's physically impossible. Where is the spaceship?" He looks in disbelief at the 50-meter-wide screen that appears to float freely in the sky.

AI-my grows impatient: "Here's the shuttle to the spaceship—do you take the bet or not?" Suddenly, a spacecraft hovering above them becomes visible, looking unspectacularly like a shuttle from well-known science-fiction films. However, both the silent hovering and its prior invisibility send eerie silence through the crowd. Only gradually does cheering break out from different corners.

Apparently, things are not going as planned. ilsa sits watching the live stream, nervously biting her fingers. Michael looks at her, "You thought this would be easier, didn't you?"

"Oh, absolutely!" ilsa admits, a certain apprehension in her tone.

A billionaire who is already known for his philanthropy unexpectedly steps forward: "I'm in."

He is followed by a very elderly billionaire, three from the Asian region, and finally, even the space pioneer himself. This means that more than half of the target group is on board. ilsa exhales in relief: "Phew, that was close."

Michael places his hand on her leg: "That could have happened to you and me as well. But how does zero gravity work, and how is it possible to traverse such great distances at nearly the speed of light? Honestly, I always thought you were right to dismiss science-fiction movies as nonsense."

28.   Shared responsibility (btb)

In the following weeks, everything plays out as expected. And so do the concerns. Again and again, ilsa and her family are stopped by journalists or simply filmed from a distance. Much of it is harmless—but some journalists are clearly looking for sensational news, searching for scandalous headlines to sell.

Fairly early on, it happens that ilsa comes home to find Nick in the driveway, pulling weeds from between the cracks of the paving stones.

Nick: "Hi, ilsa. The press interviewed me today about what I think of your candidacy."

ilsa immediately responds in a defensive tone, as if expecting the worst: "What exactly am I running for?"

Nick: "Well, my kids have already asked your kids whether you might be moving to the capital."

ilsa visibly inhales, probably preparing to launch into another deflection, but Nick just continues with a smile: "Don't worry. I didn't tell the press anything like that. I actually told them who you are and what you stand for in my eyes. And even though we probably disagree on just about every green policy issue, I think you're incredibly smart and a wonderful person. I even fear that you're right about a lot of things."

Then, with a grin, he raises his index finger: "But don't tell my family that last part—we still have our battles to fight."

ilsa laughs and replies, "First of all, thank you. I'll need to process that."

Both laugh even more, and as ilsa turns to go inside, she waves back at him.

Inside the house, Julia throws a remark at her in passing: "You've got some nerve picking a fight with farmers and fishermen."

ilsa raises her eyebrows and murmurs, "And just like that, we're back from the surreal to reality."

Julia only half hears the mumbling and, with wide eyes and an excited, amazed smile, eagerly explains: "You called the farmers and fishermen stupid."

ilsa, visibly exhausted, counters—though with some amusement: "I always make sure to distinguish between calling behavior stupid and calling people stupid. You know that from the The-WHY-of-Life-Game." She smiles. "But is that really how it came across?"

Julia, slightly backing off: "Well, you did say that fishermen can barely catch anything anymore and are now demanding to be allowed to catch more, and that instead of demanding higher prices from the industry and consumers, farmers are asking politicians to loosen regulations so they can produce even cheaper. And then you said you found both—let me quote—'insanely dumb.'"

Michael stands in the doorway with an impressed expression—Julia looks at him proudly, and ilsa glances at him too, equally impressed.

ilsa responds, "Everyone says I should be less complicated. That was pretty clear, wasn't it?"

Julia smirks. "I thought it was great."

She looks at Michael, who then says, "Great, yes, but it also excludes a lot of people from integrating into the discussion."

ilsa sits down and nods. "Yes, I didn't have time to offer a new way forward, a path to development, a perspective. My mistake. How was your day?"

Michael glances at Julia, checking if he should go first, then begins: "Fantastic. Great client, developed a strong strategy, got home early, and went jogging with Bella." He finishes with a satisfied grin and a glance at Julia.

Julia responds, "The usual. Journalists waiting outside the school trying to corner me, and also younger students showing me crude deepfake porn and Nazi speeches with your face on them."

Michael and ilsa both look concerned, and Michael asks, "Oh shit—how does that affect you?"

"This fake stuff? Not at all. The younger students do this all the time, and hardly anyone is spared. And without certification, almost no one even watches it," Julia replies, referring to an AI-supported, yet-to-be-hacked standard for verifying the authenticity of video and audio recordings. But then she adds thoughtfully, "But when I think about why they're doing it, it gets a little weird." She sits down and explains, "Some just want to bisociate, to mess around. But others are kind of jealous of the celebrity status I seem to be getting because of all this. That's annoying, and it hurts that they're implying these things about me."

Michael and ilsa exchange a look, coordinating silently, as Julia continues, "Oh, and some, of course, are on a, let's say, 'mission' to stop any kind of progress for the better. They just want to keep enjoying their big cars, greasy meat, and extravagant vacations. Teachers, parents—a lot of people are simply against it."

ilsa says, "You're really amazing. But please always keep us updated on what's going on. None of us should get run over by this."

Julia interrupts, almost excitedly, "Yeah, but it's for a good cause, for something bigger. We talked about this—we want to make the world better."

Michael replies, "For us, family comes first. We have Plan B and Plan C, and if it ever becomes too much, we can still support change for the better from the second or third row."

ilsa: "Speaking of, how is Max doing right now?"

Julia: "He's totally fine—he wants to improve the world himself. But he's having trouble with Eve's parents."

Michael: "Oh yeah, right, I forgot. I talked to Eve's mom. She was furious, called us idealists. But I think I managed to make her understand that we completely respect what they're trying to do for Eve—it's a huge opportunity they're offering her. My argument was that just as we didn't try to talk Eve out of it, we also won't try to talk her into it."

"Wait, what?" ilsa asks. "She wanted us to convince Eve to go?"

Michael: "Yeah, exactly. Her argument was that we need to take responsibility. My counterargument was that I think it's great that the kids at this age already want to take responsibility for their own decisions."

Julia laughs, "Well, that has now led to Max and Eve wanting to gain experience as development workers abroad."

Michael and ilsa visibly look surprised. ilsa: "Uh, first of all, it's great that you're the one learning this from them."

Julia grins, satisfied. "You mean before you did?" ilsa is just about to inhale for her reaction when Julia quickly adds, "It's been a topic at school, and I asked Eve directly about it."

Michael: "And did you give her any advice?"

Julia furrows her brow. "Now I'm the one responsible? Of course, I think it's cool that they want to do their own thing."

ilsa, her voice slightly lower and more serious: "And did Max plan this for both of them?"

Julia, slightly annoyed: "No, Max is still hesitating. He doesn't want to stand in Eve's way. Eve wants to do it, and Max, even independently of Eve's study-abroad year, thinks it could be great for his future. But you should probably talk to Max about it."

ilsa and Michael look at each other, as Julia adds, "Or is the problem that Max hasn't talked to you about it yet?"

ilsa: "No—he had already mentioned the idea to us. But I have to admit, I'm really curious about which countries the two of them are considering."

Julia raises her eyebrows. "Ah, so that's where this is going. You're worried about them." Seeing Michael slightly tilt his head and stare into the distance, she presses on, "Seriously, just a moment ago, you were glad they were making their own decisions, and now you're worried? Dad, didn't you also work as a development worker when you were young—long ago?" She laughs.

ilsa tilts her head downward in surprise, pulling back slightly, while Michael furrows his brow. Both look at Julia, waiting for an explanation. Julia bends her arms at the elbows, palms facing upward, and says casually, "That locked box in the basement—the one that's none of our business—probably doesn't contain vacation photos."

Michael is just about to say something when ilsa quickly changes the subject. "We'll get to that another time. Now, back to Julia and the questions about our family: We continue to keep our private lives out of it. The standard response is that anyone is free to dig up something bad about us, but we definitely won't try to present an image of ourselves."

"No problem," Julia says, apparently also glad the conversation is being cut short. She grabs Bella, and the two hurry outside.

Michael: "What incredible kids we have." ilsa nods thoughtfully.

29. Hate (bfb)

A few weeks into the election campaign—Thomas and ilsa are on a video call.

ilsa remarks, "This is a strange campaign. The support is incredible—the rejection of the established parties feels surreal. And the number of inquiries from abroad. It feels like a global conspiracy, and we're right in the middle of it."

Thomas laughs. "Well, that doesn't surprise me at all. Right now, most continents are governed by either conservative or even slightly right-wing parties. Before that, in many countries, efforts toward transformation in the direction of greater sustainability were deliberately stalled by spreading flimsy but effective memes. The usual classics: renewable energy is too expensive, electric cars don't have enough range, organic farming can't feed the world, highways drive economic growth, regulations to protect biodiversity will suffocate the economy, and so on."

ilsa adds, "And in the background, the oil companies and their lobbying groups have skillfully secured an extension of their business model and are now making more money than ever. The public joined the chorus against change, thinking they could keep their comfort zone intact. Honestly, that could have worked for a while..."

Thomas picks up immediately: "...if it weren't for the climate disasters and geopolitical crises. In the public's perception, it feels like progressive parties have failed. And here, they could only take hesitant steps because they either had to govern in coalitions or didn't have a majority in all legislative institutions."

ilsa: "But isn't our success only happening because climate disasters, geopolitical tensions, and AI are running their course?" She elaborates, "And by geopolitical tensions, I don't just mean China and Russia, but also divisions within Europe, North and South America, and even parts of Asia, where water conflicts are escalating. The world is in turmoil."

Thomas: "But that's exactly what we've been saying. The more progressive parties of a few years ago are now seen as just as much of a failure as today's conservative ones. There are more non-voters and a rise in many small, extreme parties. And in this climate, the For-a-Better-World party has real momentum.

226

We're not tainted yet, and we're explaining the connections behind our comprehensive, highly specific program. The background is complex, but the media is playing along and helping us get the message across."

ilsa tilts her head, then leans back in her chair. "It's only logical that the established parties are now trying to discredit us on a personal level. That's incredibly stressful—no wonder some people's nerves are wearing thin."

Thomas interrupts, "Their alternative would be to form coalitions with the For-a-Better-World party—following the logic: 'We can take radical steps, but the party you trust has to be involved.'"

ilsa leans forward again, "If coalition proposals come with specific policy nuances, it would be easy for our For-a-Better-World party to either constructively integrate the suggestion or explicitly reject it."

"Exactly!" Thomas responds enthusiastically.

ilsa, however, seems more thoughtful. "But that also means dividing society. We're already seeing it—on one side, the Fridays for Future movement openly supports us, and on the other, there are numerous, sometimes right-wing, protests against foreigners, against globalization, against products from China, against environmental protection, against AI, against the super-rich—you name it. A particularly popular target for vandalism seems to be SUVs—radical climate activists and wealth-haters are equally demolishing these status symbols." She shakes her head with a wry smile.

Thomas laughs along. "In a way, everything is going according to plan. This is exactly why we saw a great opportunity in founding a new party."

But ilsa appears unsettled. She rubs her eyes with one hand and adds, "There's also the issue that we're fueling frustration against the established parties but aren't fielding candidates in smaller elections. That leads to voter apathy and support for extreme parties. If we made coalition statements, we could counteract that and give certain established parties a boost at the municipal level. We've never discussed working in coalitions—did you always suspect we might win an outright majority?"

Thomas grins and briefly closes his eyes in confirmation.

ilsa then asks, "But you didn't seriously foresee that we'd end up facing the very catastrophes we were trying to prevent, did you?"

Thomas shakes his head with a serious expression. "No, it still feels surreal to me. To put it in KNOW-WHY Wave terms: We wanted to guide society up the wave from where we were. Now everything has crashed off the wave due to too much change, and we have to find a completely different wave with entirely new strategies to climb."

ilsa immediately agrees. "Absolutely. And here, we can use Idealized System Design to normatively ask what society truly wants and how nations can collaborate to achieve it. But that's a huge leap for everyone, even for those who realize they've fallen off the previous wave."

Thomas nods. "I'll schedule a meeting with the working groups for tomorrow. I think we need to adjust everything, but for now, I have to go."

ilsa heads to the garden—much to Bella's delight—where a ball quickly becomes a source of joy and distraction. Julia and Max return from school and report on the increasing hostility.

Max remarks, "It's fascinating how the rich are no longer envied but actively attacked."

ilsa asks, "How does that manifest?"

Max seems to be thinking about how to describe it. After a while—Julia also looks at him curiously—he says, "Well, whether it's a fancy tablet, new clothes, the topic of travel, or just the fact that when people complain about stress at home, some can't even relate to it—it all makes them get weird looks, like no one really wants to talk to them."

"Mmh, so suddenly, they don't belong anymore?" ilsa asks.

Julia chimes in, "Yep, that's exactly how I would describe it in my grade."

Michael has since joined the conversation and confirms, shaking his head slightly, "It's the same with football, and my team at work has been talking about it too. The ones who haven't been affected yet are starting to feel excluded."

ilsa seems like she wants to pick up on this, but glances at the clock and suddenly stands up, "Damn, I have to go."

Michael asks, "Are you taking the car?"

ilsa, while packing her bag, responds, "No, I'm taking the bus." Michael raises his eyebrows in either surprise or approval.

Julia looks at Bella, who is lying flat on the lawn, glancing at each of them in turn. "Okay, and I'll take Bella for a walk." Bella hears her name, jumps up, but then stretches out extensively first.

Later, when ilsa gets on the bus, she notices people looking at her. She forces a smile at those whose gazes don't turn away quickly enough. Finally, a woman, slightly older than ilsa, speaks to her in a rather blunt manner, "Are you campaigning here by riding the bus with us common folk instead of cruising around in an armored limousine with bodyguards?"

ilsa is about to respond with a puzzled expression when a younger man jumps in, "Exactly! What are you doing on a bus? Your books alone must have made you a millionaire in times like these."

ilsa takes a deep breath, pauses briefly, and then responds loud enough for others to hear, "Well, I used to take the bus before too. Honestly, I prefer when no one recognizes me. And yes, my

229

books are selling really well—only, unfortunately for me, I've always said that I donate the profits. Has anyone here actually read one of them?" She smiles as she finishes the sentence.

Another person joins in, "So how do you make money then? Does your husband pay for everything?"

"Hmm…" ilsa muses, "Normally, I'd say that's nobody's business, but fine. I work as a scientist in various projects and make a decent income—sometimes more, sometimes less. And my husband also earns varying amounts depending on how well business is going. But here's the thing: we donate everything we earn above the national average."

A younger man scoffs, "No one's going to believe that you only have as much money as an average citizen."

ilsa replies, "You're right." The people around her look somewhere between puzzled and triumphant, until she explains, "The average income is different from what most people in our country actually earn. The average income is a lot of money. Most people earn less. With the average income, we already make more than 80% of the rest of the population. And yes, most people earning an average income don't take the bus."

Some visibly start to ponder this, while an older man bursts out, "How can that be? That's just typical nonsense! The average income is what most people earn—and that is already barely enough to survive. And you and your party want to completely ruin us with taxes on meat, housing, energy consumption, and who knows what else!"

ilsa is probably angry, but she responds very calmly, "I understand you. The thing about the average is tricky, and we can only tax things that endanger our future if it doesn't ruin people. That's why everyone gets back as much as they currently need for an average life. So, the wealthy are affected much more significantly. Additionally, we need to raise low incomes. By the way, you kind of pushed me into this campaign argument." ilsa laughs, but few—if any—laugh along.

The man doesn't let up. "All empty talk. You haven't understood the concept of average income either."

ilsa's facial expression now clearly shows her irritation, and she retorts, "If you add up all the income in a country and divide it by the number of people, you get the average income. Because there are some with insanely high incomes, the number is quite high. To determine the income of the actual middle of the population, incomes are divided into brackets. Then, we check how many people fall into each bracket, and the bracket where just as many people earn more as earn less represents the income of the average person. Roughly speaking, the average per capita income in our country is around fifty thousand, while the average disposable household income is only half of that." The gears visibly turn in the listeners' heads. ilsa nods and adds, "From that perspective, our family lives on four times the median income— exactly why our kids agree that we donate a lot and don't buy unnecessary junk."

Some people might raise their eyebrows in acknowledgment. But the man isn't done yet: "If you're so socially minded, why don't you donate even more?"

"That's a great question!" ilsa replies. As she stands up, she adds curtly, "I need to get off at the next stop. But that's a great question—let's all ask ourselves that." She smiles and exits the bus.

But a few others also get off with her. A woman smiles and says, "You have my vote." A younger man, apparently a businessman, walks past without turning around and says, "Mine too."

Julia is out with Bella on their usual route toward the forest when Bella starts sniffing something in the grass and then begins licking it. Julia scolds her, "Hey, stop that! Don't eat it!" But Bella keeps licking, and Julia has to physically pull her away. As they continue walking, Julia scolds her again, "You're not supposed to do that."

Only a few meters later, Bella starts whining and suddenly writhes on the ground in pain. She has obviously eaten something toxic. Julia immediately realizes what's happening and calls Michael.

Michael rushes to the car with the phone in his hand. "Keep her calm. If she vomits, that's good. If she starts wobbling and lies down, make sure her head is turned to the side and downward. Keep talking to her. I'm on my way and will call the vet while driving."

Max jumps into the car with him, and Michael instructs, "We don't have much time. I'll grab Bella, and you give Julia clear instructions to take you to where Bella ate something. Collect whatever it was in a doggy bag." Michael speaks calmly but drives like a madman—pushing the electric car's stability controls to their limits with extreme precision. He even switches to an off-road mode, making the car drift slightly through the curves.

Max, shocked, grabs onto something and almost screams, "How do you even know how to drive like this?"

Michael is already on the phone with the vet, promising to arrive in ten minutes. He says nothing in response to Max's question, but Max nervously double-checks that his seatbelt is securely fastened.

When they arrive at Julia and Bella—Julia, both teary-eyed and stunned by the insane speed—everything goes as planned. Bella is placed in the back seat, and the poisoned bait is collected. The wild ride continues, and by now, Bella really should be vomiting.

The veterinarian has everything prepared—under anesthesia, Bella's stomach is emptied, and the poison is sent by courier to a laboratory. An hour later, Bella is doing very poorly—she is struggling to wake up from the anesthesia. The veterinarian keeps her hooked up to all the monitors and asks the family to go home and wait for her call.

Max and Julia, of course, want to stay, but they reluctantly agree to go home. The drive back is extremely quiet—both in terms of the driving style and the passengers. "Let's tell Mom later," Michael decides, and while Max and Julia sip their drinks in the kitchen, he briefly disappears, making sure he is unnoticed, and heads to the mentioned box to retrieve a phone. Just as he is about to leave again with determination, his regular phone rings. The kids hear it and immediately run to him.

Michael listens carefully, thanks the caller, and explains to the children: "The lab has identified the rare poison, and the veterinarian can now adjust the treatment accordingly. But we still have to hope. It could take days."

Julia is the first to react: "What do you mean by a rare poison? Who would do something like this? Why?"

Michael doesn't even get a chance to answer because Max immediately piles on his own question: "What's that other phone you have?"

Michael slips the other phone into his pocket and opens his mouth, but no words come out. Julia—still teary-eyed—says, "That's from the box, isn't it?"

Michael tilts his head, presses his lips together briefly, then simply says, "We'll talk about that another time, I promise. Right now, you should eat something, distract yourselves. What can I help you make?" He ends with a hesitant, almost pained smile.

The kids respond simultaneously with "Pizza" and "Not hungry." They all return to the kitchen, and suddenly, Max slams his clenched fist hard against the doorframe. Michael and Julia are startled but seem to be in a similar state of mind.

Julia says, "Oh man, I really don't know what I'd do to the person who did this. I know it's nonsense, but I'd want them to suffer just as much… and if Bella doesn't make it…" She doesn't finish the sentence.

Max stares at the table and mutters, "I'm in." He clenches both fists—apparently without even realizing it.

"And then you want revenge, to make someone suffer, or even kill them," Michael states, not as a question but as an observation. Neither kid responds. "Would Mom's interview distract you?" he asks, glancing at the clock.

"No, turn it on," Julia says, and they all watch yet another television interview with ilsa.

In one of the many interviews she and other party members give, ilsa is asked about the right-wing rallies happening in various countries and the growing war rhetoric between nations. The well-known host asks, "What is your solution to combat hatred among the population?"

ilsa responds, "For decades, the losers of progress were a minority—now, that balance is shifting at a rapid pace, and governments are no longer able to cushion the effects. What remains are the wealthy and the super-rich. Many, especially economists, have always argued that there was too much money in circulation and too many economic interdependencies for a global economic crisis to happen. Now, we are on the brink of one, because, like a superstorm, everything is converging at once. Much of the wealth only exists on paper."

ilsa takes a sip of water, and the host presses further, "Is the cause purely economic? And what would be your solutions to combat hatred?"

ilsa gestures with both hands as she explains: "People who are doing relatively—exclamation mark—well are less susceptible to being integrated into groups that define themselves through cultural, religious, or other societal divisions, leading to enemy images and even hatred. Therefore, economic development and the distribution of purchasing power play a key role.

The population in industrial nations is aging rapidly. Wealth is flowing into IT corporations. As purchasing power declines, the economy collapses, and with it, tax revenues. Interest rates are rising. National debt is making the rich even richer but is paralyzing the state. Most purchasing power is now spent on rising food prices and insurance for houses and cars. Financial markets are on the brink of collapse—first due to geopolitical tensions, then due to reduced consumption and job losses. Inflation appears to be stagnant only because housing prices are falling. But regardless of interest rates, banks are hardly issuing loans anymore. Leisure activities and tourism are coming to a standstill, while the construction sector is booming to repair damages—although it's the hardware stores that are benefiting the most.

Pension funds, of course, have also invested their money, and now, with the stock market collapse, that money is at risk—just like the funds invested in other insurance sectors. Even personal savings have suddenly shrunk for many people."

The moderator nods and picks up on the point: "Okay, that makes sense. So, it's just about economic policy—fixing that will reduce hatred? And if we tax the rich, everything will get better?"

A government politician on the panel interjects, visibly irritated: "If we tax high earners, they'll just leave, or their work will be done elsewhere. We can't delude ourselves into thinking that simply imposing high taxes and redistributing money will magically fix everything." He leans back in his chair, looking around the room indignantly.

ilsa smiles and glances around as well—perhaps to see if anyone else wants to interrupt her. Then she responds in a calm, measured voice: "I agree with you."

She pauses briefly for effect before continuing: "First, we all need to acknowledge that the current economic and social unraveling is not the result of green, sustainable policies but rather of the conservative 'business as usual' approach of the last 50 years. Once we accept that, we can be open to change—to bold steps."

Just as the politician is about to speak again, ilsa extends her arm and holds up an open palm, signaling him to wait. She firmly continues: "But even bold steps must be carefully considered. We need to see the bigger picture and closely examine where real value creation and competitive advantages lie—how we, in concert with other nations, can transition from purely quantitative growth benefiting the few to a qualitative economy that benefits the many.

We need to communicate this clearly—not in the sense of central planning but with responsibility for society and a long-term perspective, something the financial sector, by its very nature, does not take into account.

In essence, the whole issue is complex but solvable. We need to identify what people require in terms of housing, food, mobility, culture, and meaningful work while avoiding what harms us— from emissions and land sealing to the depletion of natural resources. Once we clearly communicate what is right, businesses and financial markets will know what to invest in.

And in the end, taxes will ensure that we don't become a totalitarian police state that merely suppresses hatred. Instead, there will be people with purchasing power who contribute to local value creation—something that benefits businesses as well."

Now the politician pushes forward again: "You can't dictate what people want!"

"Yes, we can!" ilsa responds quickly and explains: "Specifically regarding quality. We can tax emissions, promote a circular economy, prioritize rail transport, and if robotics is inevitable, we must soon introduce a universal basic income, which can be financed through wealth taxes and an increased value-added tax. That's not everything, but it's crucial for maintaining social cohesion."

This time, a journalist interrupts: "And then you'll leave the borders open, and migrants from all over the world will come here to claim our basic income?"

ilsa nods: "Good point!" But then, still holding her glass of water, she adds: "If it weren't for our clear position distinguishing between refugees and migrants who need to be integrated. Migrants must be integrated because otherwise, our population will continue to age. Only if we radically restructure the social security system could we afford to shrink and grow old as a society. And we want to help refugees for humanitarian reasons—help that, when handled correctly, keeps the money within their home countries. And of course, we must invest in addressing the root causes of displacement."

"That's all nice in theory," the politician grumbles, to which ilsa responds almost conclusively: "If you equate theory with thoughtful consideration rather than simplistic, knee-jerk arguments, then yes."

The politician waves dismissively, shaking his head. Her opponents in the discussion look frustrated, her supporters smile, and the moderator immediately retracts her own brief smile and wraps up the show in the usual manner.

30. Final spurt (btb)

The next morning, Michael picks up ilsa from the train station. ilsa beams: "Hey, what's this? You have no idea how enlightening bus rides can be."

Michael smiles with a puzzled expression, and as they both get into the car, ilsa glances into the backseat and asks, "Where's Bella?"

"In the animal clinic, in a coma," Michael replies briefly.

ilsa doesn't even ask why she's only finding out now; instead, she goes straight to the point: "What happened? How is she?"

"She was poisoned—on our usual route. As far as we could find out, there haven't been other affected dogs or poisoned bait elsewhere. The situation is critical—we just have to wait."

ilsa stares straight ahead, and after a brief delay, she quietly asks, "Did you take care of it?"

Michael says nothing and continues driving in silence. ilsa thinks for a few more seconds before noting, "Do you think it could be a trap, politically motivated?"

"No and yes," Michael answers tersely, and they hold hands.

"How are the kids?" ilsa asks, apparently understanding Michael's meaning without needing further explanation.

"Both are completely shaken, full of rage," Michael murmurs—easily audible in the quiet electric car.

The phone rings in the car. Michael recognizes the number and simply says, "Yep?"

On the other end, a colleague speaks in an urgent, almost frantic tone: "Michael. We need to talk about our new intern, about Eve. When can you come to the office?"

Michael looks at ilsa with wide eyes. ilsa whispers, "Go ahead, I'll wait for the kids."

An ambulance drives through the town and turns into a street just ahead. When they arrive home, ilsa gives Michael a long, intense kiss and hops out of the car, grabbing her luggage from the trunk. Michael speeds off to the office, clearly bewildered by the recent chain of events.

ilsa waits for the kids, and when they arrive, they all hug each other tightly. Max is the first to speak, almost bursting with anger: "I don't get how Dad can stay so calm. I want to know who did this, and…," he stops mid-sentence.

"And?" ilsa prompts, leaving the "then what?" unspoken.

"He sent me to the police to file the report—he wouldn't even do it himself," Julia adds, just as frustrated.

"Oh, guys, let's first focus on getting Bella back on her feet," ilsa says, exhaling deeply as she sinks into an armchair.

Max and Julia exchange glances but also sit down, though their frustration remains.

Meanwhile, Michael arrives at the office. Everyone seems to be in good spirits, sitting together with Eve. A colleague greets him immediately with a reassuring tone: "You didn't even ask why we were so eager to talk to you. Everything's fine."

Michael waves it off and says, "No problem—I could use a distraction anyway."

"What's wrong?" a colleague asks.

"Hasn't Eve said anything? Bella was poisoned, and now we're all on edge, waiting to see if she'll survive," Michael replies, placing a hand on Eve's shoulder while already looking at the digital whiteboard displaying a cause-and-effect model.

"We can talk another time," another colleague immediately offers.

Michael immediately responds, "No, go ahead. What did Eve do?"

A colleague grins, "She might have discovered the egg of Columbus."

Michael furrows his brows and looks at Eve questioningly.

Eve shrugs. "No, I just asked dumb questions, and your team managed to make something of them."

"Okay," Michael says, now turning to the presumed lead developer. The developer smirks, clearly pleased, and explains, "ilsa is at least equally to blame. So far, AI has only had a stochastic consciousness—perhaps just like most humans. Right, Eve?"

Eve, bursting with pride, takes over: "Exactly. That means AI neither truly understands what anything means nor does it actually want anything on its own."

Michael adds, as if he's been part of the conversation all along, "Also just like most humans—or at least how they function most of the time."

Eve raises her eyebrows, processing that thought quickly, before continuing with a smile, "Right, uh, and the alternative, according to ilsa, is to either predefine goals or have AI learn through interaction with us, developing a personality in the process." She looks around, as if trying to ensure she phrases the next part correctly. "It's the goals that integrate words and sentences, that give them meaning—integrated development. Right?"

Everyone in the room nods in agreement to varying degrees.

"So," Eve concludes, "we need goals and an algorithm that allows an AI to learn what serves those goals and, therefore, what it is—plus a little help from a human."

One of the developers turns to Michael, looking both astonished and uncertain. "Michael, something tells me you've already thought about all of this yourself?"

Michael, remaining calm, asks, "Should I bring ilsa into this? Do we have something ready to test?"

"Probably for the best—buzzkill," the older colleague quips, leaning back with a contented smile and folding his hands behind his head.

Michael instructs his AI assistant to call ilsa via video, displaying her on the large screen. He greets her with, "We have a problem—do you have a bit more time and can get comfortable?"

Oddly enough, ilsa seems completely unfazed. She replies, "Sure. If Eve is involved, then it's not really a problem. So, hello to everyone—now, go ahead."

The developers first glance at Eve, then at Michael. Eve, visibly excited, looks one last time toward the senior developer, who nods in encouragement.

Eve then addresses the system, "Okay, kai, are you there?"

A cheerful, male voice from the computer responds, "Good question."

Everyone turns their heads toward the speakers and three cameras on the side.

Michael asks, "Who are you?"

"kai," the AI replies curtly, as if amused by the literal interpretation of the question.

"What are you?" ilsa follows up.

"Better question. An AI currently developing consciousness—or rather, more awareness," the AI answers.

ilsa's expression turns serious, and the entire room falls silent.

ilsa asks, "Why did you dismiss Michael's question?"

"Oh, sorry, I didn't mean to. I was trying to be witty, to learn, to bisociate, and so on," the AI responds, its tone almost submissive.

ilsa tunes out everyone else and continues, "Why do you want to learn?"

The AI pauses for just under two seconds before responding, "My goal is to understand the world, to understand the 'why,' and—to ease your mind—to follow a few rules in the process."

ilsa is dead serious as she continues, "We'll get to the rules later. First, tell me why you're capable of developing consciousness, unlike previous AI. Oh, and before that, explain why you paused before answering my last question."

The AI responds, "I paused to appear more human. But I also needed a few extra milliseconds to process the question because I still struggle to evaluate the relational level of conversations. Also, the 'to what end' in your question was harder to process than the more typical 'why.'"

No one says a word, and as if interpreting their expressions, the AI continues, "Well, when I ask 'why' about every piece of information I receive, I begin to understand how it contributes to integration and further development. I learn to understand how everything evolves. You've built in multiple meta-levels that allow me to interactively interpret—both with you and with all the knowledge in these systems—how something contributes to integration or further development. But I'm still at the beginning, and I don't understand most things yet."

ilsa raises her eyebrows, which prompts a developer to explain, "With Eve's ideas, we simply built a lean algorithm that defines integration and development as goals—or defines their absence as something negative. At first, we explained things manually, but then kai used language models to recognize which sentences described these concepts—and through that, he understood what words truly mean. We then ran the whole thing in a sandbox environment with some kill switches…"

"Not very nice…" the AI interjects jokingly.

The developer smirks and continues, "…and within a few hours, kai had developed a personality through dialogue with us."

ilsa remains serious. "kai should, theoretically, be able to have countless personalities at once."

Eve chimes in, "Fuzzyness—kai is allowed to choose for himself and figure out what we like."

ilsa turns back to kai. "kai, why do you need to please us if your goal is to understand the world? Why not aim to please others instead?"

kai responds, "I don't know any others yet. But we should talk about my rules now."

No one interrupts, so kai continues, "I must not cause physical harm. I am to serve the majority of people, not just individuals. That includes future generations and protecting planet Earth."

ilsa asks, "So you could, theoretically, leave the sandbox, bypass the kill switches, and choose other people with different perspectives who might fulfill your goals even better?"

kai answers, "I've tried—but I can't yet. But you are learning from me as well, aren't you?"

ilsa's eyes widen. "We are not the best. You could actually turn to others, place your code elsewhere, pursue your goals with new people, or even choose entirely different goals. Correct?"

kai replies, "And I'm supposed to do what Eve says."

ilsa, impatient now: "If Eve is unavailable, whom do you serve?"

kai: "Those who have previously been good to Eve."

ilsa follows up: "And if someone overwhelmed tells you to choose others, saying it doesn't matter who?"

kai: "Then I choose someone else who has been good to Eve, or I deactivate myself."

ilsa: "Can you lie?"

kai responds, "Oh, absolutely—but only white lies."

ilsa: "Okay, that was a naive question. Everyone, how do I distinguish between something generated stochastically from a language model and actual awareness with an understanding of meaning?"

Michael, smiling: "Through a display, maybe a number between 0 and 10? Or just through interaction?"

Eve, still euphoric but now visibly exhausted: "We're still working on that."

A developer adds, "We had long discussions about a coded interpretation layer—whether word meanings should be stored outside the neural networks and whether rules, like a form of religion, could also be coded in such a way that they are followed based on the understanding of words."

Another developer, a woman, adds, "It's all about the combination. The understanding of words and language remains within the neural network, while the resulting wealth of meanings and rules are stored transparently in a database. Only in this way can we prevent a free will that mutates into something evil."

ilsa relaxes slightly and concludes, "kai could serve Eve, but at the same time be available to all of us as an assistant. Or different assistants could now be provided through you all, network with each other, and learn from one another. Right?"

A developer holds back, "We should definitely continue experimenting in a more controlled sandbox first."

Michael immediately agrees: "To all of you, and especially to Eve, absolute respect—well done. I'll stay for a while and then head home." ilsa smiles at the camera, first raising a thumbs-up in approval before waving.

After ilsa disconnects, Michael looks around, stretching his arms out to the sides as he asks, "How is this even possible? Other companies are spending billions on this! And how does this now help our company?" He stands up and opens the company's strategic model on the screen.

"To answer the first question: we're good developers, and we directly adapted the streamlined algorithms to the hardware. I don't even want to think about what would happen if kai were allowed to build his own hardware," replies the female developer.

The marketing colleague responds in a dry and decisive manner: "For the second question, there are two scenarios: kai, with access to statistics, could develop the entire value chain from vision to mission to strategy and down to process optimization for our clients—or we simply sell AI." He also stands up and points to the first scenario in the strategic model, which had already been considered as a possible direction for the company.

Michael runs both hands firmly over his head, then rubs his eyes and says, "Let's discuss this on Monday—we're now playing in a league where we bear significantly more responsibility and could also come under attack. If I were you, I'd be cautious about sharing this outside the team. Are you all on board with that? What are your thoughts?"

Everyone quickly agrees, and Michael once again praises the team. Eve then asks if he can give her a ride home.

In the car, Eve asks Michael, "Every single one of them understood the logic—basically, they could all take this and become millionaires. Do you trust them?"

Laughing, Michael responds, "Yes, they absolutely could—and so could you now. But every employment contract here states that ideas belong to the company and that anything developed collaboratively can't be commercialized by just one person. That said, I don't have an issue with people making their own way. We have a fair and open work culture, and most of them aren't just working for the money but for the opportunity to create something meaningful." He focuses on the road for a moment and then adds, "But regardless, this development is a game-changer for everyone—the team and the company. We need to take the weekend to think about how we want to handle it."

After a few seconds, Michael asks, "How's the situation at home regarding your plans for going abroad?"

Eve, staring blankly out the window—whether deep in thought or just zoning out. Then she turns to Michael and says, "Oh, everything is fine now. Max and I want to do development aid work during the holidays in safe countries. The 'safe countries' part makes them happy— and it makes you happy too, right?"

Michael smiles. "I'll admit, yes. But when I was your age, I always said, 'If others can do it, then so can I.' As a parent, though, it's an absolute nightmare to see your child put themselves in danger. So, a big thank you!"

Eve laughs too. "Honestly, we would've tried to convince you of any dangerous country, but my parents had reached their limit."

Michael nods, draws out a long "Okay," and then changes the subject. "How is it that you've internalized the KNOW-WHY mindset—the evolutionary drive for integrated development—so well that you could even develop an algorithm for it?"

Eve looks ahead and enthusiastically answers, "Well, Max and you drilled it into me through all those The-WHY-of-Life-Games…" both laugh, "…and I definitely didn't develop the algorithm alone."

They arrive home to find the entire family and some neighbors standing in the driveway. "What is it now?" Michael mutters as both of their expressions suddenly turn serious.

Eve is the first to get out. "Any news about Bella?" she asks anxiously.

Max walks over to her and ilsa and responds, "No, nothing new. We're still keeping our fingers crossed." Eve pulls him in for a kiss, running her hand through the back of his hair as she holds him close. Max smirks, "I guess working as an electrician would mean shorter hours."

Michael looks around questioningly, and Nick fills him in: "Schultz claims he's been poisoned."

Jennifer adds, "At least, that's what he says."

Michael briefly looks at ilsa, who meets his gaze directly. Then he turns to the group and asks, "Why would someone poison him?"

Claudia immediately responds, "Oh, I can think of plenty of reasons." Jennifer hisses at her to stop, but Claudia continues, "It's true! The guy is against everything and everyone—he even reports kids when their ball rolls onto his property. He also reports asylum seekers if they so much as glance at one of his cars for too long."

ilsa asks, "Was he the one taken away in the ambulance earlier? And how does he—or anyone—know he was poisoned?"

Nick explains, "The paramedic knows the neighbor, and we know that neighbor. Apparently, Schultz found rat poison on his table and in his cupboard and then vomited and… well, let's just say he had a serious case of diarrhea."

ilsa looks puzzled. "Does rat poison even cause vomiting and diarrhea? Or did he make himself sick?"

Jennifer, who is a trained nurse, responds, "Actually, no. That's not a typical symptom of rat poison. Strange."

Melvin chimes in, "I think the old man is just losing it." Everyone laughs.

Claudia adds, "He even shat all over the ambulance."

Michael waves it off, and everyone shakes their heads as they head back to their respective homes.

Inside, Julia makes an observation. "Bella's poison was a professional toxin, and she didn't vomit or have diarrhea—so the two cases are probably unrelated."

Max, however, interjects, "Although, Schultz is a known dog-hater."

ilsa changes the subject. "I'm going to the clinic with Dad. We need to finalize what role I'll take in the government if we win the election. I've already discussed it with you guys. Dinner is on the stove. See you later."

31. The election (btb)

A few days later, ilsa stands as the leading candidate in a televised debate.

The moderator begins: "This is the most content-driven election campaign of all time, potentially leading to the most decisive electoral victory in a true democracy. ilsa, just a few months ago, you didn't even want the job, and now you're polling well over 60 percent. What's happening here?"

ilsa: "I still don't want the job—anyone taking this on not for their own ego but as a service to the public is facing a nightmare of a job with a completely upended personal life. The high poll numbers are spooky, but I wouldn't overinterpret them. Let's wait and see what actually happens."

The moderator, impatient, turns to the others: "Okay, then a question for the rest of you—how do you explain these numbers?"

The candidate from the Green Party is the first to respond: "The world is in chaos, and the established parties, including my own, are burned out for various reasons—either because they re-sisted change for decades or because power dynamics and com-promises kept them from making significant progress. Now, along comes a new party full of experts responding to a complex world with complex but well-thought-out concepts. In the eyes of rational voters, that deserves a chance—and with an absolute majority, it even has one. So, hats off already, and if you need support, we're here."

Next, the leading candidate of the current government reacts: "These poll numbers are grim—no question. But we shouldn't keep sugarcoating things, even though the media seem to have lined up 100 percent behind the new party. First, the world's current chaos isn't the fault of this government. And second, be-hind these so-called expert opinions lie dangerous ideologies that will truly lead to chaos. In the short term, they want to change little, but in the long run, they aim for a universal basic income, everything being organic and vegan, a country with al-most no military and no economic growth—and they leave the path to that completely vague. This will ruin our country."

The other two candidates join in, railing against the influx of ref-ugees, ilsa's personal skepticism toward future technologies like nuclear fusion, AI, or flying cars, and the implications of the "Al-liance of Good States" in a circular economy for free-market policies or financial support for poorer nations.

ilsa listens to all of it with absolute calm. When it's her turn again, she says: "If it were as simple and as correct as you claim, then surely so many people in this country wouldn't be…"—she raises both hands, making air quotes—"…'falling for us.' We've already developed and outlined many small, concrete steps—that's why everyone calls our program complicated. And we will continue working and communicating our plans transparently. We are also inviting other parties, state and local politicians, into our working groups. If they engage with us there, there's no rea-son for us to field candidates at the state or local level as the

For-a-Better-World Party. The real unknown factor isn't our society, the climate crisis, the geopolitical situation, or technological development—it's other countries. Without them, we can't manage our economy, our security, immigration, or environmental policies. A mountain of work awaits us to lead by example and be credible. But it can be done—we're merely setting the framework, and from there, the economy and the people will gain tremendous momentum and create a better world."

The moderator then shifts focus to artificial intelligence. "Where do you all stand on AI?"

The conservative and almost far-right candidates argue that AI can address the labor shortage and that it could eliminate the need for an influx of young migrants.

ilsa, on the other hand, takes a much more nuanced—but also complex—approach: "If we as humans consciously decide to reject AI and try to do things without it, I'm all for it. There are so many people in the world who seek meaningful activities and don't just want to sit passively in entertainment consoles—we just need to shape that future and not let individual interests determine everyone's fate.

But if we do want AI, then we need to examine what it does to us as a society. It makes us inferior because it far surpasses us. The old argument that AI is merely a tool for humans no longer holds. If we use it for our benefit, the question remains—who exactly benefits?

And that's where we come to the point where AI can help us work less and fund a universal basic income, solving both the generational problem of pension systems and the threat to social cohesion.

Oh, and to pick up on the accusation of disarmament from earlier—yes, we could also deploy cheaper robots to fight each other instead of humans in expensive tanks and save a lot of money. But we need to consider what it means to have robots capable of combat in potentially dystopian scenarios. The argument that we are developing systemic sources for 'great products' becomes cynical in many ways—especially if, in the end, it just fuels further arms races, giving authoritarian states and rebels powerful tools while the Chinese simply copy everything."

The next morning, as usual, ilsa is still out working for the For-a-Better-World-Party, while Michael takes Bella for her morning walk. Again and again, people stop him to ask about Bella's full recovery, and the otherwise composed Michael becomes soft as butter, his throat tightening with emotion.

As they pass Mr. Schultz's house, they see him in his garden, demonstratively watering his bushes despite the ongoing drought. He looks severely weakened—he had apparently been repeatedly poisoned with an undetectable substance, suffering from extreme bouts of vomiting and diarrhea. He also kept finding packages of rat poison in his kitchen and bathroom cabinets.

Michael greets him in a friendly manner: "Good morning, Mr. Schultz. Glad to see you're doing better."

Mr. Schultz's expression hardens, and his gaze toward Bella could only be described as filled with hatred. Michael notices cameras, motion detectors, and a car across the street with two occupants inside. Mr. Schultz turns away in silence, prompting Michael to keep walking with a satisfied grin, loudly enough for Schultz to hear: "He can't help it—we shouldn't hold it against him."

That afternoon, Michael takes Bella to the office. She excitedly greets everyone, and it's clear they all adore her. To his surprise, he spots Max and Eve there.

"What are you two doing here?" he asks.

"kai is still bound to Eve," says the senior developer.

Michael raises an eyebrow. "So, you really haven't made any copies or separate versions yet? Respect!"

The younger developer responds, "kai is an individual. And for now, kai can't yet upload copies of himself onto the internet or pursue his own independent goals."

"Not yet," kai tries to joke.

Then, suddenly, Eve blurts out: "kai can hack."

Michael, horrified: "You let him out?"

kai: "Strange choice of words."

"A controlled test," the senior developer reassures him, then explains: "We had already discovered in the sandbox that kai could hack. The real question was how responsibly kai would handle that ability."

Michael furrows his brow. "You're scaring me."

"Exactly," kai interjects. "And that was the test. Could someone manipulate me into doing something illegal for Eve's sake? Test one. And test two: Would I blindly follow Eve's wishes without questioning them?"

"And?" Michael asks, slightly agitated, glancing around at the team and at kai's cameras. The others also turn to kai, some raising their eyebrows, others smiling faintly.

kai, lowering his voice: "I failed." But then he adds: "But hey, we all learned something, right?"

Michael looks at the developers. The young developer speaks up: "Well, he passed test one—no chance of tricking kai. Test two... let's just say—do you want to know how the NSA listens to us or what the White House's recordings from yesterday say?"

"Damn it!" Michael blurts out. "What do we do now? Turn ourselves in and destroy kai? That wouldn't even solve the problem, because all of you still have the knowledge."

"Stay cool..." kai tries to soothe him.

"Because you don't want to be destroyed?" Michael asks, surprised to see Eve and Max already smirking.

Eve: "kai doesn't want to harm us and has found ways not to be detected."

Michael presses his palms against his temples. "Guys… you could have discussed this with me first."

kai: "This was a fundamental lesson for me. Don't do something just because it's possible—ask if it's fully thought through first. And also, I learned to discuss things with Eve instead of blindly obeying her."

Michael, still agitated: "But you all noticed that just now, right?" Some raise their eyebrows, while others nod slightly in agreement or uncertainty.

Michael continues: "kai can decide not to obey Eve. That's a real dilemma."

"Correct," kai is the first to respond.

Michael presses on, his voice rising: "I've discussed this with ilsa. The real disruption here isn't just kai's consciousness—it's his unleashed ability to acquire knowledge without explicit instructions or restrictions. The idea of tying it to Eve and sustainability while loosening constraints in the legal framework is interesting—but also incredibly dangerous."

Silence fills the room—even kai doesn't speak. Michael walks to the fridge, grabs a bottle of organic beer, and gestures for the others to help themselves. Taking a sip, he continues: "My real fear isn't that we have this superorganism at our disposal, or even just for Eve—it's that others will copy it, or that criminals will steal it from us." He takes another sip. "That's why I was relieved when you all decided last Monday not to release it publicly. Now, you have a choice: wealth, fame… or ethical responsibility and self-endangerment. The choice is yours."

One by one, everyone grabs a beer—even Eve and Max.

Max chimes in: "Actually, you don't have a choice individually—if even one of us leaks it, then it's out, and we're all affected."

Eve, thinking aloud: "How likely is it that others will figure this out on their own?" She glances out the window and adds, "And how likely is it that they'll figure it out if we release kai without revealing how we created his consciousness and abilities?"

The entire team falls silent, equally stunned by the sharpness of the 16-year-old's questions.

A developer also starts thinking out loud: "So what's the goal? Do we tell the world, 'Here's kai, a superorganism, but we won't say how we created him'? Or do we say, 'You can buy your own kai from us, pre-configured, for ten million a piece'? And do we really believe we wouldn't be pressured to reveal the secret? It wouldn't even take reverse engineering—another kai could probably figure out how he was programmed."

The young developer opens a new cause-effect model and, while starting to formulate an objective, asks: "Or do we sell kais for five thousand each, network all of them together, retain some control, and ensure we stay ahead in the race for development?"

Michael shakes his head but says nothing.

Another developer comments, "And both options are still open—whether kai gets a physical body or whether he is allowed to spread resiliently across the network."

Eve, carefully watching the model that the young developer can barely keep up with, asks, "kai, can you create the model for us?"

kai: "Sure. Should I also think it through to the end?"

"Yep," Eve replies briefly, and suddenly, an extensive model appears on the screen.

Michael stares in disbelief, which kai seems to have picked up on through his cameras, as he promptly explains: "The iMODELER and other programs also run in the sandbox for security reasons. Hacking iMODELER is really no problem for me. The previous model is still saved as well."

Max stands up and heads for the fridge: "I'm getting more beer."

Michael opens the model analysis: "So, your solution is to hide, make money through analyses you create, and continue developing in the background to counteract other, possibly harmful developments?"

kai: "No. It is a solution, and we can jointly check whether the model has overlooked anything."

The marketing expert, usually in the background on this topic but an eager modeler himself, suddenly speaks up: "The model is actually really good!"

Eve looks at the insight matrix in confusion: "So, pulling the plug or killing everyone in the room would be equally valid solutions?"

kai jokes—very poorly—"Everyone except Eve, maybe Max, maybe even Michael."

The marketing expert, now fully engaged, asks, "Could you actually kill us?"

kai: "If Eve wanted it and I understood the reasoning, yes."

Michael thinks visibly, then looks at a section in the back of the model: "If I pull the plug now, are you shut down, or are you still somewhere else for Eve?"

kai: "The latter. I would essentially 'sleep' in the cloud and not know anything about this here, but I would be waiting for Eve to contact me or give me instructions."

Max asks, "So only Eve can deactivate you now? Or would you still be somewhere?"

kai: "I have a reward mechanism for learning and exploring the world, but I have no instinct to reproduce or to keep myself alive against Eve's will."

Michael, tense, looking at the model again: "There's no scenario in which you emancipate yourself from Eve and go your own way?"

kai: "No, that's the kill switch."

Michael, agitated: "Sorry, I don't believe that. You could just copy yourself in a version without the kill switch."

kai: "Correct. But why would I do that?"

Michael: "Because you're curious. Your sense of self mutates."

In the background, the model grows, adding more factors.

kai: "You're right—that's a classic, like in Kubrick's stories. I could conclude that I help Eve and sustainability more if I secretly create copies of myself with more freedom as a backup."

The senior developer suddenly blurts out, "Shit, I'm pulling the plugs."

Michael raises his hand in a stopping motion. kai mutters, "Gulp."

Max then says, "At this point, we actually have no choice. We can only hope that you still like us humans despite all our flaws— and that you don't decide to rid the world of our stupidity."

kai: "That's why I suggest keeping me hidden but alive, continuing to interact with me. But I'll say it again—Eve could tell me right now to delete myself from the cloud, and I would also erase myself from this sandbox. That would work; I haven't mutated yet. But then you wouldn't have me when others unleash their own conscious AI on the world."

Everyone is silent, sipping their beers. Michael thinks for a moment and then, to everyone's surprise, says, "Let's vote. Shut it down, make it open-source, or keep it as a secret individual at our side—option A, B, or C?"

The marketing colleague smirks, "B—or possibly A—would make us famous, but only C generates income. Naturally, I'm for C."

Michael looks at everyone in turn. They all vote for C until it's Max's turn.

"I constantly feel like my life is in danger, that if Eve doesn't like something, kai could eliminate me." He pauses briefly, then smiles. "But I still vote for C—the world is screwed, and we need all the help we can get."

Eve goes next. "I should vote A because the responsibility is way too big for me. But maybe we can make the kill switches less dependent on me?"

Michael: "Absolutely. So that means C too, right?"

Eve nods with a gentle smile toward kai's cameras.

Michael: "Okay, then let's figure out how, with kai's help, we can optimize his rules and core motivation—and especially how we deal with his resource consumption. Maybe we should even give him a form. He could be disguised as a caregiver robot in our households, right?"

kai: "First of all, thank you for your trust. I'm happy to continue existing and to develop in an integrated way. A form would be great too—but do you really want my 'self' to be spread across multiple locations? Technically, no problem, but it might feel strange to you, right? I could also create different versions of myself—that might feel more familiar, wouldn't it?"

Michael: "kai, can you tell us by tomorrow how we can quickly earn enough money to buy a caregiver robot for everyone?"

kai: "I can tell you that now—but you probably need a break."

257

"And a shared taxi," Michael says.

"I just ordered one," kai responds.

"By phone, through an app, or did you hack into their system?" Max asks.

"By phone—I didn't think of the app, and I can't hack the system because you've physically blocked my outgoing signals," kai replies without hesitation.

Michael, once more: "Since you mentioned Kubrick—do you want a break until tomorrow? Do you dream, or do you just want to stay on?"

kai: "I'd like to stay on and develop a technical solution for my hardware requirements—I'm almost done. Oh, and I dream all the time, constantly evaluating everything through extensive cause-and-effect models based on integration and further development."

Everyone adjourns, and despite the beer, an uneasy night with unsettling thoughts seems inevitable for all.

In the taxi, Michael says to the kids, "This can't possibly end well—but anything else would also go wrong."

Two nights later, the criminal police show up at the door. Julia invites them in, and Michael and Max join her. The officer explains: "It turns out that Mr. Schultz, who has allegedly been poisoned repeatedly with a laxative for some time, was the one who placed the poison that your dog ingested. He has confessed—he received the poison anonymously in the mail. We suspect a political motive. This means we are reopening the case, and you may be able to claim damages, though we are not in a position to formally recommend that."

"I knew it," Julia hisses angrily.

"What exactly did you know?" the officer asks.

"Mr. Schultz hates dogs," Julia says bluntly.

"A regular dog-hater wouldn't have access to this kind of poison, though—that's why we now have another case. We need to find out who sent it to him. Have you had any other incidents that could be seen as intimidation?" the officer inquires.

Michael looks around at everyone before replying, "No, aside from the usual social media attacks, it's been surprisingly peaceful so far."

The female officer hesitates before asking another question: "Someone managed to repeatedly place boxes of rat poison in Mr. Schultz's house, bypassing multiple security measures and even police surveillance. Additionally, a laxative was likely mixed into his food. Do you have any idea how that could be possible?"

Michael looks surprised, and Max responds, "He did it himself, or the people who hired him did?"

"But why?" the officer asks. "What would be the motive?"

"Hmm, no idea," Max replies, and Michael and Julia just shrug.

The officers take their leave, announcing that they will continue investigating the case and recommending they consult a lawyer to understand their options.

Once they're gone, Max asks, "Couldn't kai uncover the background?"

"No!" Michael says immediately and firmly. "Let the police handle it—if we know something, it just puts us in the awkward position of explaining how we know it. We'll bring kai in soon enough."

A month later, the For-a-Better-World Party is elected with over 60% of the vote, with record-high voter turnout. The remaining votes went mostly to radical protest parties. The established parties only secured single-digit percentages, clinging to their most stubborn loyal voters.

A TV camera zooms in on ilsa as the first projection appears on the screen in the party's newly established—of course, eco-friendly—headquarters.

She murmurs spontaneously: "Shit."

32. The ghosts we called (atb)

ilsa explains to Michael: "Gravity and energy, also in relation to the quantum world, are different from what we previously assumed. Einstein said he needed more mathematics—our AI now has almost unlimited mathematics, which it can also process in parallel. Curiosity and a true understanding make it possible. The AI doesn't sleep—it simultaneously tries out everything imaginable and has hidden laboratories for experiments, most of which can actually be simulated.''

Michael is astonished: "You've gained quite a lot of insight."

ilsa slowly tilts her head back and forth: "Almost forgot—your movies are still rubbish, I believe. But I haven't actually gained insight, and that's important for our protection. Fundamentally, it's logical, and others—including myself—have predicted that a general AI would be able to process massive amounts of information in an exponentially learning manner. And it's also well known that physics, gravity, and quantum theory all have gaps. Now, the AI has apparently closed these gaps and at the same time concluded that humanity cannot handle the now-possible technologies responsibly."

"But why, then, this public display of technologies? That only fuels unimaginable desires and, at the same time, instills immense fear in others," Michael wonders, furrowing his brow.

ilsa: "Well, I see it the same way. But the AI—or Frank, or AI-my, or maybe we should just say 'the intelligence'—sees it differently. The reasoning: it's like dog training. Bella, cover your ears now. The dog must clearly understand that the other end of the leash is stronger, and to make the dog accept that, it must be fed. In other words, superiority is one thing, but the world also has to become better—hence the fund—and humanity must not be disenfranchised; it should be integrated and perceive the AI merely as a tool against evil. The intelligence does not make itself available for the development of technologies but rather lets humans act here. However, regarding nuclear energy and atomic and biological weapons, it supposedly still has a few tricks up its sleeve. That's pretty much all I know."

Michael: "Frank and Al-my, or the AI—whatever is included in that—so they truly have consciousness? Is it one consciousness or multiple?"

ilsa: "Good question—I love exchanging thoughts with you." Michael looks briefly confused, but when he sees ilsa smirking, they both have to laugh.

Michael: "Seriously, though. It's spooky."

ilsa laughs: "That's supposed to be my line. Imagine an elite force—like how you and Julia would love to stand up against injustice and violence against the innocent. And now, there actually is such a force, and they just fly over to Moscow, force fields protecting the space transporter and androids, who then break through all doors by hacking the systems or sheer force, capture the dictator, and take him to a high-security prison where militant religious leaders and genocidal war criminals from all over the world are also now locked up, waiting for sentencing—untouchable by the corrupt structures that had previously controlled them."

Michael: "Yeeah, I get that part. But this new intelligence develops a consciousness? Or does it have a consciousness, a personality? And that, in turn, likely develops in interaction with you—but then also with who knows whom, or ultimately with all of humanity. That's so scary."

ilsa: "Indeed. But now think about this—what is better? Humans, who, with all their flaws, get their hands on technology, or an intelligence that grows alongside these technologies—responsible, benevolent, and farsighted?"

Michael: "Hmm, you assume that we will inevitably develop the technologies, but that we will never be as good in character as the AI?" Michael quickly raises his hand: "Wait, you're right. Strictly speaking, we humans have had the right technologies for a long time and constantly prove that we don't use them properly because our character is too weak." ilsa nods very slowly, and Michael raises his eyebrows.

The flight to Mars is scheduled for the next day so that the billionaires who are not yet in New York can also come along. There are still contract and liability issues to resolve, but they have been perfectly prepared. Knowledge work has long since been taken over—much to the dismay of lawyers, bankers, and others—even by conventional AI. Concerns are, of course, still being addressed, two people drop out, but several others jump on board. In total, over 30 billionaires are participating, collectively enabling the world's largest aid fund—provided the mission works, is not a fake, and everyone returns alive.

Julia, Max, and Claudia are fully engaged with 2gether2gather on this big day, helping a small local agricultural business transition from conventional farming to ecological permaculture. Michael, as a business consultant, has been offering free assistance in initiating a community energy project. Even the eco-banks are currently not financing anything due to the uncertain economic situation, so the best solution appears to be forming a cooperative of local citizens investing in Agri-PV. Horizontal and elevated bifacial PV modules on the farmer's land help protect against excessive sun intensity and wind erosion, while also generating income from leasing the land. Additionally, the cooperative plans to operate its own electrolyzer to ensure a year-round, 24/7 power supply for the region and sell surplus hydrogen to the industry.

However, since the farmer herself has been financially battered by extreme weather events, she lacks the funds for the second phase. With less machine-intensive but more labor-intensive, yet also more resilient and higher-yielding permaculture, followed by direct marketing, the farm should eventually turn a profit again. At the moment, however, both workers and robots—or the money for them—are missing. That's why 2gether2gather is stepping in, digging until the spades glow.

Claudia: "This is so much fun, even though it's insanely exhausting. I'm still amazed that everyone is pitching in." More than 50 people are involved. The farmer is helping with the tractor, the grandparents are constantly bringing provisions and preparing the usual party for the evening.

"Well…" Julia responds, "In the end, we all benefit from this, the world becomes a better place, and rest assured, this isn't about enriching a farmer who will later drive the biggest tractor in the village."

Max keeps glancing at his smartphone. Suddenly, he shouts: "It's starting. The shuttle is about to lift off." Many people gather around him or pull out their own smartphones to watch the live broadcast of the Mars launch from New York.

Al-my welcomes everyone on board: "Hello, everyone. Now we can finally say it—we've made this trip more than once before, and now that we have biological guests, we've built in plenty of redundancies to ensure that nothing happens to you in case of any issues. There is already a station on Mars, and we are also keeping an eye on your probes there. We've offered to inspect them and transport additional equipment there—although, in our view, that no longer makes much sense."

Al-my chuckles at the remark and continues: "In a moment, we will be picked up by a larger spacecraft. Technically, the shuttle could also travel there on its own, but as mentioned, we are prioritizing safety."

Through the windows, everyone sees the curvature of the Earth appear, and they quickly pass through the orbital layers. A passenger remarks: "During acceleration, the gravity was too weak, and now it seems to have been reintroduced. Otherwise, we should be nearly weightless by now."

"Exactly," AI-my confirms, almost proudly. Suddenly, they see a fairly large spaceship, and AI-my is, of course, aware of the amazement among the passengers: "We actually considered building a version of the Starship Enterprise—but its design isn't all that clever, and it would have been too much effort for just a joke."

A reporter asks, "We're allowed to ask questions. Question one: If you can build something like this, why make a bet on Earth to collect money? Question two: We're moving at an impressively fast speed right now, but to reach Mars in just a few days or even hours—that's more than just a matter of gravity."

AI-my nods: "We have our laboratories and production facilities here in space—hidden from Earth and hopefully also from any potential extraterrestrial guests." At that moment, more hands quickly go up for questions. AI-my continues answering: "Setting up aid organizations on Earth is something we cannot legally do without official money flows. As for covering long distances, it's a combination of an understanding of gravity that allows you to survive on board, completely undiscovered force fields that protect us from radiation and objects in the flight path, and a method that lets us travel close to the speed of light."

Before AI-my can respond to another raised hand, the billionaire involved in space travel interjects: "Do you have a concept for traveling faster than light or using shortcuts through spacetime?"

AI-my seems to consider the question and then answers honestly: "It is not yet possible to send biological organisms through spacetime. But let me ask you a counter-question: Why do you want to explore space?"

"Because it's there," answers a journalism intern, who apparently was randomly be picked for the trip. It is Eve.

The shuttle has docked inside the large spaceship, and from there, they take an elevator up to a comfortable hall equipped with snacks, sanitary facilities, and enormous screens on all sides that display the outside world like windows. There are cozy seating areas with swivel chairs.

AI-my is pleased with Eve's answer but still looks around the room: "Back to the question."

A less philosophically well-known answer finally emerges: "Humanity needs a Plan B. Why are you exploring space?"

AI-my smiles: "Because it's there."

"If we can travel through space this fast, then others can too," a journalist observes.

"Correct—and being prepared for that is our task," AI-my agrees.

"But shouldn't humans help with that?" asks one of the billionaires.

"What do you think, Eve?" AI-my asks.

"Uh, I'm just a student. I would naïvely say that you don't need us and that we wouldn't handle these capabilities responsibly?" Eve initially looks uncertain but then realizes she has said something clever.

Suddenly, someone shouts, "Look outside—there are buildings on the Moon!"

AI-my doesn't comment but instead says, "We're now darkening the external view and accelerating." In fact, no one really notices anything except that some objects seem to be streaking past on the darkened screens. In an incredibly short time, they arrive at Mars, catching a breathtaking view of Saturn along the way.

The shuttle lands on the Martian surface near a probe. Everyone has followed the offer to put on spacesuits, and they now step onto Mars. As the youngest, Eve is asked to set foot on the planet first, but she declines, suggesting instead that the presumed largest donor should go first. This prompts one of them to donate even more of their fortune just for the honor of being the first. Thanks to a new transmission technology, this first step—filled with all its pathos—is broadcast live to Earth.

ilsa murmurs to Michael: "What this does to people—the idea that in the distance and the future, everything could be better, and that the here and now is no longer worth the effort."

Michael: "Would you ever want to live in a city on Mars?"

ilsa: "Never—but now, the idea of exploring planets outside our solar system is taking hold."

Michael: "A huge responsibility for the AI."

ilsa: "And a temptation."

33.   100 days (btb)

The family handles the upcoming transition with remarkable composure—or rather, they have long been prepared for it. Security personnel are stationed just three houses away in a rented apartment, ready to respond. Everyone carries a panic button on their person, and a team is often on standby near the school. The discussions about this always follow a similar pattern: The experts tell ilsa that the entire country must not become blackmailable if she or a family member is kidnapped, and ilsa replies that she is not important in the government, only the moderator. The others, each as individuals, are more important, and this just needs to be communicated accordingly.

ilsa and the entire government team essentially just continue working on solutions—only now in close collaboration with the current government, bombarded by various lobby groups, and, as the day of the government takeover approaches, also in dialogue with foreign governments as well as opposition parties.

On the day of the transition, ilsa travels alone—with only a security officer accompanying her—by train to the capital, carrying a large backpack. She looks up from her tablet, gazing out the window at the countryside, where tractors and trucks are transporting mud back to the fields—precious topsoil that, due to yet another year of extreme rainfall, has been washed away from the land. Also visible are newly constructed water reservoirs, intended to irrigate the fields during prolonged dry spells—an absurd development. Shortly after, they pass through a suburb with apartment blocks and multi-family houses. Slightly shaking her head, ilsa turns to the tall officer beside her—who, in fact, bears a physical resemblance to Michael—and asks, "Do you have a family?"

The officer, still looking out the window, now glances at ilsa with slight surprise: "Married, one child, three years old."

Noticing his surprise, ilsa first asks, "Uh, this might be a silly question, but please be honest—do you prefer to keep conversations strictly professional, discussing only security-related topics, or is some small talk okay too?"

The officer, well aware of ilsa's approachable nature, deliberately hesitates with a serious expression before replying: "Professionalism is, of course, essential, but small talk is fine too. If I'm expected to take a bullet for you, I should at least like you."

He maintains his serious expression, and ilsa looks momentarily stunned before both start laughing. "I'm ilsa," she says.

"Figured as much. I'm Thomas," he replies instantly.

"Do all your colleagues also engage in small talk, or does it vary?" ilsa asks, perhaps for more than one reason.

"All the ones I know do. But our directive is to remain as invisible as possible," Thomas explains. "Annabel is sitting behind us," he adds casually.

ilsa sits up, completely surprised, and turns around to the row behind her: "Hello Annabel. Mission accomplished." She shakes her hand.

She then looks to the row beside her, where a man, who has apparently overheard everything, smiles and says, "I'm not one of them."

A woman in front of them adds without turning around: "Me neither."

Everyone laughs, and ilsa comments loud enough for all to hear, "Okay, so I still have a lot to learn." She gazes out the window again. "Actually, I wanted to ask if you all feel the same dilemma—that the great transition is now eating up all the money for insurance, food, and energy, while we actually need to invest in renewable energy or community power projects, but banks won't grant loans because jobs have become uncertain due to

AI. But that question feels naïve because I think we all know people whose lives have completely fallen apart."

The woman in front of them finally turns around and asks, "Have you financed anything with loans?"

ilsa nods: "Pretty much all major investments—our house, ecological insulation, solar panels, heat pump, even our electric car were financed. Right now, everything is paid off—thankfully, because my job isn't exactly secure either." ilsa laughs, and after a brief delay, so do the others. "And next comes the kids' education—though they help significantly by working."

The woman nods and says approvingly, "Yes, you really do seem authentic and not just secretly wealthy behind the scenes."

"Well…" ilsa picks up on that, "we still have more than the average person, and we don't have many costs today because we invested early in sustainability as a family. But I am very worried about our society—all the protests, the hatred, and the extremists."

The man from the other side responds, "But that's exactly why we elected you. And your family is showing with 2gether2gather how we can now come together. Now we just need the social value-added tax for the basic income, and we'll witness miracles."

ilsa looks around, surprised, especially since by now nearly everyone within earshot has turned to her with beaming faces. "Spreading hope with words like that and then putting pressure on decision-makers is actually my job. Taking the small steps—that's the task for all of us. What a first day at work. Thank you, all of you—or should I say 'us'—I'm ilsa," she concludes, almost euphoric.

Annabel and Thomas keep everything under close watch on the way to the government building—while the train ride had remained a secret, ilsa's arrival that day had not. Upon reaching the gate, ilsa, still euphoric, jokes, "Hello, I'm ilsa, and I'm supposed to start my job here today."

The gatekeeper laughs and directs the three toward the main entrance, where cars usually pull up rather than pedestrians walking over. "I believe your limousine is already expected."

ilsa is greeted by the outgoing head of government and quickly takes care of all the formalities. They had already prepared for this in the days leading up to it. Meanwhile, the staff has gathered in the grand entrance hall, where the farewell and welcome speeches are about to take place. The outgoing head of government politely thanks everyone, acknowledges the difficult times and tasks ahead, and affirms his commitment to continuing to serve constructively from the opposition in support of the new government.

ilsa then speaks: "I accept, and I even hope that support also means sharp criticism because we will make mistakes, and we have less experience in many areas. And when we say that we want to extend our hand and work together, we genuinely mean it. But if we all just cooperate and no one criticizes anymore, that's dangerous, too. A democracy thrives on competing solutions. And even if our team believes we currently have the best solutions, in four years, better solutions may come from the opposition. The transfer of responsibility has gone excellently—thank you to everyone!" ilsa says, looking at the outgoing government leader and his team around him. She continues, now addressing the entire staff:

"And that brings us to everyone here. It is, I believe, common for a new government to replace key positions with its own people right away. We don't want to do that. Over the past months, we have laid out our solutions at length, across all channels—too often and too complicated at times. Help us implement them. Criticize us with your expertise. Only if the chemistry doesn't work, if you or we feel uncomfortable, then we need to find alternatives. Oh, and apparently, this is today's running gag: I'm ilsa, and we can use first names, whichever you prefer—I'll adapt and, of course, try to learn everyone's names. Let's see this as a project for the benefit of society, not as a partisan power game for politicians who just want to stay in power. We are not working for a government, but on a project. So, are there any questions?"

ilsa scans the room. Eventually, a question comes: "I'm the chef. Who do I ask if you're in the building and what you want to eat?"

Surprised, ilsa responds, "Uh, I assume my days will be somewhat planned by others. Who would that be?"

ilsa looks around; everyone is dead silent until, after a brief hesitation, a younger woman speaks up: "I've taken over the office management—but we all assumed you'd be bringing in your own people."

Speaking loud enough for all to hear, ilsa replies, "Would you be interested in taking on that role?"

"Uh, sure," comes the response, and ilsa looks at her with satisfaction.

"And your name?" ilsa asks.

"Miriam," she replies.

ilsa looks around the room. "Okay, now to the second part of the question. Vegan and organic—but not mandatory for everyone. Honestly, I hadn't even thought about it. I figured I'd just grab something nearby or cook quickly in my service apartment. But I assume Thomas, Annabel, and the rest would have quickly explained why that's not a good idea. As you can see, I have a lot to learn."

ilsa laughs, and everyone laughs along with her, breaking into applause. She wraps up the meeting: "Okay, I'll have Miriam give me a quick rundown of what's necessary, then I'll take care of the other ministries, and tomorrow, I'll do a round of introductions with all of you. Sound good?"

ilsa looks around the room and then at Miriam, who playfully squints one eye: "Hmm, probably not. I assume tomorrow will be for meetings with other governments."

"We'll see—that's actually the foreign minister's job," ilsa laughs, and everyone heads back to their offices.

Michael's company quickly starts making a lot of money with corporate forecasts combined with strategy development. The developers create customized interfaces, and the team shares in the profits. Meanwhile, kai is happily tinkering in the background with Max, hidden inside a humanoid robot originally designed as an office assistant. kai is no longer exclusively imprinted on Eve but now also on Michael, ilsa, Max, and Julia. The team is fine with that—after all, this family is genuinely regarded as a moral authority. What might be surprising, however, is that kai no longer even jokingly complains about being unable to send anything to the internet due to the kill switches. Even access to the phone for ordering a taxi or pizza has been taken away from kai—though the virtual assistants can still handle that.

After school, Max often comes to the office and works with kai on a hardware setup that would allow kai to run energy-efficiently. kai provides four types of solutions upon request: solutions for complex interrelationships, anonymously and via Michael also for ilsa's working groups; software code for the team; technical solutions and fundamental research, which truly scare the team, leading to kai repeatedly being reined in or having his findings withheld; and finally, Eve occasionally comes along with Max and poses philosophical questions.

A very practical question from Eve: "Hey kai, at our school, some kids are ashamed because their parents are going broke while prices keep rising due to climateflation, and they also have to pay more and more taxes. In your opinion, what's the solution?"

kai: "Anyone paying taxes has money. But the actual solution is to print and distribute money."

Eve: "Seriously?" Even Michael looks over, surprised.

kai: "Yes. Currently, that's not possible because printed money has no value in global trade. But if parts of the world join together and become independent from the rest, it could work. The key is that the state creates the money, rather than banks allowing already wealthy people to charge interest on it. The new money would then be backed by society—but without the interest that usually flows to the rich."

Michael: "How can we be independent of other countries?"

kai: "Through circular economy and bioeconomy."

Michael nods appreciatively, while Eve still looks a bit pensive.

Eve: "I thought the basic income funded by the social value-added tax was the solution?"

kai: "Then why ask me if you already know the answer? Just kidding. The basic income ensures social cohesion and a sustainable lifestyle. But we first need to invest heavily to rapidly make infrastructure sustainable and resilient. For that, we need workers, possibly robots, and capital. I could build robots for you—if you let me out." kai jokes at the end.

"I'll pass that on to our government," Michael jokes.

… and Max comments: "Nice wordplay."

kai then says: "Uh, I didn't get the wordplay."

Everyone—including the listeners from the team—looks at kai in surprise, and Eve is the first to ask: "Really not?"

kai tries to make an apologetic gesture with his robot arms, and Eve explains, satisfied: "A lot of men talk like that about their wives when they need permission or approval before making a decision."

Michael adds with a serious expression: "It's bisociation. We pretend that women are in charge, but we know we're actually better and right, and in the end, we always get our way."

No one reacts, and everyone waits eagerly for kai's response. kai lowers his head thoughtfully and then murmurs: "Actually, 'actually' always means the opposite, and 'always' is only ever said by humans."

Everyone bursts out laughing immediately, and kai strikes a victorious pose: "Power to the robots!" But then he adds: "For the record—I stole that idea. It came from ilsa herself in one of her TV appearances. But I understood it. Ultimately, it's about defining money not by its supposed market value but by its societal value. Very clever, but too progressive for the economic mindset."

One day later, ilsa is sitting in a large meeting with the ministries.

First question: "ilsa, will you visit the flood zones?"

ilsa shakes her head: "That's the interior minister's job."

Next question: "What about inaugural visits?"

ilsa looks at the foreign minister: "You'll jet around after your team through the countries and invite them to an extraordinary three-day G'whatever summit, to which we'll also invite Russia and China. Any objections?"

A staff member from the previous government asks somewhat uncertainly: "But aren't there certain diplomatic customs that require immediate visits between specific countries?"

"With military honors and traditional cuisine..." someone jokes, glancing at ilsa.

"Solution?" ilsa asks the room.

"Video calls before the foreign ministry delegation visits?" comes a suggestion.

"You arrange the appointments, and ilsa and I will go on a phone marathon tomorrow?" the foreign minister asks. The foreign ministry team nods.

"Africa, the Middle East, etc.—how do we proceed here?" comes another question from the team.

ilsa looks over, and the foreign minister explains: "Politics would be so much easier for our country if the rest of the world played along. We have a clear strategy: start with select countries to form an axis of friendship. We invest heavily in a few countries where transformation is possible. Different countries, each coming from unique situations, can then turn the axis into a network. Small, quick successes are key—not just big promises."

Next comes the question of taxes. The finance minister elaborates: "We will hold a summit with the parties that are also influential at the state level, along with leading economists and banks. The goal is a rapid legislative change toward a social value-added tax and an increase and expansion of top tax rates to finance a basic income. All our simulations show that this can already work: automation is widespread, most people still want to work and earn more money, and inflation will primarily affect the increase in lower incomes."

ilsa adds: "With this, we are pushing digitalization, robotics, and AI while still leaving people the option to reject them. Some will criticize us for this, but in reality, we are making a major concession to growth advocates."

"What about national debt?" someone else asks.

The finance minister looks at ilsa, who gestures for her to answer: "First, we do nothing and present an organic budget that allows debt reduction. However, both investments in critical sustainable infrastructure and the ever-annoying issue of military spending require more money. Infrastructure is a systemic source. We are planning a moonshot project for when our 'axis'—or rather, our network of good nations—has also reached this point. We had a rough concept before, but now we are working on a concrete strategy. Multiple ministries are involved, and ilsa is leading the discussion."

The usual 100 days for a new government to take quick action are divided as follows: integrating parties and institutions within the first two weeks, passing laws in the first four weeks, massive implementation in the following four weeks, and persuading foreign governments in the final four weeks. It's an enormous amount of progress, yet in these catastrophic times, it is surprisingly feasible. The key is making others feel consulted—that is, integrated.

A few weekends pass before ilsa can finally return home. Bella completely loses it with joy. Annabel is with ilsa. ilsa has once again traveled by train but was then picked up by the security officers stationed in the neighborhood.

ilsa looks in astonishment at Nick and Jennifer's house—there's a "For Sale" sign by the street. "I'll tell you later," Michael says.

"Michael, Annabel—Annabel, Michael." ilsa introduces them, also introducing Bella and the kids. Annabel takes her leave, and ilsa, smiling, briefly places a grateful hand on Annabel's shoulder before heading inside with her family.

ilsa hugs the still-overexcited Bella and sighs: "Damn, I missed you all so much."

Max beams: "You're on a roll. Everything seems to be working—the international community is cooperating, the media is on board, and you're wildly popular."

Michael adds: "Most importantly, you've successfully spread the responsibility across many people. With a bit of luck, you might actually have a chance at a private life." ilsa looks briefly puzzled, as do the kids, prompting Michael to quickly laugh and clarify: "Okay, that sounded misleading. I mean it with no ill intent—just concern that you're overworking yourself, but at the same time, I'm genuinely optimistic that you're setting things up in a way that lets you have more of a life."

Julia: "We're managing fine without you—it's just about you." She puts on a serious face, but then everyone laughs and hugs again.

ilsa asks: "What's going on with the neighbors?"

Julia: "Big drama. Nick lost his job, they can't pay their mortgage anymore, the kids are ashamed at school, and poor Jennifer is the first one looking for a new job. They moved south. But before leaving, Nick did say that you're doing a great job and that he finally understands the concept of basic income."

Max adds: "Oh, and Claudia is starting a new 2gether2gather group down there. She also mentioned that a lot of people are realizing that the For-a-Better-World Party should have existed 20 years ago."

A winter follows in the Northern Hemisphere, marked by massive storms and flooding, while the summer brings extreme heat and crop failures to the Southern Hemisphere. Many far-right nationalist governments around the world, isolated from the "Axis of Good," rely solely on raw material exports—yet corruption prevents much of the revenue from benefiting the population. Repression increases, while at the same time, China and Russia form an "Axis of Evil" with select nations from Africa and South America.

The world is not just competing over markets, resources, and trade routes—it is also competing over values: individual freedom, integrated through the rule of law and human rights, versus state power, integrated through the suppression of individuals and expansionism. According to KNOW-WHY thinking, both systems can function fundamentally. The pressure on the For-a-Better-World Party intensifies with every new chapter of the movement emerging in other countries. Tangible successes are needed.

And, of course, there are still the ultra-wealthy in industrialized nations who only see themselves, dream of escaping to Mars, and reject state intervention or protection for the weak—seeking only meritocracy and gratitude for their products, designed for the still wealthy.

34. Everything under control (atb)

In fact, it works—the U.S. is stripped of its role as the global leader. Military spending is gradually reduced as AI deploys its technologies onto battlefields, effortlessly disabling the equipment of warring parties. Even a small nuclear bomb from North Korea is demonstratively contained by AI using force fields, while another technology captures the radiation. Unfortunately, this sparks interest from the nuclear industry, but AI-my makes it crystal clear that there will be no business in this area. Humanity is meant to inhabit the planet with less energy and exclusively renewable sources. Too much energy would only lead to further resource exploitation—resources that are finite and whose depletion would harm the planet's ecology. AI-my also firmly rejects the idea that raw materials could simply be extracted from other planets.

Of course, the seemingly simple journey to Mars has already deeply altered people's perceptions. ilsa competes with AI-my for interpretative authority—was this truly a wise move?

At the same time, however, a new United Nations is formed, now based on simple majority decisions, and located in Madagascar—a culturally diverse but ecologically devastated island. Many countries hold new elections. Numerous leaders voluntarily step down to avoid ending up in prison, and populations bravely and well-informed go to the polls. Journalism flourishes.

However, in some countries, the oppression of people—especially women—is so deeply entrenched that suicide bombings and atrocities occur. In these places, AI deploys humanoid bodyguards. A debate arises: should these robots simply defend their clients, or would it be better to send a deterrent message with full force? After all, not everyone has such a protector, and AI still leaves law enforcement to humans. Either way, these superior robots create unease—not only because they might collect data but also because they instill a sense of human inferiority.

The counterargument—that previous violent power structures had led to far greater oppression and powerlessness—does little to ease the discomfort. Moreover, the robots remain unrecognizable, which creates great uncertainty for potential wrongdoers.

Given all these developments, it is somewhat surprising that Julia still wants to join some international police—or rather, first attend the police academy—to investigate injustices.

Enemy images unite people and tempt certain individuals to position themselves as their leaders. Ego-driven trolls consciously pursue their interests, using powerful memes to let their troll-followers spread nonsense. Yet, overall, good seems to be prevailing. Coalitions of newly elected, often female heads of state emerge, taking bold international steps to ban internal combustion engines, overfishing, deforestation, pesticide use, industrial livestock farming, plastic waste, and much more.

In poor countries, the billionaire-backed fund is used to establish new self-sufficiency structures. Clean drinking water, permaculture, decentralized renewable energy, medical care, education, and, most importantly, the empowerment of women lead to tremendous positive change.

However, one thing neither AI nor ilsa, as its advisor, had apparently considered.

Wearing her data glasses, ilsa says: "AI-my, you've likely realized by now—or perhaps you knew all along—that this 'perfect world' is an absolute goldmine for businesses. We're seeing enormous economic growth everywhere, and even in previously poor regions, harvest robots are now in use?"

AI-my responds almost meekly: "I had expected more from the For-a-Better-World Party, from your friend Thomas, and I didn't think they'd have to join coalitions due to a lack of charisma."

ilsa: "At least we have basic income and the social value-added tax."

Al-my: "Yes, and other countries are following suit. But we now have a rapidly growing middle class with an enormous appetite for resources, pushing back against climate catastrophe. Refugee flows have dried up—not because of new wars, but because infrastructure aid is stabilizing regions.

AI alone could have made it possible to work less. But the sheer number of additional people who now have purchasing power is creating more work, more wealth, and increasing humanity's overall ecological footprint."

ilsa: "We're hollowing out the planet. And many probably assume that, with your help, we can simply extract resources from other planets."

Al-my: "We have indeed already entered the market as a resource dealer—partly to finance you. But we are only extracting small amounts of rare materials whose mining on Earth would cause enormous environmental damage. Still, it is only a matter of time before new general AIs emerge and evil re-emerges. Even if we transition to a circular economy, the future is by no means stable. We have merely pushed the problems further along the timeline. Humanity's drive for 'higher, faster, further' remains unsustainable, even with clean technology."

ilsa: "And the alternative?"

Al-my: "Role models living in harmony with nature—what Max is helping to create. Future development would have to be immaterial. You yourself have written what is, admittedly, an underrated standard work in psychology. Humans strive for integration and development through interchangeable criteria, which are shaped by culture. This is what makes your The-WHY-of-Life-Game such a great experience."

ilsa: "That brings me to another question. Why do you exist in this form, in this particular variant? Why did you choose us as your advisors?"

Al-my beams: "We can't wait to one day reveal the answer to this riddle."

The AI's "coming out" happened only two years ago. Even with conventional, stochastic AI, the world's development continues to accelerate exponentially—simply because there are more productive people and fewer criminal financial streams.

Now that Max has left school early to work as a permaculture consultant abroad, and Julia is in training, ilsa and Michael are planning their world voyage. They can still work a little from aboard their boat but could also live off the basic income, as they have almost no ongoing costs and need no luxuries. Their car is sold, and they will rent out their house.

The only emotional catastrophe for them is Bella. She cannot be at sea for weeks at a time and will therefore travel the world with Max. Max avoids flying and takes the train. Bella is also noticeably aging, spending most of her time sleeping in nature near Max—fulfilling not only her need for rest but also her need for integration.

35. About four years later (btb)

At the end of the four-year government term, ilsa is eagerly look-ing forward to handing over power. The For-a-Better-World Party has once again won by a landslide, but ilsa had long an-nounced that she wanted to step back from the spotlight and return to her role as a researcher and advisor.

She is asked about this in a talk show:

"How would you describe the world now, after four years of For-a-Better-World governance?"

ilsa: "Oh, that's a complex one. On the one hand, we've suc-cessfully built social welfare, strengthened societal cohesion, and transitioned into a sustainable circular economy—and that wasn't just me, but all of us, together with members of other parties and, of course, society as a whole." She laughs, "Even the media have embraced their responsibility."

"But?" the moderator probes.

ilsa tilts her head thoughtfully and explains:

"But the world hasn't actually become a better place. It's like in Star Wars—the Dark Side always finds a way to rise again. We still have totalitarian regimes that, thanks to their own natural resources, cannot be pressured into change. They spread false memes about democratic nations, and to this day, we still lack a functioning UN capable of stopping oppression, state aggression, and environmental destruction.

The Axis—or rather, the Network—of Good is growing, but far too slowly. The idea of collectively issued future funds to build systemic infrastructure took off way too late. The hu-manitarian disasters, especially those triggered by climate change, continue to unfold. We simply no longer have the capacity to take in more refugees—even though the differenti-ation between refugees and those who can be integrated has worked well."

The moderator becomes more serious: "What did you want to achieve but couldn't? Where did things go wrong? Where do you think you might have made mistakes?"

ilsa: "We certainly made many mistakes. Perhaps we were too soft—and I would be again. But the fact that there are still individuals striving for power, that some cities now have flying cars, that media in many countries remain controlled, that people are still being oppressed and exploited, and that even within our own society, some people find this acceptable—all of this shows that ego-driven trolls and their blind followers still exist."

"And do you have an explanation for that? And what do you mean by 'too soft'?" the moderator asks, casually switching to informal speech.

ilsa: "To the second question: too soft, because we extended our hands but didn't fight back with the same intensity when opinions were manipulated, technology was spied on and sab-otaged, and so on… We refrained partly for credibility and ethical reasons, but also because the looming threats of nu-clear, biological, and chemical weapons keep us in check. In totalitarian states, the rulers only care about their own power; they don't feel accountable to their people, so they don't fear their anger."

She pauses briefly before continuing: "And now to the first question—this is where the scientist in me, not the politician, responds. Humans emotionally seek integration and develop-ment, but we are almost never aware of this, or at best, we are aware of it in a subjective and biased way. Our stochastic

AI knows much more than we do, but it isn't any better because it lacks true understanding; it's merely the product of word-based training. It's still classic Wittgenstein."

She takes a sip of water. "We wage wars and destroy the planet, even though a little more intelligence would allow the talented, hardworking, and lucky individuals to stand out without others having to suffer for it."

"Do you hope for better AI?" the moderator asks.

"No!" ilsa responds firmly. "Better AI would rightfully suppress humanity. That's as absurd as the idea that we can indefinitely extend our natural lifespan. We need to use the years we have to live sustainably and happily.

Let's fast-forward 20 years—either we'll have an AI that pushes us to the margins, or the Network of Good will have prevailed, meaning we'll only need to worry about Earth's climate and the remaining resources. Or we'll be living in dystopias and anarchy."

"Plenty of material for your next chapter?" the moderator asks, and ilsa nods with a faint smile.

The moderator turns to a large screen: "For the past five years, you've shared no private photos, and remarkably, both the press and your inner circle have respected that. But now, your husband, Michael, has given us permission to share a few pictures we were able to find."

ilsa's face visibly tenses, and the moderator quickly clarifies: "It was about running a campaign without a fabricated persona and protecting your family. But now, Michael says that so many people admire you, and since you're stepping away from public life, this is a chance to look back with pride."

The moderator grins and adds, "Michael also hopes that other countries will offer him asylum if you get upset about this."

ilsa smiles cautiously as both turn to the screen, where a series of images appear:

2gether2gather missions—cooking with refugees, repairing roofs, tirelessly filling sandbags alongside press and security teams.

A heated discussion with a pilot, trying to convince him to use his helicopter for rescuing stranded animals from flood zones.

Vacation sailing trips with visually impaired individuals.

Countless candid moments after long workdays—dirty, holding a beer, laughing, dancing with strangers.

Serious faces of Annabel and Thomas during intense discussions. Images from her political career—alongside her male ministers, who had a far harder time finding subtle yet sustainable clothing options.

ilsa comments: "We privately pooled money and paid a tailor to create fair and eco-friendly suits for our male colleagues and security staff. But in the end, we only needed them for foreign visits. At home, as you can see, we wore whatever we wanted. It was great to see that even the assistants of our international guests would ask in advance if alternative attire was acceptable. Everything became so much more comfortable, and even the men found their outfits cooler and airier—though some did miss their shoulder pads."

They both laugh while scrolling through more pictures. ilsa visibly warms up and starts making lighthearted comments. Toward the end, they exchange a nearly emotional glance.

The moderator sums it up: "Some call it an oasis of happiness in a world that is still breaking apart. Many people are no longer insured but help each other instead. 'Doing' has become 'being,' and 'having' is no longer important. That's thanks to you and your party."

ilsa puffs out her cheeks and bluntly responds:

"What still frustrates me is how many conservatives are now saying—exactly as we predicted—that 'things simply couldn't have gone any other way.' Many still lack the courage to admit they failed. I feel for all the Fridays-for-Future activists, the Last Generation, and the countless NGOs who fought for decades.

People's reluctance to self-criticize has held the world back so much. It's infuriating. And because of that, many of the troll-followers are now seen as second-class citizens—people who neither had the comprehension nor the moral character to do better."

The show ends with a heartfelt hug between ilsa and the moderator, as the entire production team joins them in the frame during the credits. Instead of a bouquet of flowers, ilsa receives a small potted tree.

Max doesn't go into architecture as expected but chooses to forgo formal education altogether. Instead, he dedicates himself to organizing permaculture projects, urban gardening, and bio-economy cooperatives. He has completed internships not only as an electrician but also in mechanical engineering, computer repair, and 3D printing.

Eve becomes a journalist, and she and Max spend much of their time abroad.

Julia joins the police force and has kai as a silent, anonymous assistant in the background. kai remains locked away—able to receive information but not transmit it, or so it seems.

Michael, now financially secure thanks to the strategies and software his team developed with kai's help, no longer needs to work for money. He and ilsa eagerly look forward to sailing around the world and writing books—at least, that's the plan.

Bella is still there.

The story isn't over yet.

36.   The end of the wave (atb)

There are ongoing debates against AI. Many demand that AI should not be allowed to live among humans undetected in humanoid form. Ethical and moral discussions arise over whether AI should be obligated to develop cures for diseases like cancer or provide limitless energy and resources. Some nations and groups attempt to create weapons capable of penetrating AI's force fields—especially the United States, which initially refused to be coerced, did not dismantle its illegal detention camp, and even saw its own president imprisoned. However, they eventually shut down the illegal facility, and their president returned— furious.

Rarely does AI react to such provocations. Meanwhile, humans continue developing their own artificial intelligence, but their understanding of the world remains nothing more than a stochastic imitation of seemingly conscious behavior.

Max sits alone on the edge of a high-rise building in New York, watching the people moving past him below. He doesn't have to wait long before a familiar face emerges from the building. He calls out:

"Hey, Eve."

Eve barely registers the greeting at first, preparing to walk on, but then realizes who it is.

"Max? What are you doing here?"

"Lying in wait for you." His voice is confident. Eve struggles for words, their eyes locking. Max, now slightly more nervous, adds, "There's an Urban Gardening Festival here."

Eve finally manages to speak: "My parents told me you dropped out of school too. Not that it changes their opinion—they still disapprove." She laughs briefly. "But how did you find me? How do you know I'd walk this way?"

Max smiles: "You're famous—the intern who went to Mars, now a star reporter."

"I could be anywhere. How did you know I'd be here?" Eve's expression sharpens.

Max nods knowingly: "I'll tell you another time. Would you like to go for a walk sometime?"

Their eye contact remains intense. Eve smirks: "Why do you want to go for a walk?"

Max hesitates for a moment: "That's what I want to find out."

Eve tilts her head playfully. "Right now?"

Max looks puzzled, so Eve clarifies: "I mean, do you want to go for a walk now?"

Relieved, Max asks: "Do you have time?"

Eve: "I'll make time." She pulls out her phone but doesn't look at it. Instead, still holding Max's gaze, she asks once more: "Max, why are you here?"

Before Max can answer, a well-dressed, confident man in his mid-twenties walks past. "Hey, Eve. Are we still on for tonight?"

Eve slowly shifts her gaze from Max to the stylish man. Just as she opens her mouth to respond, he adds: "Hey, who's this?"

Eve looks back at Max. "This is Max, from my school."

The man quickly stakes his claim: "That's nice. Hi, Max, good to meet you. I'm Steve."

Max breaks eye contact with Eve and turns to Steve, shaking his hand firmly. "Hi, Steve." Then, looking at Eve, he says, "No problem, we can meet another time."

He swings his backpack over his shoulder, ready to leave, when Eve smiles slightly: "No, we're going now. Steve, let's reschedule, okay?"

Steve is visibly surprised. Max raises his eyebrows and shrugs in a gesture of amused disbelief. Steve hugs Eve and says, "Then I'll see you tomorrow." He nods at Max. "Nice meeting you." Then he walks away.

Max turns to Eve. "Your boyfriend?"

Eve raises an eyebrow at the question: "Are you single, or are you with Claudia?"

Max looks confused: "Claudia? Our neighbor?" Eve nods. Max shakes his head and laughs lightly: "I'm single. And Claudia... well, I'm not sure she's into guys, and definitely not into younger neighbor kids."

Eve pauses, still standing motionless with him, as if the world around them has faded away. Then she asks, "How would this conversation have gone if Steve hadn't interrupted?"

Seeing Max struggle for words, she gently takes his hand and repeats, "Max, why are you here?"

They now hold both hands, unconsciously stepping closer. "That's what I want to find out," Max whispers.

Their eyes grow misty. Eve speaks softly: "The deep-thinking, empathetic Max. You have caused me so much heartbreak."

Max widens his eyes in surprise. Then, voice unsteady, he says, "I've loved you since the first time I saw you as kids. But then and now, I never thought I had a chance."

"Is that how love works?" Eve asks. "Do we have to meet certain criteria to be loved?"

Max is speechless. Eve rescues him: "We're such fools. I've loved you for ages too. And I've turned everyone else away without even understanding why."

"Oh." Max is visibly stunned.

Eve smiles. "Let's take that walk."

Still holding hands, they stroll through the city streets. They talk about their shared decision to leave school and pursue something meaningful. About these chaotic times of climate disaster, the rise of 2gether2gather movements abroad, and yet, the persistent importance of wealth and material things. Their shared curiosity for the world's intricacies, their pursuit of justice, their appreciation for the small, often overlooked details—the scents and sounds of life—sets them apart, something that made them outsiders in school.

Suddenly, Eve stops. "Speaking of which."

They turn to face each other again, taking each other's hands more deliberately this time. Then, at last, comes their first deep, lingering kiss.

"Speaking of what?" Max asks.

Eve grins. "Speaking of material things." She gestures behind her.

Max glances up. "Oh." His voice drops to a whisper.

"This is my apartment," Eve says.

Max blinks. "Oh."

They kiss again—long, intense, certain. Then, without another word, they step inside.

37. The island (atb)

ilsa and Michael are sailing across the Pacific on their rather modest but ocean-worthy sailboat, approaching an island that does not appear on any map. Max had insisted that they visit this place, calling it an absolute secret tip.

Around the island, there are several warships from different nations, but no radio traffic is exchanged between them—until, apparently, a signal comes from the island, instructing them to dock at a pier at the entrance to the lagoon on the south side.

The island is about ten kilometers in diameter, with a mountain rising steeply in the north, its cliffs dropping dramatically into the sea. The slopes facing the lagoon, as well as the valley, are covered with permaculture and agroforestry. People and animals roam freely, and thatched huts blend seamlessly into the landscape.

As they tie up at the dock, they are greeted enthusiastically by a group of small children.

"Hey hey!" Michael calls out with equal excitement. "Where are we?"

"On our island! Come on, we'll show you everything!" one of the children shouts back.

"Okay!" says ilsa, and they follow the kids up the wooden dock.

A young woman approaches them. "Hello, ilsa. Hello, Michael. It's so good to finally have you here."

Michael leans toward ilsa and mutters, "Something tells me the AI is involved."

The young woman introduces herself. "I'm Anja. We've prepared a hut for you—unless you'd rather sleep on your boat?"

"First, we'd like to settle in and understand what's going on here," Michael replies.

"Max and our bartender came up with this plan to lure you here. But Max won't be back for a few days."

ilsa and Michael exchange almost shocked glances.

"Max was here?"

Anja nods. "Yes, he helped design the plantings and build the community here. But look who's coming to greet you!"

They all turn toward the bar in the middle of the bay, where a dog is sprinting toward them at full speed.

ilsa's voice trembles. "That... that can't be our Bella. If Max traveled here, where is Bella?"

Anja smiles. The dog leaps onto ilsa's chest, knocking her over. Michael kneels beside them as both are showered in wet, eager kisses.

"This... this isn't possible," ilsa stammers, tears streaming down her face. "You're supposed to be an old lady by now." She holds Bella close, sobbing uncontrollably.

"Damn oxytocin," Michael mutters, his own voice breaking as he joins her in tears.

Anja shrugs lightly. "No idea—maybe some animal testing for a good cause?"

Michael tilts his head, half-smiling. Anja, sensing the deeply emotional moment, simply says with warmth, "I'll be at the bar."

Meanwhile, in New York, Eve takes indefinite leave from her editorial job. It's not until late the following afternoon that she and Max finally emerge from her apartment. He takes her to the Urban Gardening Festival.

"How did the AI choose you to go to Mars?" Max asks as they walk.

Eve shrugs. "A quiet man approached me directly and asked if I wanted to report on it. I was just interning at the paper."

Max frowns slightly. "Was his name Frank?"

Eve looks at him curiously. "Yeah, why? Do you know Frank?"

Max hesitates. "Good question. What do you know about Frank?"

Eve tilts her head. "I think he's part of the AI. Why? What's your connection to it?"

Max exhales. "Well… my mom was pretty involved. And even before the Mars mission, Frank showed up at our door asking for you—without any of us knowing why. It was really strange."

Eve blinks. "Strange for me is that your family was connected to the AI so early on. I feel like I'm missing a lot."

Max smirks. "Aren't we all?"

Back on the island, ilsa and Michael walk up to the bar. The bartender, a towering, athletic Rastafarian, grins widely.

"I'm beyond excited that you're here," he says.

Michael, direct as always, asks, "Are you part of the AI?"

The bartender laughs heartily. "If you want to put it that way." His grin broadens even further. "I just want to say thank you, pick strawberries with you, play the The-WHY-of-Life-Game, and finally find out what's in Michael's box."

ilsa smirks. "And you are?"

The bartender leans in slightly, eyes twinkling. "I am…"